THE GIRL NEXT DOOR

A psychological thriller

LISA AURELLO

THE GIRL NEXT DOOR

Lisa Aurello

ISBN: 978-1-5136-1855-5

Cover design by Indianboy

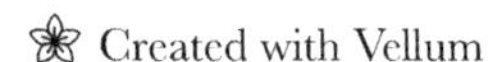

A woman with good shoes is never ugly
~ Coco Chanel

Prologue

Late September

IN THE LAST minute of her life, Cate Caldwell was thinking about donuts and high heels. Donuts because she'd been goaded into eating a piece of a maple-glazed Cronut and now she felt bloated from all that grease and sugar. High heels because she was in love with her new Saffiano leather pumps.

There were other things drifting through her mind as she got off the Metro-North train. The upcoming all-breed show in Florida the following week, for one. Cate had high hopes about their prospects. If they could take a ribbon in Miami or even just win another major in the hound division, Harper, her lovely Afghan bitch, would be an AKC champion for her second Westminster. Cate and her mother knew dog flesh, and they spotted a winner in Harper while she was still nestled with her littermates.

Plus, it was decision time for window treatments for the front of their newly acquired English mews house, or she wouldn't have them in time for the holidays. She'd narrowed it down to the plantation shutters or the white-on-white linen Roman shades.

A little over an hour ago her husband, Mason, had texted, reminding her to pick up his dry cleaning—he wanted to wear his navy Armani to the ballet the next evening, and he was out of town until midday tomorrow. She'd be in the city all the next day, so she needed to get the suit tonight. She was rushing because she left the office late today, and the dry cleaner closed at seven. It was now 6:39.

Walking briskly through the commuter parking lot toward her car, she was distracted by her thoughts and paid no heed to what was going on around her. Though her silver M4 was in sight, her eyes were riveted on her textured leather shoes. Prada makes perfect.

From a parked car came a single muffled report. The kill shot was fired out of the Sig Sauer P226. It hit Cate squarely in her left temple, the hollow point expanding on impact and pureeing her brain as efficiently as a Ninja Master. Though it took only seconds, the kinetic ballet of the bullet as it disrupted synapses, shattered bone into lethal shards, and blasted its way into the cerebral cortex caused massive tissue damage, all while the victim was still upright. She was dead before she face-planted into the concrete, breaking her perfect nose to pile onto the other indignities wreaked upon her supermodel-like face and body.

She had no time to see her own end coming, no time to effect a transition, not even a fleeting moment to consider who delivered her this fate. If she had, she could probably figure it out quickly. But Cate didn't even have *quickly*. She jumped from one moment of cognitive clarity to the next of dead as a doornail.

When she fell, the momentum of gravity sent one shoe flying off her foot, and it landed in the middle of the sidewalk, sitting jauntily cocked and waiting to greet returning commuters. It was to their misfortune that it wasn't the only thing that was awaiting their witness.

Though it was dark out, and people were rushing to their cars, eager to get home after a long day, Cate's death stood inconveniently in their way. Because a silencer was used, bystanders merely saw a woman drop to the ground. It was only when they got near enough to her that they were able to see that half her head was destroyed. One brave but misguided commuter crouched down and half-turned the body to ensure she was beyond human help: one arctic-blue eye stared back at him; the other one was distorted from internal pressures.

"Don't touch her," a woman yelled at him.

The man got to his feet. "I had to check to see if she needed first aid. She doesn't," he added in a quiet voice.

Several people called 911 from their cells, pleading for an ambulance. By then the killer was already driving away from the crime scene, late to meet someone for dinner.

TWENTY-NINE DAYS earlier (late August)

THE CAR DOOR swung closed with a muted thud. After a casual glance around the lot, the man pointed the key fob at the vehicle and locked it. Noting that the car parked immediately next to his was the same make, model, and color made him smirk. Yet another one was parked a few cars down. Turning, he adjusted his tie and sauntered toward the entrance to the restaurant, his eyes continually scouring his surroundings. If he noticed anyone he knew even in passing, he'd abort and leave the premises.

The old trope said the best way to hide was in plain sight so he tried to blend into the background: he wore a navy suit, his dark brown hair was neatly combed back, and he wore a bandage over the tattoo on his middle finger. He kept quiet, avoided eye contact, and left his Porsche back at the office, instead taking his assistant's four-year-old silver Honda.

His problem was that people tended to notice him. His natural good looks, combined with a body he earned with obsessive dedication to weights and running, kept attention, especially of the female variety, coming his way. True, his looks served him well in multiple ways, but in others they were a huge pain in the tit.

Glancing at his phone, he saw he was early. Once inside *Rasputin's Inn*, he scoped out a secluded table in the rear of the dimly lit dining room, away from any windows. Pointing with his chin, he politely asked the hostess—the one who approached him so quickly she teetered on her high heels—"May I have that corner table?"

Greedy eyes roamed him up and down, accompanied by a covetous smile. Or more accurately, a leer. "Of course, sir. Follow me."

Trailing behind her, he could tell she was swaying her ass more than was natural. Even though he was used to women flirting with him, today he found it irritating. He was trying to fly under the radar, for fuck's sake.

The table was cloistered from the view of most of the other tables yet positioned so that he could still watch for her entrance. "Thank you," he told the hostess. She stepped aside slightly to allow him to sit, but he had to wedge past her to do so—her obvious intention. She probably didn't see his eye-roll at her ploy. Lately, he had even less patience than usual for aggressive women.

"I'll send a waiter over to take your order." Her smile stretched wide, revealing a scarlet lipstick smear on her right front tooth.

After a curt nod at her, he sat back and picked up the menu, but his eyes were on the room. Scanning left to right, he made sure there weren't any familiar faces. Someday soon they'd be able to do away with this covert shit, these clandestine restaurant meetings, but not yet. Patience was requisite and happened to be one virtue he had in abundance.

The cafe was alive with the din of chatter and boisterous laughter as diners streamed in and out in even exchange. Crowded and noisy suited their purpose.

About five minutes later, she appeared in the doorway. As soon as she walked inside, he recognized her. Since it was easier for her to disguise herself, they'd agreed she'd be the one to do it. Sporting a wig and sunglasses, she was incognito, but it didn't matter what she wore—not to him. He knew her in and out: her gait, her body, and her posture. He knew her in other ways too. He knew her, in fact, down to her DNA.

Patient as always, he watched as she slid her sunglasses down her nose, and her eyes panned the interior. He held up a finger, and as her gaze zeroed in on him on the second pass, her expression changed, and she began to thread her way toward him. He stood as she kissed his cheek in greeting before they sat down across from each other. Their close proximity allowed him to stare into her eyes—he needed her to believe that he thought her a goddess.

"So?" She placed her shades on the table and looked at

him. Her eyes held a glint of what he interpreted as nervous anticipation. His probably did too.

He tried to smile. "It's zero hour. We need to do this or kill it."

"So to speak," she whispered. "It could go bad."

"It could," he agreed, maintaining his neutral expression. "We could move to plan B instead. Just take off."

"We could... but... why should we?"

He said nothing, studying her face. She wore a solemn expression, but her eyes reflected her resolve. In fact, her entire demeanor evinced her purpose: brows pinched, hands folded, spine oaken. The woman knew what she wanted.

"After what she's done..."

Reaching across the table, he covered her hand with his own, trying to convey affection. "I know. I just want you to understand that if we go ahead with it... it could all go south on us—you're right about that. We're aiming for a big win. The bigger the reward, the greater the risk."

She laughed quietly. "I wonder how many times you've said that to me in the last few months.

Now he chuckled too. "More than once, I'm guessing?" Head down, his eyes fixed on the table. "I just want to make sure you fully comprehend what the risks are going in—"

"No, I get it," she interrupted as his eyes rolled up to hers. "I do. I know the risks... it's going to be so difficult for a while..." She swallowed hard, and he could see the muscles in her throat contract. He felt a little sexual tingle. "Even so, I think we should go for it. Starting all over would be a bitch... and then there's the payback. I want it too."

"That's important to you, I know."

Her face went slack. Leaning back in her chair, she

crossed her leg under the table, bumping his knee. "Why isn't it to you?" Her tone had crisped from a few moments ago.

He didn't answer her right away. Sliding his tongue over his front teeth, he tilted his head, taking a moment to check her out from head to heels. The heels alone made him hard. An erotic image popped into his head: drilling her from behind when she had nothing else on but those shiny black stilettos. "It is," he insisted as he expelled the breath he'd been holding. "So it's a go—win or lose. Hopefully, we'll get the win."

She smiled and nodded, reaching for her glass of water.

Decision made. They'd waited long enough. One bitch would be dead before the next month was out.

The other one would take the fall.

Chapter 1

Dutchess County border, NY, September 10th

"PYSCHO KILLER, *qu'est-ce que c'est, fa fa fa fa fa fa fa...*"

Jane squealed, cranking up the volume of the car stereo to duet with the Talking Heads. The sinister sky was about to rip open and deliver its wrath, but she wasn't paying too much attention to the impending storm. She was busy feeling good.

Cool relief sluiced through her bloodstream like a fast-acting sedative now that the dreaded meeting was over, and she was on her way back to the city. After so much time, she finally felt calm and even slightly giddy now that it was behind her. The looming prospect of today's appointment had been stressing her out for weeks, and her anxiety level had steadily climbed to the point of physical illness: nausea, headaches, and a rash on her forearm that might or might not be poison ivy. While getting dressed this morning, she'd noticed that her nails were chewed down to ragged nubs—an icky habit she'd managed to break years ago.

Bright-siding all of that *agita* was that she lost another five pounds because of it. The charcoal sheath dress—size-ten and form-fitting—she'd purchased last month was actually a little loose on her today. For a former fat girl, size ten was a triumph in and of itself, but Jane was still shedding weight. With every pound gone, she felt more empowered and in control of her own fate.

As she cruised around the bends of the scenic roadway, she thought with a measure of disbelief about the turns her life had been taking—one-eighty pivots in almost every facet of it. At twenty-five, she was an efficiency expert wunderkind and up-and-coming *it* girl. Well, that was the joke since she worked in IT. Everyone called her and Melanie the MT *it* girls.

But old habits die hard, and no sooner had she acknowledged her cautious optimism than the usual doubts and self-loathing scurried back in like cockroaches when a light is flipped on—feelings she endlessly recycled from the landfill of her personal despair. *He* was the reason for it all: both her fragile hopes and disbelief that anyone could appreciate her, much less a man like him. Jane wasn't stupid: she knew she was unlovable and had known it ever since kindergarten—maybe even before that. Maybe the self-knowledge had germinated in utero with the first cell divisions. Probably.

Useless. That's what her mother used to call her. Her father preferred pigheaded.

It was much more than about looks, though that was important. When Jane was in high school, her mother used to nag at her to wear some makeup or maybe consider more fashionable clothing. In her high-pitched voice, she'd badger her daughter relentlessly: *Jane, you could be passably pretty with a little damn effort. Maybe you can try a shorter skirt? You could get away with it if you borrow my high heels—they'll make your legs look less heavy. How about wearing a little makeup today? God forbid, you try to look nice. I got a new lipstick shade that might possibly work on you. Give it a try, why don't you?*

Jane wanted to fight back at her critical mother with one of the few talents she possessed—her extensive repertoire of word missiles—but bit her tongue till it bled out the salt in her, keeping the insults from flying from her mouth like RPGs.

Maybe she could look better, but Jane felt it was important to display on the outside the way she felt on the inside. Disguising her congenital hideousness behind makeup and clothes seemed patently dishonest.

Jane's shortcomings included major personality deficits as well. She recognized it and had long ago come to terms with it. Though she had a wry sense of humor, it was often misunderstood by others. Patience was also something Jane found in short supply in herself.

Honesty, though. That was crucially important to her—one of the few attributes Jane both respected and possessed. And she was brutally honest about herself. Looking at her own reflection used to fill her with cold dread and bolster her self-hatred, yes, but it was liberating at the same time. She didn't have to worry about losing popularity over some imagined high school infraction because she never had it to begin with. An author Jane read in high school, Zora Neale Hurston, said it best: *the game of keeping what one has is never so exciting as the game of getting*. Not that Jane ever tried to get it, nor did she even consider the possibility, but she could recognize the authenticity of the sentiment. Not only is it not exciting to try to keep what you have, but it also must be massively stressful.

The clique girls had to deal with such bullshit high-school drama on a daily basis. Jane didn't.

She also didn't have to worry about what she was going to wear every day because it didn't matter. Jane was plain and overweight, yeah, but she embraced it, instead spending her energy on honing her sarcasm and wit into something as sharp as a surgeon's scalpel. Those glossy, popular girls at school with perfect bodies were like an alien species to her, one that she couldn't even entertain the notion of belonging to, but in some ways, she actually felt sorry for them. The strain of keeping up their pretenses must have been almost unendurable because Jane was pretty sure that underneath all that makeup and fashion were other ugly girls.

Lately, though, things had begun to change for Jane, both outer and inner alterations. Today, wearing the new dress that she hadn't yet dared to wear to work, her hair styled in soft waves, and light makeup meticulously applied, she was actually pleased instead of horrified when she took a peek in the mirror. It inoculated her with a small burst of confidence, a word that wasn't listed in her personal dictionary until very recently. She smiled again, thinking of the main reason for her surge of self-esteem and the reason she was going to all of this trouble.

Scanning the sky through her Subaru's windshield, she decided she would probably just beat the monster storm bearing down on New York City. Her gray suede pump pressed a little harder on the accelerator as one of her favorite Radiohead songs came on the radio.

About twenty miles back, a black SUV had begun to pick a fight with Jane. There was no reason, no provocation other than asinine sport. It kept passing her and then slowing down—passive aggression, highway-style. Jane tried to avoid road rage by keeping clear of the vehicle but the other driver seemed to be out looking for trouble. For the last mile, however, the SUV stayed away.

Just as she passed a busy exit, navigating a sharp curve, she saw it. It was unmistakably a bald eagle, sitting on the grassy swale off the wide shoulder. Jane's eyes remained glued to the bird as she drove past. She'd never seen one in the wild and at so close a distance and wished she could pull over to take a photo, but it wasn't safe and she wanted to get back to the city before the nor'easter hit. She said a quick prayer that the bird wouldn't venture onto the road. She'd heard that the eagles were coming back to New York in greater numbers.

Then it happened.

Jane was in the left lane to pass a compact car going just under the 55-mph speed limit. The black SUV came roaring up behind her, then zigzagged first into the right lane in front of the other car and then back into the left lane just ahead of Jane's vehicle, leaving her no out, no choice, but to swerve to avoid a high-speed collision.

Her panic made her overcompensate and she lost control, the car sailing over the narrow grass median. She saw the pickup flying directly at her, saw the horrified shock in the driver's face, in the whites of his eyes, a terror that he surely saw reflected back at him in Jane's expression. At the moment of impact there was a thunderous boom, followed by shrill screeching as two fast-moving opposing forces collided head-on to an abrupt stop.

It all went down so fast that she never even got to project the scream that lodged in her throat, making it impossible for her to breathe past it.

Her world became incomprehensible pain… and then spiraled into oblivion.

Chapter 2

"Looks like a head-on," the young state trooper shouted over the roaring wind as he hurriedly approached Peter Perez, the first paramedic to leap out of the ambulance.

Trooper Birkin, on scene four minutes after the call came in from a passing motorist, had just swallowed the last delicious bite of an overstuffed burrito when he got the call, and this accident scene was doing his digestion no favors. High-speed car collisions were never fun to look at, and this one was pretty grisly with both vehicles twisted into such a damn mess, as if the hand of God himself reached down and scrunched them into a gruesome sculpture, complete with organic components. Mixed-media art. He snorted a laugh at his own black humor. Birkin was seriously not looking forward to having a look-see at the bodies inside the mangled metal. If the Gs could do that to steel…

Lucky for him, the EMTs reached the site less than ninety seconds later before Birkin was forced to make any assessment himself. He radioed in for a medevac to stand by, waiting only for the paramedics to confirm life in either vehicle. From the looks of both, it was doubtful. He just prayed there were no kids involved. That would ruin his whole night and follow him into sleep. Head-ons were always the worst, trailed closely by T-bones—and of course when bikes laid down. Nasty business.

As Perez and his partner got to work, Birkin again got on the radio, asking for backup, and set about securing the scene and detouring traffic, which would start to get heavier with the evening rush hour approaching. The wind was blowing something fierce, and his eyes and nose were running nonstop, commingling and making it difficult to see a bloody thing. The heat had been oppressive all day, humidity making the air heavy like goo, and now a nor'easter was about to drop, the sky already dark as midnight at barely three o'clock. Looked like all lanes of the highway needed to be shut down since the debris field spread across the median, extending to one lane in both directions. Maybe they could keep the outer lane open each way? Regardless, rush hour was gonna be a hot mess. Wet mess.

Perez yelled to Birkin as he checked inside the compact Subaru SUV. "I got a pulse, single female occupant. We'll need an airlift to Danbury or Westchester, stat."

Birkin radioed the update as Perez's EMT partner checked the cab of what was left of the pickup. He shook his head when Birkin came over to check. "One occupant, male, deceased."

"You sure?"

The paramedic shrugged. His usual unfazed expression slipped a tiny bit. "Can't live without a head, last time I checked. Dog's alive, though."

Birkin grimaced, glad he didn't go do it himself. "A dog?"

"Yeah. Needs medical attention. Can you drop it off at

the closest vet until we notify his next of kin? The dog would go to them—if it lives."

"Yeah," Birkin said, "I could do that. Would you bring it over to my squad car?"

"Can do. Here comes the chopper." He whistled. "That was fast. Looks like he's putting down over there... where the median widens a bit. I'll have to bring the woman there first and then get the dog. Sit tight."

Birkin nodded and shifted his attention to detouring traffic. What a crappy end to a long day.

IT WAS ALREADY a busy night in the emergency room at Westchester General and only promised to get worse as the storm hit and traffic accidents began streaming in. One was arriving ahead of the storm. As they wheeled the young woman in, the team was already in place.

Emily Lopez was on her first shift in the ER. Last month she'd requested a transfer down from neonatal, having watched three preemies die in a single week. Though the other nurses and even a few doctors assured her that it was an unusually high mortality rate for the department, Emily couldn't hack it. She could deal with blood and gore but not dead babies.

When the EMTs unloaded the gurney from the ambulance, Emily was by the door to do escort and get details. She took one look at the young woman's nose that was hanging off her face and Emily felt her stomach acids gurgle. Poor girl. Taking a deep breath, she forged ahead. The ER might take some getting used to as well.

They got the young woman situated in the farthest cubicle, hooked up to an IV drip, and were prepping her for surgery. Emily was assisting until Chrissy came on shift and relieved her in triage, so she was able to grab a quick bathroom break. Afterward, she headed over to reception to help out there since she was currently an ER floater and went where needed. As she approached Rosie at the desk, a young man rushed in. He wore business attire and an urgent expression.

"Can I help you?" Rosie's calm was in direct opposition to the man's panic.

"Uh, yeah. I just heard my friend was brought in here. Car accident?"

"Your friend's name, sir?"

"Jane Jensen."

Emily looked at Rosie. "That's the young woman who just came through ten minutes ago." She shifted her attention back to the man. "Your name, sir?"

"Er… Ed… Jensen." At their look, he added quickly, "No relation… just a coincidence. Is Jane going to be OK?"

"So you're not a relative of Ms. Jensen?" Rosie inquired.

"Uh… no, a friend."

"I'm sorry, Mr. Jensen. We cannot release any information to anyone other than relatives. Do you know a family member we can contact?"

"Shit, no. I don't. Can you at least tell me if she's going to make it?"

Emily watched Rosie shake her head. "I'm sorry, sir, but we cannot. Only family members. You can help tremendously if you can have one of her relatives contact us."

Running his hands through his hair, he spun around. "All right, all right. I'll try to get in touch with one of them.

Can you take my name and number and ask her relative to call me with her condition in case you reach one first?"

Rosie nodded, her voice hesitant when she said, "I suppose I can do that."

He had to look at a paper in his wallet to give her a contact number. He wrote down Ed Jensen, followed by one of the numbers he'd taken off another piece of paper and handed it to the woman. She accepted it with a frown, her hackles gone up for some reason.

"Thanks," he grumbled as he turned to walk out and under his breath added, "for nothing."

AS SOON AS he stepped through the hospital doors and walked outside, the man who called himself Ed Jensen took a moment to try to collect himself and organize his thoughts. Standing under the awning as the storm beyond quickened, a panic like he'd never known before rolled through him—he tried to power through it. What the hell should he do? Just wait to see what happens?

Damn it. He stomped his foot so hard on the ground that sharp needles of pain radiated from his heel and shot up his leg. Raking his hands through his hair, he grabbed fistfuls of it as he whirled around in place. Go back and try again? Damn it all to hell—he should've said he was fucking family.

He knew it was stupid to come to the hospital in the first place—security cameras were everywhere. But this shit wasn't supposed to happen. What if she died? The plan would have to be changed. Things were already going horribly wrong before it was even off the ground. He began taking deep breaths and holding them for as long as he could.

He stood there for a long minute staring into space before he snapped back to reality and made his way to his Porsche.

He felt like choking someone to death, and he knew just whose throat he was itching to strangle.

Chapter 3

Her brain was on fire.

Jane couldn't move, couldn't do anything to stop the explosive violence happening inside her brain. The pain was unbearable and like nothing she'd ever endured. It forced her outside of her body, right into a hallucinatory state.

There was less than nothing that she could do about it. The paroxysms were ceaseless, excruciating, and growing in severity. She needed it to stop, but she didn't know how to make it. She couldn't even scream, and she didn't know why.

Sounds were coming at her. They started as a low murmur, gradually increasing in volume as if traveling closer from a long distance but at a fast speed. Through a tunnel maybe. She couldn't identify them.

A bright light was bearing down on her. Headlights? The light shone directly into Jane's eyes and it hurt too. She tried to turn her head away from the offense but couldn't move an inch. Her head was immobilized. She grimaced and her face hurt from even that small motion.

Every inch of her throbbed, she realized, as consciousness unfolded over her, revealing itself piece by piece.

"Jane? Can you hear me?"

The disembodied male voice was deep and suddenly loud. Jane wanted to answer him but was somehow unable to. She attempted to nod but was quickly reminded of her inability to move more than a quarter of an inch.

"Jane?"

She couldn't answer; she tried, but nothing came out.

"Jane, I'm Dr. Lavelle. You're in the ICU of Westchester General. Do you know how you got here?"

"No," she finally managed, the word croaked out. Her throat was a parched ruin. Desiccated like a desert arroyo in deep summer. She yearned for cool, clear water. Nothing else would slake her thirst.

"Do you remember what happened?"

Jane scrabbled through the jackhammering in her head for the answer that she should know. "I-I… I'm not… not sure."

"Do you know your full name?"

"I…Water."

She heard him say something in a lower voice. Asking for ice chips… Someone else must be in the room. "Your name?" he asked again.

"Jane. Jane Jensen."

"Good. What's the last thing you remember, Jane?"

"I…I don't know. School, I guess. It's over."

"School is over?"

"Yeah. For the year."

"And?" the doctor prodded gently after a pause.

"And," she repeated, "now… it's summer."

"Summer? Of what year?"

Her hand, IV tubes dangling from it, reached for her forehead to rub it, as if that would trigger her memory but stopped when it touched bandages. "I'm not sure. I think... I think I... ninth grade?"

The doctor's words came through the dark slowly. "All right, Jane, there appears to be some memory loss and—"

"Why?" she interrupted, rising panic in her tone.

"Please don't become alarmed," came the soothing voice. "You were in an automobile accident, and you've sustained a head injury. It's not uncommon to experience some temporary memory loss."

His volume dropped to a near whisper, but she could still hear him despite the distant murmur of other voices. "Right now, I can only say it seems to be more extensive than anterograde amnesia—the inability to create new memories after the traumatic event. We'll have to wait and see—"

"Is the baby OK?" Jane's rusty voice spoke over him, panicked.

The room fell silent except for the hum of machines. "Baby?" the doctor echoed. "Was there a baby in the car with you?"

He turned to the nurse standing just behind the resident trailing him today. "Can you check to see if there were any passengers in her vehicle?"

Then he turned back to her. "Jane, don't be alarmed. Everything is being taken care of.

The doctor continued speaking in a low volume, not to Jane but to the resident he had shadowing him, probably believing that his patient was barely lucid. His voice remained in a monotone, no doubt hoping to reassure her since she was conscious, however minimally.

He must have assumed she couldn't hear him but she did, every word. She just had a hard time responding.

"There seems to be some long-term memory involvement as well." He patted Jane's hand. "In all likelihood, you will recover all or most of it as you heal. Right now, we're going to help you feel better and begin to get back to yourself. For now, I just want you to rest.

"OK." Her voice was so faint that the doctor had to bend over to hear.

Dr. Lavelle exited Jane Jensen's ICU room, stepping just outside to speak with someone. Jane could hear a female voice and though the conversation was murmured, somehow, she heard the words.

"Lois?"

"Yes, Doctor?"

"I want Ms. Jensen to be closely monitored for the next twelve hours. Understood?"

"Yes. Should I put organ procurement on alert? Her driver's license indicated her as a potential donor."

"No, that's premature at this point. Right now, keep her stabilized and watch closely for significant swelling—that's the most immediate danger and almost inevitable. I'll be back to check in on her within the hour." He paused for a split second. "Do me a favor, Lois. Check the intake report on Ms. Jensen to see if there is any mention of other occupants in the patient's car. We ran a pregnancy test and it came back negative, but the patient mentioned a baby. I'm fairly certain she's delusional, but it's worth a check. I hope to God there's no child at home waiting for her."

"Of course, Doctor. I'll be happy to look into it."

Neither of them heard Jane's moan at the mention of organ donation. A single tear slipped down her cheek as she thought of her own imminent death and the fact that there was no child at home waiting for her. Or so the doctor said.

The only thought running through her head at the moment was her resignation that it was her time to die. And she didn't want to go.

Chapter 4

The call came in at 5:25 p.m., as Melanie Bartholomew, Jane Jensen's coworker and only real friend, was getting ready to leave the office for the day. She'd been sitting with her brown riding boots propped up on the open drawer of her desk, totally spacing out as she tried to decide whether she should go straight home or treat herself to a new pair of shoes. She'd met a live one at *Bar None* the past weekend who'd persistently asked for her phone number and his parting words were a promise to call. Then again, Mel had been on the cusp of blackout drunk so maybe he wasn't all that hot anyway—besides, everyone looks hot at last call. Maybe she hadn't even given him the right number.

Even without the potential of a date, there was no wrong reason to buy a new pair of shoes. Leaning back, she ran her fingers through her short black hair. She loved the silky way it felt after a new haircut. Hair salons had the best conditioners.

"Mel?"

Nate Thompson's deep voice calling her name snapped Mel out of her reverie. "Wassup?"

"Phone call on line four. A woman. Wouldn't say who it was. Do you want to take it? Sounds like a bill collector." He lifted his brows as he wagged his finger at her.

Melanie narrowed her eyes and shot him a filthy look. "Shoes aren't free, asshole." He knew she was kidding. They were always going back and forth like that since Mel was fairly obsessed with shoes—a walking cliché in that respect—and her desk was always surrounded by shopping bags. "Yeah, I'll take it." She picked up the phone and pressed the line button. "Hello?"

"Is this Melanie Bartholomew?" a nasal voice on the other end of the line asked.

The skin on the back of Mel's neck prickled. "Yes, this is she. How may I help you?"

"Ms. Bartholomew, you are listed as next of kin for Jane Jensen, of 1632 Kipling Road, Riverdale. Is that correct?"

Mel's heartbeat picked up like flapping bird wings. "Yes," she managed to choke out clearly, "that's correct."

"I regret to inform you that Ms. Jensen has been involved in a serious automobile accident and has been brought into Westchester General's ER. She is currently undergoing surgery, and her condition is critical."

The shock of the news was like a gut punch and Melanie doubled over, huffing out the last breath she took. "Oh no… my God. OK. Um… I'll get there as soon as I can."

"Thank you. It would help if you could provide us with Ms. Jensen's personal and insurance information."

"Yes, yes. I'll do my best. Thank you. Westchester General, you say?"

"That's correct, ma'am."

"OK, right. I'll be there as soon as I can get there."

The moment she hung up, she started moving in every direction before sitting back down.

Calm down and think, Melanie.

Panicking wouldn't help Jane; she needed to have her wits about her and proceed with a plan. She slapped her hands, palms down, on the desk. First, get Jane's insurance information. The hospital asked specifically for that. Joe Carroll in HR would have access to it. She picked up the phone again and punched in Joe's extension, praying he was working late. On the tail end of the third ring, he picked up.

"Joe? Thank God you're still here. It's Melanie in IT. Listen… I'm going to need Jane Jensen's insurance information…"

"TAXI!"

The yellow cab switched on its *unavailable* sign as it passed her. Bastard. Mel flipped her middle finger at the driver. She knew the weasel totally did that on purpose so he wouldn't have to pick her up. She'd been standing in the rain for ten minutes now, trying to get a freaking taxi and her gorgeous boots were getting ruined.

"You know what? Screw it," she said aloud and decided she'd get to Jane faster if she just took Metro-North. Grand Central Station was two and a half blocks away and she was already soaking wet. She'd just slosh right over there now and get the next train out. It was stupid of her to try to get a cab in the rain anyway. If there's one lesson every person who visits Manhattan learns soon enough, it's that it's impossible to get a taxi in the rain—it might be easier to win the lottery. Either half the fleet disappears into some underground bunker or everyone on the isle of Manhattan comes out in the rain to hail cabs as some sort of secret pagan ritual. One or the other.

At any rate, the train was faster. She was just in time by a comfortable margin of about fifteen seconds to catch the 6:19 express. While she sat by the train window watching scenery fly past, she thought about the conversation she'd had with Jane last year. They'd gone out for drinks one Friday evening after a hellacious workday. Total lightweight that she turned out to be, Jane got tipsy from just the one glass of wine she'd drunk.

She wasn't intoxicated enough to be sloppy so Mel ordered her a beer to chase the wine. What the hell—Jane needed to let her hair down. Wearing her usual style of clothes—baggy and often brown—Jane stared at the table, making designs with the water ring that leaked from her frosted glass. She'd had something on her mind. "Mel, can I ask you a favor?"

Sloshing back her Negroni, Mel held onto a chip of ice to crunch. "What's up?"

"Um…uh," she stammered while watching her finger move in furious figure eights on the table, "I was just wondering if you would mind if I listed you as next of kin on my personnel records."

The combination of Campari and vermouth was easing Mel into a friendly buzz, but she was still sober enough to consider Jane's request. "Why, Jane? Don't you have any family nearby?"

"No, not really. My parents moved west last year. To Arizona. I don't have too many friends in the area either but… If it's too much of an imposition, that's fine. I just thought it would probably—"

"No, it's fine, Jane. Sure, I'll be happy to be your next of kin."

"Really?" she asked as if she were astonished Mel said yes.

"Yes, really. Now..." She emptied her glass. "Another drink?"

Mel disguised her feelings behind alcohol, but she'd been touched by the request. She also felt sorry for Jane. God, it must be tough to have no one close by. Such a lonely existence that Mel could barely fathom—she hailed from a family of five and everyone lived in the same city, more or less. In fact, sometimes more was less, and she wished they lived farther away so they could irritate her only by phone. Disconnecting a phone call was much easier than slamming a door in someone's face, if significantly less rewarding.

Never realizing that anything would come of it, today it did when Mel got the phone call from Westchester General. Mel just prayed that Jane's injuries weren't so severe that her life would be permanently altered. What had that hospital woman said? Her condition was critical... but not much else. Mel would have to wait and see.

As monolithic apartment and office buildings gave way to suburbia through the windows, Mel saw more trees and Tudor architecture and knew she was approaching her stop. Less than one minute later, the train pulled into the station, and she hurried to gather her belongings. Armed with Jane's medical insurance information and her mother's telephone number, Mel headed out into the chill autumn rain.

WHEN MELANIE BURST through the automatic doors at the hospital entrance, she looked like she'd rolled around in a mud puddle for fun. She was so wet she could feel rivulets of water trickling down along her spine and into her undies via her ass crack. Trying to ignore the icky sensation, she looked around to get her bearings.

The hospital lobby looked like a five-star hotel, with lots of plush beige software complemented by matte metal hardware and punctuated by smoky glass everywhere in between, all of it illuminated by elegant underlighting. If Mel were there for a less tragic reason, she would have appreciated the decor way more. As it were, she tried to focus on finding the right area and person who required the information she possessed and who could give her some in return. A security guard with a beer gut and bloodshot eyes directed her down a long hall to the reception desk at the ER.

She got to the desk. "Jane Jensen. I'm here for Jane Jensen. Is she going to live?" Mel could hear the breathless panic in her own voice though she was employing all of her resources to remain calm.

The woman behind the computer screen shook her head. "Are you her next of kin?"

Mel nodded vigorously.

"You'll have to wait to speak to her surgeon. Meantime, you can fill out the paperwork." From the side of her desk, she picked up a clipboard with a wad of forms and held it out.

Reluctantly, Mel accepted it and spinning around, found and perched on the edge of a vinyl-clad chair to fill out Jane's insurance and personal history minutiae to the extent possible.

When she finished the final one, scrawling the last few lines in her illegible script, she returned them to the woman and looked at her questioningly. "Is there no update on her condition?"

The admin perused the paperwork. After a minute or so, she looked up and answered Mel's question with one of her own. "Does Ms. Jensen have any relatives nearby?" At Mel's stern look, she hurried to add, "It's just that although you are designated as next of kin, you indicated on the paperwork that you have no relation to the patient."

She only had to remember that bar conversation to answer so Mel shook her head. "Right… uh, no. She doesn't. Her parents live in Arizona, and she has no one else. That's why she listed me."

"I'm afraid only relatives can be provided the status and visiting privileges of our patients, ma'am."

"Well, I'm her stepsister. Why isn't that enough?"

"You just said she only had her parents…"

"Well, I thought you meant biological family, but I'm as close as you can get without the blood tie," Mel lied through her teeth. "So… now can I know? Or see her?"

The older woman, her hair bright red with two inches of snowy roots, frowned and regarded Melanie through narrowed eyes. Her hair color reminded Mel of a strawberry shortcake ice cream bar she'd buy from an ice cream truck back in the days when she'd put anything in her mouth. The vanilla ice cream center was ringed by the red stuff. Or was it the other way around? Trying not to stare, Melanie waited patiently for the woman to consider her bald-faced lie. After a long minute the woman shrugged, obviously deciding she really didn't give a rat's ass.

"Not right at the moment. She's just out of surgery and in recovery, but when she comes out of the anesthesia, her surgeon will be doing an assessment to see if she's sustained any brain damage. I assume they'd like to speak to you at the very least and then possibly they'll let you in to see her."

Melanie nodded, using her boot toe to try to scratch the back of her leg. It was going to be a long freaking night. "Is there a cafeteria or somewhere nearby where I can get some coffee?"

"Cafeteria's on five but it closes in a half hour. There's a Starbucks half a block away that's open until midnight."

"Ah, excellent," Mel huffed out on a long breath. "First good news I've heard all day. Thanks." She gave the woman a big, toothy grin because Mel had long ago learned that it never hurts to make new friends. "May I get you one too?"

The woman returned her smile, revealing a mouthful of crooked teeth that somehow harmonized into a pleasant grin. "No, thank you. I'll never get to sleep tonight if I have coffee now. By the way, I have a note here attached to Ms. Jensen's file. Someone came in earlier wanting information on your stepsister's condition. A friend named Ed Jensen, no relation to the patient he said? He asked that someone from Ms. Jensen's family contact him with her condition and left a number."

"Oh, OK. I'll take it. Thanks."

As she walked away, Mel mulled over that last bit of information. *Odd*, she thought. But she had no time to dwell on it right now. She'd call him later when she had more information to impart. Right now, she pretty much had zilch. But the question continued to nag at her.

Who the hell was Ed Jensen?

Chapter 5

The phone rang only once before the woman picked up. "Hello?"

The man spoke rapidly into her ear. "It's me. I'm on a burner. Just tell me that it wasn't you who caused the car accident..."

A throaty laugh sounded in his ear. "It was a stroke of genius, baby. Are you happy?"

Closing his eyes, he sucked in a deep breath through clenched teeth, trying to slow down his pulse, relax his seizing muscles, and untangle the chaos of his thoughts. "Am I happy?" he finally said with exaggerated calm. "No. I'm the opposite of happy."

"Why, baby? It fit in perfectly with our plan."

"No. It isn't at all what we planned," he said in a low rumble, trying but probably failing to mask the malignancy he felt... and then because he couldn't help himself he added, "What the fuck did you think you were doing? We never talked about causing a car accident."

"I saw an opportunity and I took it. You know, carpe diem. I thought you'd be pleased..."

"Why would I be pleased over your taking someone out in highway carnage?"

"For crissakes," she screeched, "this whole plan is about taking someone out. Or did you forget all of a sudden?"

He pulled the phone away from his face and jammed his finger in his ear—her strident voice actually hurt his eardrum. Fighting for calm, he kept his tone modulated. "Shh, keep your voice down. We do not need to add to the body count, do we? What is wrong with you?"

He was pacing now but it wasn't helping. If anything, his temper was on the rise. He had to spew it to release some of the volcanic pressure—Krakatoa-sized. In his head, he yelled at her: *you stupid cunt. What were you thinking?* Aloud, he only said, "We had a definite plan…"

"Look, an opportunity presented itself, and it was too damn good to pass up. I was driving home from my meeting with her—just as we planned. Everything went off without a hitch and I wasn't recognized. By the time I left, I figured the stupid bitch was long gone since I met with Pernod afterward but on the way home, I stopped at a gas station right off the highway, and lo and behold, there she was. I just thought that if I could cause her to have a fatal accident, it would work to our advantage. And it was so ridiculously easy. Too easy."

"You also killed a complete innocent. You know that, right?"

"You mean the man?"

"Yes, I mean the man," he echoed in a high-pitched voice, mocking her. He couldn't help it—he was furious with her. They had a carefully crafted plan, and she deviated from it. That's how mistakes were made and stupid people got caught. He did not intend to be one of them. Lucky for her she was on the phone miles away and not in front of him—he was that angry.

"Yeah, well… that was unintended. He was just in the wrong place. It's called collateral damage."

Because every word she uttered was high-octane fuel for his wrath, he pulled the phone away from his ear for a moment to rein in his fury as best he could. It would serve no purpose, and they had to make this work, had to keep going with the plan. After a few deep breaths, he returned it to his ear and gentled his voice. "Whatever. I was trying to get Jane Jensen's condition but the hospital wouldn't release any information. I don't suppose you have any way…?"

"No, but with any luck if she doesn't die, she'll turn into a vegetable. That way we won't have her death on our conscience but things still go our way. Wouldn't that be lucky?"

He huffed out his breath, and a bitter little laugh hitched a ride. "I'm tempted to call the whole damn thing off now, thanks to your improvising. These kinds of things have to be meticulously planned, or we'll get caught. Please remember there's a lot at stake—our futures, to be precise. You just can't go and do things off the cuff. I thought you were smart enough to know that."

"Too late to call it off. Pernod's already got the cash, and he's planning on doing it soon. I wouldn't know how to get to him in time since it's difficult to reach him. Just relax, okay? It's almost done."

"Yeah," he scoffed, "relax. Just please do me a favor and don't fuck up anything else. All right? Answer me."

"Yes, all right, all right."

"And by the way, pick up your own drop phone and use that to call me at this number in an emergency. Do not, I repeat, do not call me on any other phone. Got it?"

Disconnecting the call—or thinking he did—without waiting for her acknowledgment, he stomped over to his duffel bag and pulled out his running shoes. He had to get this mounting frustration off him before he exploded, and running was his therapy, the endorphins his drug of choice. He loved being outside, feeling the power of his legs, shoving his body beyond its natural endurance. After switching out the shoes, he started his run while still in the building, almost taking the heavy glass door off its hinges with the violence he used to swing it open on his way out.

From his pocket, he suddenly heard her screeching. "I really don't understand why you are so upset about it. I honestly don't. Hello? Mason?"

Chapter 6

Jane was falling deeper…

Deep and fast into a black hole and there was no way to arrest or even slow her descent.

Her head still throbbed in fiery pain but with each layer of deeper unconsciousness, it bothered her incrementally less. She heard muffled voices that kept receding into the distance until they were silenced entirely. She thought maybe one was her mother. Earlier her parents had been here, she thought anyway, unless she was dreaming. Her mom had been holding a baby.

"It's your daughter, Jane," her mother had said, her voice oddly flat. Devoid of any emotion.

"My daughter? I don't have kids—*I'm* a kid."

"You're ten years old, and this is your baby," came her amplified voice. Why did it sound so loud? Jane's mother continued, "What will you name her?"

Jane was confused. Was this really happening? She thought she was speaking to a doctor who told her she'd been in a car accident. He'd said something about her memories when she told him she was in ninth grade.

Almost fourteen, not ten, Jane realized. Her mother was psycho. But that was nothing new.

And Jane didn't have a daughter, for God's sake. She would have remembered that. Why was her mother even here? It's not as if she cared about Jane—she'd never cared. Jane couldn't figure out why she'd start now. Or maybe they'd grown close and she just couldn't remember?

There was someone else in her life… but Jane couldn't recall exactly who it was. Someone she wanted with her. She had a friend… somewhere. Maybe that friend would come help her. What did the doctor say about her memories? She couldn't remember exactly what they'd discussed. Her head ached so much, and a metallic tang filled her mouth.

And now there were these rolling waves of darkness, like standing on a beach at midnight and not seeing the ocean but knowing the waves were coming at you. It was kind of terrifying—what if there was a really giant one that would take you out? That's sort of how she felt now, but she thought maybe the waves, ominous or not, would bring sleep if not oblivion. The pain increased and receded with each wave that rolled over her.

She needed sleep. Or was she dreaming right now? She couldn't tell what dimension she was in, but she kept hearing her mother's voice, always needling her about something. Going in and out like the waves. The waves were gentle, though, unlike her mother.

The darkness rolled in like an approaching storm. When it finally reached her, it came like a power blackout… and it came at her, consumed her, and she ceased to feel any pain nor have any thoughts.

Her last thought was of death—her own. It stood to reason that the encroaching blackness was death itself. Unless she'd already died? But if she had, why was she still having thoughts? And hearing her mother's voice. Hell? Why was she dropping from some great height? Jane could almost feel the speed picking up as if she were falling down a deep hole, going faster with each unit of measure. She kept sinking into it, unable to stop or slow her momentum as she fell and fell until she hit bottom—defying gravity with a soft landing—at a depth where everything shut off: there were no thoughts, no dreams… no nothing.

A black hole.

For all intents and purposes, Jane was dead.

Chapter 7

Melanie finally tracked down Jane's surgeon, and he told her what happened. Following her surgery, Jane's brain swelling began to worsen despite the surgical team's best efforts to prevent it, so her surgeon made the decision to medically induce a coma. Brains need less oxygen when unconscious so coma is a helpful tool in treating a TBI, he explained to Mel. If it got worse, he might have to perform additional surgery, removing part of her skull to relieve pressure that can easily damage the brain further or even kill it. The first twenty-four hours were the most critical for an accident victim, so Dr. Lavelle ensured that Jane Jensen would be checked on every fifteen minutes—without exception, he'd told the ICU staff. He was making every effort to lead Jane Jensen out of the woods, he assured her, but he made sure she understood the severity of the situation. The patient was on the bridge between life and death—she could go either way.

A few hours later, Mel had stepped out of the ICU suites and spotted Jane's surgeon speaking to the redheaded admin or nurse—Mel wasn't sure of her position. He told her he was ducking out for a nap. "Were you able to get any information on Ms. Jensen's family?"

The older woman grimaced. "According to her stepsister who was listed as her emergency contact at her job, there's no one in the area."

Mel smirked. Meet Melanie, Jane's brand-new stepsister. Her ears perked up at the next comment.

"...so no kids then?"

"No, Doctor."

"That's a relief. I assume if she had pets or anything, her stepsister would see to them."

"I'll double check with her if I see her again."

"Thanks, Lois."

Mel about-faced so they wouldn't catch her eavesdropping. She began to walk the other way, deciding to grab a breath of fresh air. Exhaustion was starting to take its toll, and she needed to stay up a few more hours, hoping to wait until Jane was out of the woods before she left the hospital—if that was even possible.

An hour later as Mel, slouched in an uncomfortable vinyl chair, was nodding off like a junkie, she felt a warm hand touch hers. Startled, her head shot up, and she saw Dr. Lavelle crouching in front of her.

"How about I find you a bed so you can catch a few hours of sleep?"

Mel smiled at the distinguished-looking doctor. "That'd be really helpful. Thank you."

He crooked his finger at her to follow him and led her to a small room with a single cot inside and a shelf stocked with bed linens and towels.

Mel smiled again in gratitude, and the moment the doctor closed the door behind him, she sprawled on the bed and was out within seconds.

The kind surgeon came back about four hours later to wake Mel.

"Good nap?" he asked her.

"Really good." She smiled. "I feel a thousand percent better."

"I had my own nap too. Let's hunt down some coffee, shall we?"

When the two of them crossed paths with a nurse in the hall, Dr. Lavelle begged the young man to get him two black coffees and find him on his rounds. He turned to Mel.

"Black coffee is the only way it's palatable—trust me. Come on. My first stop is your sister."

The amazing nurse bearing coffee found them before they'd even gotten on the elevator. Mel watched as the doctor downed the small cup of bitter coffee in two gulps, and then he seemed instantly energized by the caffeine. The elevator arrived and they got in and punched six for ICU. Outside of Jane's room, he eyed her chart and gave Mel a big smile.

"She made it through the night. Our girl has a fighting chance."

Mel grinned back and wondered if it was bad etiquette to plant a big smooch on the surgeon's lips. She decided against it.

After Jane survived the first day post-accident, Dr. Lavelle became more confident about her prognosis. She remained in the drug coma, however, since there was still significant swelling. Mel finally had to go home, but she told Lavelle she'd return after work or early the following morning.

It took almost three days for the brain edema to reduce enough to bring Jane out of the coma and would take another seven days to get her from the ICU to a regular room, but her condition continued to improve daily. Though she had other serious injuries, the main threat to her life had been the cranial pressure due to the swelling, so as that eased, she was upgraded from critical to serious and finally to stable. They told her it was a sure thing that her youth helped her recovery.

Twenty-five was a good age to be.

ALTHOUGH MEL WAS ALLOWED to visit throughout, Jane had been unconscious the whole time so when Mel stepped into the room late on the third day, she was more than surprised to see her friend's eyes open and tracking her movements.

She felt the relief all throughout her body at seeing Jane conscious but also fear that she might be… different. Would she even remember Mel? The doctor said she'd lost a lot of recent memory. She forced her voice into an upbeat tone. "It's about fucking time your snoozefest ended. Here you've been getting all this beauty sleep while I've been trudging all over New York City." She leaned in to peck Jane's forehead. "Boy, it's good to see your pretty eyes open, Jane."

Jane's lips pulled into a slight smile. "Thank you. I'm so sorry to impose on you so much…" she managed in a rusted voice and then cleared her throat.

Melanie shook her head, her glossy hair swinging with the motion. "Stop it. I was kidding. I'm just so glad to see you awake." She carefully eyed her friend. Jane was super pale, but her eyes were animated and that made Mel feel better. "How do you feel?"

A rueful grin appeared on her face. "Like I was run over by a truck… which essentially I was." Her face fell right after she spoke the words. "A nurse told me the other driver died. I feel so bad about it... like it's my fault."

"How is it your fault? It was an accident. I seriously doubt you set out to collide head-on with some poor schmo on the road with you. Why were you upstate anyway? Do you remember?"

Jane tried to shake her head but had limited movement with the neck brace. "No clue. My memory is all screwed up—recent memory, that is, because I can remember pretty much everything up to ninth grade and then a few scattered memories here and there afterward. It's really weird..." Her voice cracked. "...and scary."

"I'll bet." Mel dragged a mauve-colored vinyl chair closer to the hospital bed, its legs scraping in protest across the tile floor, and she lowered herself into it. "What does the doctor say about that?"

"He says I'll probably recover most of my memory as my brain continues to heal. He said it's likely I won't ever remember the accident itself and the immediate aftermath... but honestly I think that's a good thing."

"Yeah, remembering that trauma wouldn't do anyone any good." She patted Jane's blanket-covered leg. "So everyone at the office told me—"

"I'm sorry," a nurse who strode into the room interrupted, "but you'll have to step outside the room for a few minutes, miss. You can continue your visit in about a half hour."

Mel glanced at Jane. "I'm going to get a coffee. Want one?" Her eyes darted from Jane to the nurse. "If it's allowed?"

The nurse just smirked and shook his head, his blond-streaked dreads swaying with the motion. "Afraid not."

"OK, I'll go have one then. No sense in both of us suffering, right?"

Jane mustered a smile. "Thanks a latte."

Groaning, Mel waved goodbye and moved toward the door.

Jane called to her. "Please come back."

Mel turned her head and winked at her friend, so happy that Jane was her old self. "Only if you promise no more corny puns."

"Cross my heart."

A shot of whiskey, Mel thought, would go nicely with the coffee right about now. And that nurse with the dreads was kinda hot. How come this hospital had so many male nurses? Mel knew where she was coming if she ever needed a place to convalesce.

Chapter 8

"Ugh."

Jane pushed the gelatinous slime away from her. It was gross and didn't deserve to be called dessert although she had to admit, it was fun to play with for a little while. The hospital food in general was so bad. The only thing she found edible was the rice. At least she could feel more pounds of ugly fat sliding off her body because of the horrid fare.

Food, edible or not, was not her major concern.

Profound depression mixed with discomfort was. The walls of her hospital room were closing in on her, and though she was getting better physically, her state of mind was worsening. Each day dragged painfully by as she lay in the hospital bed, the time measured either by the variegated light outside her window or the subpar meals she was served three times a day. It had gotten so bad that even though the food was putrid, she looked forward to the arrival of the meal tray since it broke up the monotony of the day.

Basically a stranger to herself, Jane nonetheless still felt like she was the kind of person who had to be doing something—either mental or physical. Strenuous. She couldn't just lie here anymore.

She couldn't escape into books because reading aggravated her constant headache. Nor could she tolerate listening to music for more than a few minutes at a time. Mel brought her laptop from work since her personal one had been in her car trunk and was destroyed in the accident, but surfing the internet also made her head pound. The only entertainment she had apart from Mel's visits—and that of a few other people from the office who dropped by, including her bosses—was television. She ended up watching a lot of home-improvement shows and true-crime dramas. When the editing was too choppy, she'd close her eyes and just listen.

She wanted out of the hospital—desperately. She was so ready.

Her memory was still liberally peppered with huge gaps, though she'd recovered some recent memories. Not a lot, though. When the very distinguished-looking Ty Renault, the CFO of MT, strolled into her room, she had no idea who he was at first. He had to introduce himself and after a few minutes, his face became more familiar. It was sort of funny that Jane was becoming inured to the shock on people's faces when she looked at them blankly, having no recognition of them at all. She even found it mildly amusing. Mel, though, she'd somehow remembered all along.

The part of the memory loss that itched at her most was the feeling of losing herself, her identity. Jane had no clue as to the woman she'd become since high school. It was a bizarre and surreal feeling. Identity is one of those things that a person doesn't appreciate having until it's gone.

She just hoped that she could go home soon and do the rest of her recuperating from her new house. Mel had described it to her in great detail, and now she couldn't wait to see it again.

On the Monday evening of the third week after the accident, the surgeon stopped in Jane's room; she was more than ready to hear what he had to say. After seeing only nurses for the past few days, his smiling face was very welcome and for the first time, Jane noticed him as a man instead of just her doctor. He was handsome—a taller, thinner, and slightly older George Clooney-type, his hair completely silver, and the bags under his eyes prominent.

"Jane, how are you feeling?"

Her hazel eyes lightened as she smiled. "Surprisingly decent, Dr. Lavelle. Really well, all things considered. My headaches are not nearly as severe and my wrist feels like it's healing." She waited a beat. "Please tell me that you're here to spring me?"

"Maybe. Ribs still giving you a hard time? Every breath you take?"

She smiled weakly. "Yes. The stalker's anthem, right?"

He laughed. "Yes, and one of my favorites, though I'm no stalker. But I am old enough to be a Police fan."

"Well," Jane said with a smirk, "not all stalkers are bad, are they? Especially if they look like Sting did way back when. How do you suppose he got that name anyway?"

"I don't have a clue as to the name. Getting back to you, on a scale of one to ten, with ten being unbearable pain, how would you rate the pain you're experiencing of late?"

"Six or seven, depending on the time of day. The discomfort and stiffness from lying in bed all day is pretty constant though. The pain medication helps a lot, though, and my headaches are getting much more tolerable."

Pursing his lips, he nodded his head. "I'll be sending you home with a script for oxycodone, which is not as strong as the pain meds you've been getting here. I'd like you to try to wean yourself off of it, however, since it's highly addictive. You don't want to borrow more problems in trying to solve those you already have. Ibuprofen might be enough to keep much of the pain at bay, so you can try that during the day and maybe take the stronger stuff at night so you can sleep."

"OK," she agreed meekly.

He lowered his hip onto the edge of the bed. "This wasn't the first car accident you've been in, was it? Your x-rays and scans showed evidence of past traumatic injuries."

She looked at him as she felt curls of panic begin to rise that she quickly flattened. "I can't... Maybe there was another… I'm really not sure, Doctor."

"It looks like you broke the same wrist before, unfortunately, so this break was more serious, which is why we couldn't use a splint. Do you remember ever wearing a splint or cast?"

She paused for a protracted moment, concentrating. "I don't… maybe."

He jotted down a few notes on her chart and then looked up again. "What about your memory? Any new developments?"

"Not really. I remembered a few small things since last we spoke but nothing major. It's weird, though. There's no, like, pattern to the recovery… like, it's not sequential or anything. Is that unusual?"

"I don't think there's any right or wrong way to recover from memory loss. As long as there's progress, I'd say we're on the right track."

"Yeah, it's just that, at first, large chunks came back,

but lately it's just been fragments here and there. It's so frustrating."

"I know," he patted her hand. "But you're doing remarkably well, so let's be pleased about that and take it one day at a time. Are you keeping the journal?"

She flushed. "I started it on a scrap of paper, but I can't find it now. When I leave, I'll buy a book and be more systematic about it."

"Good." He arched his unruly eyebrows. "Well, I've come with good news. I'm discharging you tomorrow. Do you have someone who can pick you up and take you home?"

"I think my frien… um…" She felt her face go hot at her slip-up… "my sister can come get me. I'll get in touch with her."

Dr. Lavelle smiled. Jane figured he knew about the lie that she and Mel had been hiding behind but he didn't call her out on it. "Very good. I'll sign your discharge papers so you can leave first thing in the morning."

"That sounds so good. Thank you for all that you've done for me, Dr. Lavelle."

"You're very welcome. I want you to follow up with your GP and I'll need to see you again when the neck brace and wrist cast come off within a week or two. I'll have my office staff contact you to set up an appointment." He stood up. "Good luck, Jane."

"Thank you, Dr. Lavelle. I couldn't have done it without you."

He chuckled as he backed out of the room.

AS SOON AS he was out the door, Jane plucked her new phone from the table. Mel had brought it a few days before, after picking up her parcels. The nurses brought her handbag to her last week, and her phone was not among the effects. It was a crushing blow because Jane had no idea of who the friends and colleagues listed in her contacts were and whose numbers were now lost forever.

The call went to voicemail. "Mel, please, please, please come get me in the morning? My doctor is discharging me." She was about to disconnect but then kept talking.

"I want out of this room. So bad. I want to go back to the new house I barely remember." She chuckled. "Call me when you get this message."

Her spotty memory was nothing to laugh at, though. What she told Lavelle was true: sometimes bits and pieces, sometimes large tracts of her memory were restored to her, often unexpectedly. Only yesterday, she was able to recall her high school graduation and remembered Sulu Stanton, her best friend in high school.

Pretty much her only friend in high school.

Packing on an extra twenty-five pounds during the wretched affliction known as middle school, Jane was already overweight when she arrived in high school. Even worse, she had never possessed a sparkling personality to compensate for what she lacked physically. The very first day, Eleanor Constantine, a girl with the shiniest long black hair and a dimpled smile, picked a fight with her in the cafeteria over a bottle of iced tea they both reached for. That incident set the tone for her entire tenure at middle school and high school afterward. There wasn't a single social success, not a one.

The thing that completely ensured her misfit status was that she was also smart, another cardinal sin on the high school popularity measurement chart. Sulu Stanton was of a similar constitution, so they relied on each other for moral and academic support, together making it through the ravages of the war zone that was high school, albeit with plenty of scar tissue. Occasionally they were joined by the bizarrely tall Tara Rehnquist, another outcast who was a year older than they were.

Jane could remember up to the first year of high school with startling clarity but very little afterward. Last week, though, Jane started to remember Melanie in more detail. When she first came to see her, Jane somehow recognized her without quite knowing why. Pretty quickly, Mel became more familiar, but in the beginning, it was frightening. The weird thing was that she was able to remember Mel but not much else about her life post-ninth-grade. Moreover, she couldn't say how long they'd known each other or even how they'd met.

Then that first memory that returned to her—and it came hurtling out of nowhere when she smelled coffee that someone was carrying in the hall—was of Mel introducing herself by way of bringing Jane a Starbucks latte and the conversation they had on her first day at MT. It was the distinctive coffee aroma, Jane was sure, that triggered the recovery of the memory. She'd gasped aloud at the ferocity of its return.

Jane liked the smell of coffee too. It reminded her of Sunday mornings when both her parents would be in a good mood most of the time, and the smell of coffee and bacon would waft through the house, sometimes even waking her up.

And she began to remember when she started at MT. Oddly, though, the years before that time were still lost to her. Her memory had no chronological order to its recovery though there were sequential pieces coming back to her. Like with Mel.

They were never meant to become friends—she and Mel—but opposites do attract and she and Mel couldn't be more opposite if they tried. Meeting on Jane's first day working at MT Systems, the two women's personalities should have clashed: Melanie Bartholomew was bubbly and popular, a pretty woman who knew how to wear clothes and was fearless. She was also ultra slim. Somewhat incongruous with her girly appearance, Melanie was also IT, and was asked to mentor Jane.

And Jane was Jane—lumpy and plain, but brilliant as all get-out. She thought IT was a good fit for her but was surprised when she was introduced to the beautiful woman named Melanie who looked like she'd be in marketing or sales, not anything technical.

At Jane's first glance at Mel, her back went up as she identified the attractive, fashionable woman several years her senior as belonging to the tribe of people who tormented her in high school.

But with Mel, kindness and beauty were not mutually exclusive. It was revelatory for Jane, a fact that spoke volumes about all the shitty people who surrounded her in childhood.

After only a few hours together, both women realized that Jane could do Melanie's job—and everyone else's in the department—with her eyes closed. Always the pragmatist, Melanie probably decided it was in her best interests to befriend Jane and worked very hard to overcome Jane's initial unfavorable impression of her. Somewhere in Mel's process of ingratiating herself with Jane, they oddly became very close friends.

Even a frumpy girl gets lots of attention, even adulation, when she makes boatloads of cash for a corporation. In much less than a year's time, Jane became expert at streamlining IT systems, saving the firm substantial time, ergo, money, in diverse departments—everything from accounting to order fulfillment to human resources benefitting. Her skills, they all soon learned—including Jane—didn't end there as she started tackling efficiency management. As soon as she identified a problem, she was able to find an immediate and genius solution to fix it.

Jane was still sort of in disbelief at how things went down. Almost from the start, her work got noticed at the company, and her reputation as an efficiency expert grew. It felt strange and good to be appreciated. Offers from competitors began to come her way—her kind of skills were in high demand in the driven corporate environment—and the positive attention (not to mention the money) began to change her. Improve her, she hoped. Nothing radical. A few pounds lost. A few new edgier articles of clothing purchased. A little more confidence acquired.

With that memory came another: her house. Her pretty little English-style house that Mel had told her all about, describing it to her in sparkling detail till Jane had a picture in her head. Then she sort of remembered it... Remembered the first time she'd seen it.

It was the biggest change in her life, her leap into real estate. Her favorite relative, her mom's aunt, had died and left Jane a hefty sum. Who knew Aunt Adele had so much money? She'd left the whole thing, nearly two million, to her grandniece, so Jane, after liquidating a huge chunk of it, purchased an expensive townhome—mostly in cash— a few months back. Her life, once so drab and pointless, became dynamic and even exciting.

Until the car accident wiped it all away.

Chapter 9

Mel called her back about an hour later.

"They're springing me, Mel! Please, please come break me out before they change their mind."

Mel laughed. "Was it as bad as all that? Seems to me you got to sleep in every day and watch television the rest of the time. Doesn't sound like prison to me, babycakes."

"Uh-huh. Try watching paint dry while you have a ferocious headache, and you'll begin to get the picture. Do you think you'll be able to pick me up?"

"Mmm, maybe. You'll have to promise to take me to that little café again—the one with the great omelets—when you're better. Your treat, of course."

Jane chuckled. "You got it. You've earned a lot more than a stupid omelet."

"Hey, I love omelets. Anyway, I was glad to do it for you. So… give me deets."

"Anytime is OK. Oh, don't forget to bring me clothes, Mel. I have nothing to wear but the backless hospital gown."

"Yeah, the hospital is going to want that beauty back.

Too bad 'cause it would be sure to bring you some attention on the streets of New York."

A loud laugh came through the line. "Not the kind of attention I desire. Besides, New York is the one place where something like that would go pretty much unnoticed. Asses hanging out are business as usual. Just please bring me jeans and a tee?"

"OK. Do I have to go by your house or can I just pick up some new things?"

"Whichever you prefer, but I'd rather have my own clothes if I have a choice."

"You do. I'm borrowing my brother's car anyway, so it's no big deal. So... what time do you need me there?"

"The doctor already signed my discharge papers, so I could leave first thing in the morning if you could go in to work late. Is that doable?"

"I think so. You know MT management adores you. I'll be there probably around eight or nine. I'm psyched to see you, Jane. Sorry that I haven't been there more often these past days but our fiscal year is ending and there have been problems as usual so it's been all-hands-on-deck—especially with you out of commission. I didn't get home before eight a single night last week."

"Oh, right. No, I understand. And Mel, thanks... for everything. Really. See you tomorrow?"

"Count on it, Lady Jane."

AS MEL STROLLED up the herringbone brick path of Jane's new home, she recalled the last time she'd been here, almost three months before. Jane had begged her to photograph her newly painted vintage townhouse for a local artist to turn into a digitized painting, and Mel had gone in the morning, just after sunrise as Jane had specifically asked, insisting the house looked best at first light. For Mel to get up that early on a Sunday morning was a true test of her friendship, but she did it, armed with her new fifteen-hundred-dollar camera, and Jane had rewarded her with a big hug, hot coffee, and a couple of hours later, an incredibly good brunch at the tiny café a couple of streets down that made a mouthwatering grilled vegetable and Jarlsberg frittata.

The 1927 attached brick-and-stucco was a charmer. As Mel fumbled with the key ring, she heard someone shout to her and looked up. The sight that greeted her made Mel's mouth go dry and her ovaries begin a lively merengue.

"Hey. Are you my new neighbor?" the man called out from just outside his front door. He was over six feet of toned male anatomy.

No, but I want to be. "No. My friend lives here." She hesitated on elaborating, unsure how much Jane would want her to share.

"Right, right. Jane. How is she doing? We heard she was in a serious car crash. Is she all right?" Coming closer, he extended his hand. "Oh, by the way, I'm Mace. Well, Mason, actually. Caldwell." He shrugged his shoulders, dragging her attention from his twinkling blue eyes right to his buff physique. "People call me Mace."

Well, hello, Mace. Mel could feel heat in her face as her heartbeat took flight. Jane had a gorgeous mofo for a next-door neighbor. Plus, he had a deep, sexy voice, the kind that is hard to resist even if a woman really and truly wants to ignore it. She sucked in a breath and used it to power a great big smile, trying to be cool despite the fact that all her female parts were tingling. "Hi, Mace," she drawled. "I'm Melanie. Nice to meet you."

Omigod, obscenely handsome up close. She could wax

poetic with adjectives about him, but even a plain description would be enough: clear blue eyes, rich brown hair, skin the color of a man of the fields but the texture of one who sits at a desk, and a ripped body—at least as much as she could see busting out of his T-shirt and jeans. *Love at first freaking gasp,* Mel thought.

"Same here. So... Jane?"

His question snapped her attention back to the conversation. "Oh, um, yeah, she's good. Fine. Coming home today, in fact."

"Is she? That's great." He smiled broadly, revealing a mouthful of teeth to make a dentist swoon. *Just fucking naturally.* "Is she... uh, you know... the same? I mean, I heard she sustained a traumatic brain injury?"

Mel nodded. It wasn't her place to divulge private information. How to be diplomatic? "Um, yes, she still has some healing to do. She's doing well, though."

"Good, good. I'm looking forward to getting to know all of our neighbors."

Uh-huh. How well? And who's our*?*

He angled his head back toward the semi-attached and nearly identical townhome next door and jerked his chin in that direction. "My wife and I just moved into our house two months ago."

That single word worked like a pin stuck in a balloon, deflating Mel's good mood instantly. *Wife. That sucks balls.* "Oh? It's a beautiful area and the architecture is amazing," she responded smoothly.

"Exactly. That's basically why we're here. My wife fell in love with the mews-style homes. Loves anything British," he said, chuckling. "Clotted cream, Jane Austen, BBC, you name it. Plus, the schools are excellent... for down the road when we have kids."

"It seems like your wife found her niche then. Looks

totally like an English village. And yes," she agreed, bobbing her head, "the schools. That's important."

Those blue eyes of his were scrutinizing her as he cocked his head like a dumb puppy. "Have we met before? You look so familiar."

Mel shook her head. "Mmm, no, don't think so."

"Maybe not," he said easily. "They say we all have a doppelgänger, right? Or maybe I met a relative who resembles you. A sister maybe?"

Scowling, Mel joked, "God, I hope I don't look like my sister."

He laughed and wagged his finger at her. "It'll come to me."

Well, that was fun, Mel thought, and started to back away. "I should go. So... good luck in your new home, *Mace*." She waved and turned, walking briskly up the path. Her interest had plummeted the instant he uttered the hated W word. Mel did not poach. Right before she gained the front entrance, she swiveled her head around for one last furtive glance back.

He'd been watching her progress, and upon getting caught staring, gave her a brief military salute and only turned away once she was inside.

Feeling oddly jumpy, Mel closed and locked the door behind her and then looked around. The house was still in some disarray from Jane's recent move-in before the accident, and Mel wished she had more time to put it to rights as much as possible before Jane came home.

OK, Melanie, focus on the task, not on the hot next-door neighbor and stop pondering how big his dick is. It's probably big though. Based on his frame. Yes, she was incorrigible and sex-crazed.

Walking into the bedroom was disconcerting since it was the only room in the house that held any furniture. Jane had told her she couldn't stand her old stuff—hand-me-downs from her parents and relatives. *"They're not even good enough for the landfill,"* she'd protested. *"Poor homeless people having to sit on that puke-colored furniture—it's cruel and unusual."*

"At least Jane isn't a neat fanatic," she muttered, taking stock of the master suite that had clothing strewn at every spot that wasn't occupied by a big cardboard box. "Let's see. Everything will be loose on her," she continued, "but baggy would be good with her medical paraphernalia." Having gathered a T-shirt, jeans, and running shoes, she was stuffing them all in her knapsack when she heard a dog bark and a woman's voice yell sharply.

Curious, Mel stepped over to the tall windows, noticing one had been left slightly open, allowing ambient noise inside. Peering out she saw her new pal Mace talking with a thin female with blond hair and elegant posture—*must be the wife*—and she had a big dog on a leash. The dog was tall and thin with long blond hair too. What Mel noticed most of all, was that Jane's rear-facing bedroom window had a perfect view of the Caldwells' patio and small backyard.

That led Mel to wonder if Jane found the married couple to be interesting theatre. If she lived here, she'd totally take a peek now and then—the architecture of these homes practically encouraged it, being in such close proximity but each house of varied dimension in the rear, creating views into each other's homes and lives.

Standing at the casement window, she studied the two carefully. The woman held her body stiffly, as if she was pissed. Her hunky husband was more relaxed but had a guarded look on his face.

Mel couldn't be positive, but their body language suggested they might not be exactly enjoying one another's company. To put it mildly.

Then again, they could be talking about something unpleasant, like unpaid bills or mothers-in-law.

She finished up her task but when she reached the stairs, she realized she forgot to pack underwear and a bra. Jane had nothing in the hospital except the few toiletries that Mel had brought her in the days following the accident. When she re-entered the bedroom, she could still hear the couple next door conversing in loud tones.

Conversing? More like arguing. Was all not peachy with the pretty Ken-and-Barbie Caldwells?

Walking to the window, Mel could hear the man say something, finishing with "your fucking dog." Hmm. So Mace doesn't like the pup? He dropped down a notch in her opinion just for that. She cranked the window closed and locked it so the chilly autumn weather couldn't make the house cold, and the Caldwells couldn't make it unpleasant.

Back to her task, she rummaged through Jane's underwear drawer to find a comfortable pair of cotton panties and bra in the top dresser drawer, noting all the pretty lingerie Jane had in there. She grinned—not so plain-Jane underneath those demure clothes. It made Mel wonder if Jane had a lover. A few days after the accident, Mel had tried calling that guy—Ed Jensen, no relation to Jane—several times but no one answered or returned her voicemail messages.

Before leaving the bedroom, she detoured to the closet to get a light jacket. Stepping into the huge walk-in—it must have been a small bedroom converted to a closet since old houses tended to have tiny closets, if any at all—she flipped on the light and looked around. Something in the back caught her eye, surprising her. Getting closer, she spotted a pair of fuck-me stilettos tucked into a corner. They were almost hidden from view, but Mel had expensive-shoe radar and her eyes homed right in on them. Her breath hitched when she saw the red soles. Whoa. Five hundred at the very least, she thought, recognizing the signature of the designer.

As she left, she chewed it over. The shoes were unlike anything Jane had ever worn—very much out of character. Maybe they weren't even Jane's? One thing Mel knew for sure: regardless of whose they were, Mel wanted to borrow them, and since possession was nine-tenths of the law, she figured Jane would be the one to loan them out. Score. Before exiting the closet, she'd checked the size: 37. What was that in US sizes? A 7, if memory served her correctly. Mel wore a US 8 so generally a 39 in European size. But what's a little pain along with a few bloody blisters for the privilege of wearing such beautiful shoes?

As her gaze passed the wall clock at the head of the stairs, her breath hitched. "Shit, it's late." She sprinted downstairs to lock up the house. Getting in her borrowed VW, she steered the car toward the hospital.

The past few days at work had been so hectic that Mel hadn't been able to visit Jane for almost a week so when she waltzed into the hospital room, she got a surprise when she saw her friend.

"Good God, Jane, I know you've just been through the mill, but I have to say, you look just, like, fantastic. Damn, girl, you must have lost twenty-plus pounds since your accident."

"Uh… thanks?" Jane laughed. "Probably there are easier ways to diet? But yeah, I feel much better today."

Mel couldn't drag her eyes off Jane, suddenly seeing her in a brand-new light. It took Mel aback. She'd always thought Jane had a pretty face but it was a little hard to see past the outer defenses that Jane had so carefully erected. She'd always dressed in a way that would keep her from being noticed, a leftover habit—no, a honed skill—from her days of being the fat, smart girl in high school, desperate not to attract attention for it was always of the negative variety... Jane had told her a few stories about her teenage years over a couple of glasses of wine. Mel had been slowly building up Jane's tolerance to alcohol.

Lately, though, Jane's style of dress had begun to change—a little bit, anyway. In the days before her accident, Jane had started to wear dresses that showed a peek of cleavage and maybe a hint of thigh, and even once or twice had styled her hair. Mel had also noticed Jane lately wearing a smidgen of makeup—nothing drastic, just lip-gloss and mascara.

Now, though, Mel was gaping at her with new eyes. Jane had a beautiful face and it was enhanced by the dramatic weight loss. Once the bandage came off her nose and her bruising cleared up completely... with the right clothes and makeup, and a cool new haircut, Jane would be a total babe. Did she even recognize that about herself?

It was curious that Mel had never seen it before. Was it just the weight loss or were there more differences? She forced it out of her mind for now and focused on their conversation. "Any new memories to report?"

Jane tried to shake her head, again impeded by the neck brace. "No, not really. Dr. Lavelle advised me to get a journal and write in it every day. He said sometimes that helps trigger memory recall and even if not, he said it's a helpful exercise in emotional recovery. So... yeah, I guess I will."

She looked up at her friend and smirked. "I'm going to be so bored, stuck at home until my injuries heal a little more and I can go back to work. Might as well pick up a new pastime."

"There's always Netflix and you can load up your e-reader with bestsellers. You have to look at it like an extended vacay."

On the heels of that comment, a middle-aged nurse sailed into the room, smiling. "Well, Miss Jane, it looks like it's goodbye forever. Are you going to miss me?"

Beaming at the petite nurse, Jane went to give her a hug. "Of course, I'll miss you, Tina... but I'll especially miss those delicious meals your chefs whipped up and brought me three times a day. Going home is going to mess with my weight-loss plan."

The nurse guffawed. "Who wouldn't miss limp green beans and lime Jell-O, right?"

"Right, limp and strangely yellow green beans."

"Wouldn't that make them yellow beans then?" Mel winked at the nurse.

"I guess I should wish you happy eating, Jane. Now you take care of yourself. Listen to your friend here and stock up on movies and books. Relax, put your feet up, and enjoy the downtime."

"I suppose. I'm still going to be bored though. It's not as if I can sit on the beach."

Mel snorted. "This is true... though I suppose you can go to a beach resort to recuperate. I mean, what's stopping you, right?"

"Hmm. I guess."

"Well, c'mon, let's get a move on."

"Yeah," Jane grumbled, "I never want to see another pastel again. Thank you for everything, Tina. Tell everyone else I said goodbye."

"I will, Jane. You take care now." She offered a sweet smile. "You were a model patient."

Mel laughed. "It's strange, though, about the pastels because the lobby is done in this industrial high-end design but when you get to the patient rooms, they look like the usual hospital fare—mauve and gray or blue and yellow vomited all over the rooms."

Jane shrugged, lowering herself into the wheelchair, and Mel steered it in the direction of the door, leaving Tina to remove equipment from the room. When they exited into the hall, another nurse hurried over to push Jane's wheelchair, so Mel walked beside Jane, and as they made their way down the antiseptic halls, Mel chatted.

"So why did you never tell me about the smoking-hot dude who lives next door to you?" she wagged her finger. "You've been holding out on me, chica."

"Really?" Jane perked up, turning her head slightly, her entire range of movement. "Either I didn't know or I totally don't remember. Probably the latter."

"I think you've never met him because he would be massively hard to forget—even with amnesia. His name is Mason Caldwell. Ring any bells?" She bent around to look at Jane's face and had to lean in to hear her soft-spoken response.

"Hmm." Jane's eyes lost focus. "No, but that name is sooo familiar. I must know him, right?" She bowed her head down and gently rubbed her temples. "Why can't I remember?"

"I know, maybe you and he began a clandestine affair right under his hated and dreadful wife's nose?"

"He's married?"

"Yep," Mel said, her face contorting. "Life is so unfair, right?"

"Oh wait, wait, wait. I know why it sounds familiar. I went to school with someone named Mason Caldwell."

"Really? Did you grow up in Riverdale?"

Jane shook her head. "No. Why?"

"Isn't that weird?" At Jane's questioning tone, she replied. "You buy a house and then your new next-door neighbor is someone you went to school with? Big coincidence, don't you think?"

She screwed her lips to one side. "I suppose… it's not *that* far, though. From Pleasantville."

Mel shrugged. "Hmm. I think he said he moved in a few weeks after you."

"I don't remember any of that… but… I think I do remember now that he was very popular back in middle and high school. If memory serves, I had a major crush going on for him."

"Well," Mel said, smirking, "don't even look at him now. He's fucking devastating. But married, of course. Some be-otch got to him before either one of us, Jane. Them's the breaks."

Jane gave her a crooked grin. "Pfft, nothing new there."

Chapter 10

"Cate?"

Cate Caldwell heard her husband calling up to her but couldn't make out more than her name. His natural voice was in such a deep register that from any remove it was hard to untangle his words into coherence. She'd been upstairs getting her laundry together so Sahara could do a few loads while they were out. She sang out, "Coming."

Now her husband's voice became louder and with evident irritation as he moved farther into the house and yelled up the stairs. The man had absolutely no patience and never had. "You are aware that attorneys charge by the hour, Mrs. Caldwell? We're supposed to be there in twenty minutes. Get your perfect little ass down here."

Cate rolled her eyes—silver-shadowed and accented with black liner. For God's sake, they had plenty of time. Shaking her head, she nonetheless rushed to finish loading all of her things into the basket. She'd asked Sahara to do their wash separately—even the dog's—because Mason liked to throw his gym clothes into the hamper when they were still damp with sweat and everything reeked accordingly. She wrinkled her nose just thinking about how rank it could get—she'd rather share a laundry hamper with Harper. Once she had the three baskets ready for laundering, she stepped lively to the front of the house, grabbing her keys and handbag from the foyer table on the way out.

~

MASON WAS WAITING IN FRONT, sitting in the retooled Porsche that he adored so much. As his wife advanced toward him, he noticed one of his male neighbors checking her out. He tried to decide if he was jealous. A year ago, he would have been, no doubt about it. Now, he wasn't sure.

When she reached him and saw the car, he grinned sheepishly. "Hop in. Weston is waiting on us to go over the paperwork."

"Is Jake meeting us there?" she asked as she folded her tall frame into the sports car.

His fingers tapped on the steering wheel, his knee bouncing in time under the dash as he waited for her to close the door and strap in. "He's supposed to, yeah. He had an earlier appointment and was planning on coming straight from there." His eyes swept over her, head to foot. "You look good. Are you going into the office today?"

She shrugged. "I thought I might, for a few hours."

He shifted the stick into first, easing off the clutch as the car leapt forward like a graceful panther. "When you signed on with them, you promised them two to three days a week. You've been doing four or five lately. Are you going full-time?"

"Eh, I'm considering it. I can't make a living out of showing or breeding, now can I?"

"Definitely not breeding," he griped, flashing her a dirty look. "What about when we sell the company?"

"I'm not sure yet, Mason. I'm trying to find my niche."

He grunted. "I'm just glad you convinced Jake to split me in as a full partner. I'm still not sure how you pulled that one off."

Cate reached over to pat her husband's cheek, her chunky diamond ring flashing fire in the sunlight. "Jake loves you, Mason, always has. I'm sure that's his motivation."

Mason looked straight ahead. "Yeah. Not sure I deserve it. He's always been a lot kinder than I am. And yet," he turned to her with a smug grin to add, "I'm not going to turn down the offer to become a full partner."

"Well," Cate said as she examined her manicure, "as you well know, it wasn't exactly Jake's idea to do that."

"But still..." His handsome face clouded momentarily. "When he finds out we're going to sell, he'll fucking hate us, Cate. That company is his baby."

"Yes," she said, smoothing her golden blond hair, the platinum highlights competing with her diamond ring for shimmer. The wind blowing in from Mason's open window was mussing up her 'do. Not that he gave a damn. "I know. But the way I see it, if not for my generous cash infusion, he'd never have been able to get it off the ground. Could you close your window, please?" She paused, looking at him expectantly.

Annoyed, he flashed her a look but grudgingly put the window up.

"As I was saying," she continued, still messing with her damn hair, "in addition to my cash contribution, without all the work you've done, all the value you've added with your schmoozing and your networking, it wouldn't be worth as much today. He's already turned down two incredibly attractive offers from bigger companies. I refuse to allow him to turn down another. I want the damn money."

Cate was unequivocal about it and once the girl made her mind up… Mason knew it was pretty much a done deal, a *fait accompli* as Cate would say in that irritating way of hers. "Well, when I'm a partner, it'll be two against one.

"Yes. Just don't let him find out before the transfer goes through, please. Today is just to go over details. I tried to get Ron to join us—"

"Ron?" he interrupted. "Our accountant?"

Cate's eyes drifted up as she blew out her breath. "Do we know any other Ron? I thought it would be good to have him there to advise us on the tax benefits of cutting in another partner—whether we should incorporate or do a limited liability or whatever."

She shrugged. "Anyway, he couldn't make it. It's not impossible we'll be able to get Jake on board for real, you know. After all, he can wind up much better off without the company. He's holding a lot of debt."

"True."

She reached over and grabbed his arm. "Let me do the talking, Mason."

He briefly glanced down to where she touched him and admired the way her golden hand with red-lacquered nails looked against the silvery tones of his suit jacket.

Running her finger down his cheek, she continued her favorite pursuit of patronizing him. "You just look pretty and keep your mouth shut as much as possible. If Jake feels manipulated into this by us—especially by you—he's liable to bail on us."

Mason shot a sidelong glance at his model-beautiful wife. She looked so much more attractive when she wasn't brimming with snark. Lately that was never. "You know, if you always try to take all the credit, you also get all the blame, apple cheeks."

"Don't call me that—my face is not chubby. And what the hell does that remark mean, Mason?" she snapped. "For God's sake, you're so damn thin-skinned."

He returned his focus to the road ahead. "Whatever. I wasn't referring to those cheeks, by the way. If it makes you feel better, my lips are sealed. I'll let the perfect Cate Caldwell, née Cobb do all the talking. You probably only married me to keep the alliterative C in your last name," he muttered.

"Wow." She clapped her hands. "Big word. Bravo. Look, Mason, don't worry about it. Jake will be fine with everything. Just leave it to me."

"Shut up already," he said without rancor. "I'm not worried. I'm pretty certain that once Jake has all that money in hand, he'll be all good about it. Lately, he's been talking about doing other things. Maybe he's splitting me in because he wants out, wants to sell. Maybe this is his passive way to manipulate that outcome, so he could forge ahead with his other pursuits."

"Yeah? Like what?" Cate prodded with piqued interest.

He shook his head, smiling. "He's on this kick… wants to sail a catamaran around for a while, see some new places. We went to sailing camp when we were kids. Jake stuck with it… but you probably know that.

"He's also been writing music again. He sold a song last month—did I mention that?"

"No, you didn't," Cate carped. "You never remember to tell me anything, Mason. To whom and for how much?"

"He sold it to a producer for a new artist to record. I don't know how much he got, but I think it was respectable, judging by his reaction. He was seriously buzzed about it."

She leaned forward. "Why didn't you ask?"

"Because it's none of my business—or yours." His face twisted into a frown, Mason looked down his nose at her—she was as gossipy and nosy as those TV housewives, for God's sake.

Relaxing back into the seat, Cate jerked down the visor mirror and checked her lipstick. "Well, well. Maybe Jake can blaze a new career path with songwriting. That would be great for him, wouldn't it?"

"Yes, it would." He met her gaze briefly before flicking back to the road. "Having buyer's remorse?"

Cate just rolled her eyes again—those crackle-glass-blue eyes that he found unnerving when they were trained on him.

He'd purposely kept his tone light, but that he'd even say such a thing probably alerted her to the fact that he was still bothered by their history more than he ever let on. This, despite knowing that she and Jake had barely dated and were never serious—Jake was just as happy to move on as Cate was when he introduced her to his cousin. But still… his cousin knew Mason's wife a little too well for comfort.

"Of course not, Mason. It's not always about you. And for heaven's sake, get rid of that garish tie," she sniped. "I don't want to catch you wearing it again. It's tasteless."

Mason shook his head, shifting into third as he picked up speed after the red light. He loved this Porsche and the way it handled. Even better, it had no long blond dog hair in it. Not a single strand. "Whatever," he said dismissively. But what he was thinking was entirely different.

Someday Cate might just have to answer for being such a twat.

Chapter 11

—Jane's Journal, mid-September

WHO AM I?

I write the question in big black letters with a Sharpie because really it is the burning question in my life at the moment.

Picture this: you wake up in a hospital bed, and you have no clue who the hell you are or how you got there.

No. Effing. Clue.

The last thing you remember is finishing ninth grade… and you're twenty-five.

You need to look in a mirror just to remind yourself what you look like. Those few details are the extent of your self-knowledge as an adult.

Scary, right?

That is exactly what happened to me.

A bad car accident stole my recent past, leaving me with memories from long ago but erasing my current life. Through some divine or cosmic providence (I don't even know if I believe in God or not), I still have my future, but the landscape is radically altered—unless or until I get my memories back.

OK, so I know my name, but I don't know who I am, what I believe in, what kind of person I am, what I like or don't like. I'm a clean slate. It makes daily life challenging. Intriguing but challenging. And lonely.

Speaking of which, it stretches out in front of me unendingly: an open road, a blank canvas with a charcoal pencil in my hand. It's time, I suppose, to start. I can't wait on life, hoping to get my memory back, because it may never happen, not fully. Instead, I have to reinvent myself in the literal sense, not in the annoying self-improvement way. So… my doctor told me to start this journal. He said it might help jar my memory and if not, it will help me organize my thoughts, perhaps even prove cathartic.

Maybe.

By writing things down, you sort of have to commit to them. They go from an idea floating through your head to a black-and-white plan. Today I decided that I have to start trying on new identities, maybe using people around me as inspiration. Or I could watch TV for ideas. I could be a domestic goddess or a DIYer. Or maybe a brilliant hacker with a conscience. Or even a criminal, like maybe a Robinhood type who steals from the rich to give to the poor—it would have to be a good criminal, I think. Or an activist who fights for the voiceless, like children and animals or maybe immigrants or something. Or a corporate cog in the wheel, my only driving ambition to make tons of money and not care whose backs I have to step on to get there.

Maybe it will be like trying on shoes. Some look just so beautiful on the shelf: sexy, expensive stiletto heels from, say, Manolo Blahnik, or platform designer shoes like

Louboutin or Jimmy Choo but when you slip your foot into that kind of shoe, they maybe don't look as good. Today, trying on the shoes in my closet, I felt like a little girl playing dress-up with her mother's shoes. Which I used to do. I only stopped when I began to detest my mother.

That I remember.

The expensive stilettos in my closet threw me. Could they be mine? They didn't fit with all the other shoes, like a pattern test for kids: which one of these is different from the rest? Definitely those. But when I tried them on, just as the glass slipper on pretty little Cinderella's foot, they fit perfectly. In fact, I paraded around the room in my underwear and the heels, getting a serious charge out of it until my ribs and back started throbbing. High heels maybe aren't so good for the body, especially one that has been bent and broken by hellacious G-forces.

But then again: if the shoes fit, put them the hell on.

Now imagine trying to find a personality that fits comfortably. It's not easy. I have to keep doing it, though, until I find the right one—the glass slipper of personalities.

It's not all bad though. Little by little, I'm getting files back in my catalog of memories. It's like gathering bits of moss, putting them away until you have a respectable amount in your basket. I have people in my life to help me, tell me things. Sometimes it's all about good facts that make me happy. Like the fact that I'm twenty-five years old—I like the age: not too young and not too old. Even better, last year my salary made it into the mid-six-figure range. Not too shabby for a person just two and a half years out of grad school.

It's scary too. Like when Mel mentioned last week that I'm basically alone in the world. Only child, parents far away. Not many friends. I wasn't popular as a kid—I totally remember that. The gods of teen misery spent a lot of time messing with me.

I piled on the pounds in middle school, gaining over twenty pounds in seventh grade. I wasn't morbidly obese, just always a little too plump.

Luckily, I did have good skin and hair but I wasn't creative when it came to fashion so I fell back on drab and nondescript—anything that would avoid attracting attention to me. Becoming a spectacle was the thing that most petrified me in school, so I kept my head down and my nose in my books. Consequently, I earned good grades, another thing that screamed "Behold an outcast!" to the top echelon of school culture. Eventually, though, I just became part of the classroom fixtures, like desks or blackboards or beakers in the chem lab. Just walk on by.

All of this past information is nice to have, but it still doesn't answer the question of who I really am. Now. The light-brown-haired, hazel-eyed woman in the mirror is a virtual stranger. I could be anyone.

The task I set myself for this week was to go through my closet. I started on Tuesday when Mel went to work—slowly and carefully. I've been in pretty much constant pain. Dr. Lavelle told me to go easy on the oxycodone, but I've been swallowing two pills every six hours because ibuprofen is not enough. But I wanted to go through my closet for two reasons: first, because I wanted to organize it. I realized it makes me uncomfortable when things are in serious disarray.

The second reason is because I thought unpacking clothes might help to unpack some lost memories, since seeing the articles of clothing might provide the jolt I need and help me get back some of the time that I've lost. Memories attach to things: clothes, songs, and maybe most of all, smells. If I can recover more memory by using those triggers, it can only help.

Unpacking, I discovered, was not doable just yet, but I was able to check out some of the clothes I have. They're all different sizes, which is weird, but I'm not healed enough yet to try them all on. Apparently, I've lost a lot of weight since the car accident.

I do know what I want in the short term. I want to be beautiful, thin, rich, and happy. That's all. Wink-wink.

I guess I want to be a good person too. No one strives to be a bad person… right? That would be a sad ambition for anyone to have.

But maybe I'm not good. Maybe life has been shitting on me long enough to turn me into a bitter, resentful wretch. Who knows?

I don't.

Here are the things that I know for certain:

My name is Jane Jensen, and I just bought my own home in Riverdale, New York. It's a semi-attached English mews-style house, circa 1927. I work at MT Systems in Midtown Manhattan, where I am the IT specialist, and MT pays me generously for the work I do.

My parents live in Sedona, Arizona, and I'm pretty sure we're all happy about the many miles between us. I was always a disappointment to them: I wasn't a beauty like my mother or an athlete like my father.

To my mother's everlasting disappointment, I had zero interest in clothes or makeup or anything remotely girly when I was a kid.

I could still hear her voice: "*You know, Jane, I was fussy about what I was wearing even before I could string a sentence together.*"

As if that was supposed to impress the ten-year-old me

who gave less than a shit about what I was wearing as long as it didn't smell bad and didn't look stupid.

I'd roll my eyes and snap at her. "*Just how old were you when you could string a sentence together, Mom? Fifteen?*" If my mother was contemptuous of my lack of femininity, I was equally so about her dearth of intellectual vigor.

I was an equal opportunity disappointer—I also remember seeing disappointment darken my father's eyes when he'd come to watch me play soccer or basketball, and I'd just totally suck at it. The teams would fight over who had to take me, nobody wanting the liability of Jane Jensen who was shit at all sports. Those early days of primary school sports were the beginning of my childhood humiliations. I wish I would forget those, but of course they are the ones I easily remember in vivid and vibrant detail. Naturally.

My father is nuts too. One night at dinner I listened to him tell his younger sister's fiancé, "*There are two things you should know about this family. First, we're all screamers. Second, we always follow the path of least resistance. It may not be the most successful way to live a life but it's how we roll… and now you're going to be one of us.*"

He'd said it so matter-of-factly and with such smug satisfaction that I busted out laughing right at the table. Everyone ignored me—par for the course. The poor guy just stared at my father as if he were insane and nodded feebly. My Aunt Kara smiled lamely, but it was obvious she wanted to slide right under the table. I thought the whole thing was hilarious.

He was actually telling the truth, though: the Jensens were a family of screamers, but unfortunately for me, I was born without the ability. I'm soft-spoken, and loud voices make me leap out of my skin. I did, however, possess the tendency to follow the path of least resistance, and that's just a fancy way of saying loser. Everyone knows that in order to succeed in life a person has to be a risk taker—the bigger the risk, the greater the reward.

Oh, right. Just in case I wasn't lonely enough because of my apparent lack of a personality, I'm an only child. I have the one good friend who also works at MT; her name is Melanie B. but everyone calls her Mel. Not Mel B. Thank God, I have Mel and that I somehow remember her. She's the only one in my adult life that I *do* remember. I know there are others but they're vague and lurking like shadows in the cobwebby gaps of my brain. When I try too hard to remember, I earn myself a blinding headache.

So anyway… three weeks ago the accident happened while I was driving back from upstate. No idea why I was there. My car was totaled. The other vehicle was pulverized and the driver, a 49-year-old man, was killed instantly. I sustained a traumatic brain injury and have recovered only about sixty-five percent of my long-term memory. My short-term memory picked up almost four days afterward when I woke up. The time in between is gone, likely forever. It feels weird.

I feel immensely awful that the man died. No one will tell me anything about him; they say it's not good for my recovery to dwell in guilt. I gathered up the courage to look up the accident: the article stated he died from multiple traumatic injuries. That could mean pretty much anything. I hope it was quick for him, I really do. The police say the accident was not my fault… that another car cut me off badly. The person who reported the accident was also an eyewitness to the collision, I believe. I guess I was lucky to have that man—or maybe woman—there. Really lucky.

Dr. Lavelle told me to start a journal—so earlier today I went to a stationery store and stood on a line that seemed to never move in order to buy this overpriced little brown leather-bound book with blank pages that—hopefully—I'm going to fill. My ribs were killing me for the effort and when I came home I swallowed two more oxys.

I started by studying myself in the mirror as I chewed my cheek in earnest. Reaching for the pen and paper, I begin describing myself:

Twenty-five. Five feet eight. Straight light-brown hair. Hazel eyes. Balanced features. Straight, even teeth—I wore braces for five years. Weight is now 138. Mel tells me I've lost at least thirty pounds—maybe even more. I was a porker, I guess.

Just like in high school. And middle school.

The accident helped me to lose weight. Maybe it was worth all the pain… but not the man's death. Nothing would be worth that.

My parents never came to visit me. They called twice but I was in a coma the first time and asleep the next. My mother was going to come to New York when she first learned about the accident, but when she realized Mel was here with me, she opted to skip it. A candidate for *Mother of the Year* she is not. My parents never want to leave the Southwest anymore.

Not even to visit their only child.

Who almost died in a car crash.

Whatever.

JANE BOLTED UPRIGHT IN BED, her heart slamming against her ribcage. The glowing green numbers on the clock said 3:18 a.m. Reaching for the glass of water she kept on her nightstand, she gulped down half of it. God.

Weird, almost menacing, flashbacks came flying at her like tornado debris. Jane wasn't sure if it was dream or memory. Probably memory. The recall was almost violent. She was sleeping, and it just came at her like an out-of-control film reel, confusing images bombarding her brain, one after the other, and now she was sitting in the dark, trying to untangle them into sense. There was this blond girl, around fifteen. Kind of scary looking—she had a leering face and big teeth—horse teeth… and she was sneering. Malevolent even. Jane didn't know who she was, but her face looked vaguely familiar. And Jane knew she hated this girl but didn't know why.

There was an ambulance and a police car maybe—lights were flashing. Her car accident?

Right on top of that, she got an image of sitting at a table, across from someone, writing. Homework with a friend maybe? And then having a shouting match with her parents. The raised voices sounded like they were underwater—Jane couldn't make out the actual words, just the strident tones. She started hoping the memories—if they were actual memories—were from her sophomore year of high school because that would mean that her memories were starting to come back chronologically.

It remained to be seen.

TODAY WAS SATURDAY, and Mel was planning a shopping day to buy Jane clothes that fit. She'd spent the night and they were making coffee in Jane's sunny kitchen.

"I had a kind of erotic dream last night."

Mel's eyes flew wide open. "Really? Tell me about it."

"There was a man—"

"There usually is in a wet dream, Jane," Mel interrupted. "Tell me something I don't know."

"I couldn't see his face… but he had a beautiful body, just, like, shredded, you know?"

"No, I don't know at all. Describe it in minute detail."

Jane laughed. "It was actually more sad than sexy. The dream. I felt l-like… I loved him… and when I woke up, I was depressed."

"Maybe someone you know?"

"Maybe. But… if I'd been dating someone, wouldn't I have at least mentioned it to you?"

"Not necessarily. You're one of those close-mouthed types who drive girls like me crazy."

Giving a small laugh, Jane quickly changed the subject. "I wonder if I've ever worn a bikini?"

Mel stood there tapping her foot while waiting for the coffee to brew. "I don't know, but you could if you want to. You've got the bod."

Jane smiled. It felt totally weird to hear someone say that to her. Last year this time, she must have been pretty heavy because most of her wardrobe consisted of brown baggy clothes, size 14, a few were even 16—baggy to cover the extra weight, she was assuming, the brown so as not to attract attention.

This morning she weighed 136 and could fit into a size-6 pair of jeans that Mel bought her. She did a little happy dance, and the thought occurred to her that maybe she should take some kind of dancing lessons. It felt strange to look in the mirror and actually like what she saw. There was now visible proof that her hipbones did in fact exist.

Do beautiful people enjoy looking in the mirror, or do they see flaws that others don't readily notice? Jane wasn't sure, but lately she'd taken to stealing glimpses in the mirror quite a lot. She liked to look at her new self though she still felt a sense of dread when approaching a mirror. Whether it was totally because she used to be fat and unattractive or it was residual fear from the accident and how it scarred her, she wasn't certain. That first time looking in a mirror in the hospital was pretty terrifying. Even without memory, she could recognize that looking at the mirror now and not hating herself was a novel experience for her.

Her hair had grown just past her chin now. Mel told her that she always wore it very short but reminded her that her hair grew very fast. It was bizarre when someone else knew more about her than she did.

Yesterday evening she went with Mel to her salon in the city to have her hair styled. As soon as Annabelle got Jane in the chair, she told her she was not cutting any length.

Jane had eyed the stylist skeptically. The woman was extreme Goth, and she was going to take style advice from her? She glanced at Mel, and her friend vigorously nodded her agreement. Two against one.

"The longer length softens the angles of your face. You're lucky to have high cheekbones and a pronounced jaw but we want to soften them just a tad. I want you to grow it much longer, and then I'll cut in some long layers. For now, I'll just trim it and add some soft bangs."

Mel was standing there, arms crossed and grinning in agreement. Her hairstylist, Gregory, was flitting about, exclaiming over Mel's marvelous cut—even though he himself did it. When Annabelle was finished with Jane's hair, Gregory started gushing over what a great job the stylist did on it.

"Honey," he said, bending down to examine Jane's face from various angles, turning it to the left and right, "I might have to do your makeup next time you come in for a cut. You have the most expressive eyes."

She smiled, enjoying the attention and wondering if this was how pretty girls felt all the time? She missed out on this kind of girl fun growing up.

"Doesn't she look beautiful?" Mel asked him.

"Yeah, especially with the gigantic white bandage stretching across my nose," Jane added dryly. "The latest in accessories."

Mel shook her head. "Jane, it's completely unnoticeable. Cross my heart. It's just that you know that it's there…"

Jane stuck out her tongue at her. "You're just a laugh-riot."

Thank God for Mel for keeping her company and also keeping her laughing. Jane didn't know what she'd do without her. She did have things in her life to be grateful for… starting with Mel.

And… next week she would finally get the bandage off and would be able to see her brand-new nose, courtesy of Dr. Philip Crenshaw, plastic surgeon extraordinaire.

Crenshaw was found and paid for by Stephen Renault, the CEO of her company. It was really nice to be appreciated… even if it's just because she saved and made the corporation tons of money. Every day she wondered what her new nose would look like. Her old one was all right but it had a slight bump just under the bridge—easily seen in all her old photos. Dr. Crenshaw was grinning when he took off the larger bandage and peeked underneath, promising Jane that she would love the results of his work. He said she'd look like Michelle Pfeiffer. Jane didn't know who that was, but she figured that the surgeon thought she was beautiful.

Her life had taken a very strange turn.

The other day she remembered that she loved animals when she stopped to say hello to an adorable little dog. She remembered that she wanted one when she was young. Desperately. Or even a cat. She'd have settled for a freaking hamster. Her parents would never let her have a pet. No siblings. No pets. Just a lonely little girl who disappointed everyone.

Maybe she'd get one now—her own dog or cat in her own house.

She mentioned to Mel that if she loved animals, then she must be a good person. Mel reminded her that Hitler loved his German shepherds.

"That's not helpful," she'd retorted.

Mel had been staying with her. She brought her work clothes and came back every night. She went home on weekends usually. Jane loved having her around. If she'd had a friend like Mel as a kid, her life would have been different. Way better.

She didn't though. Jane's friends were fellow misfits and would have made for memorable literary characters.

Here was the epiphany for today: despite everything that was going on, she realized that she was sort of happy. Happy and appreciative of nice people in the world, especially all of those who'd helped her put her life back together. Someday she'd pay it forward. The only thing that would make her life even better would be to find someone to share it with. A man. Jane was lonely and felt like something important was missing.

Getting her memories back would help her peace of mind, though. She wanted to go back to the life she had before the accident. She wanted to pick up that life where it had left off on the dark highway that night. She felt as if she lost a big piece of herself, leaving it like detritus—accident debris—in the darkness where no one could see it.

"Earth to Jane. Where'd you go?" Mel was standing opposite her, arms crossed, and eyeing her intently.

She snapped back to the conversation and gave Mel an apologetic smile. "I'm sorry—what did you say?"

"I asked you when you bought those gorgeous high heels and why didn't you tell me?"

"High heels?"

Mel leaned in close and narrowed her eyes. "Jane. In your closet, you have a pair of Christian Louboutin shoes that look virtually brand new. They are fucking gorgeous, and I want to borrow them more than I want breath."

Chuckling, Jane rolled her eyes—Mel and her shoes. "I honestly don't recall… amnesia, remember?"

Mel wagged her finger. "You've been holding out on me. Sexy lingerie and fuck-me six-hundred-dollar stilettos. I smell a man."

"I wish."

Mel screwed her pursed lips to the side and studied her friend. "Could you possibly forget a lover? I guess you could forget anyone, right?"

"I guess. I hope if there was somebody that either I remember him soon or he gets in touch… but let's face it: if he was a decent guy, he would have shown his face long ago. I mean, he would have to know that I just dropped off the face of the earth and come looking for me." She looked at Mel with earnest eyes. "Right?"

Mel hitched her shoulder. "I suppose so." Shifting her weight to turn to check on the coffee's progress, she added, "But you will let me borrow the shoes. Right?"

Chapter 12

Cate Caldwell was running late. She'd stayed at the office much longer than she'd planned, and now she was hauling ass to get to the dry cleaner before it closed. Mason needed his navy suit for tomorrow night's ballet and neither of them would have time to get it tomorrow. Cate would've been home hours ago—but for the late-afternoon shit-show at the office.

Cate had never planned on straying from her marriage but these things sometimes happened organically. The thing was… for Cate, it was just another fun fling—one that was turning out to be anything but. If she'd known what a whiny bitch Jared was going to become, she'd never have gotten anywhere near him. Cate had no intention whatsoever of leaving Mason, so Jared had to get over himself and soon. It was just a one-and-done kind of thing. A one-night stand that overstayed its welcome. That was it as far as Cate was concerned, but Jared was proving clingy.

Now she was scrambling to get the suit from the cleaners in time, cranky from eating all that refined donut sugar and anxious to get home. The only bright part of today was getting to wear her new Prada pumps, and she had a hard time keeping her eyes off the shoes—they might be her favorite pair of all. Cate knew the value of good shoes, the way they empowered her. She supposed it was like that for all women—which was why women loved new shoes so much. That and a good new haircut can make the world a shinier place. Note to self: make a hair appointment with Andre next week. Her eyes dropped down to watch her feet as she moved through the lot.

Her pretty pumps were the last thing she ever saw.

THE CALDWELL homicide investigation was assigned to Detectives Fitzgibbons and Kelvin of the 50th Precinct. The swing shift was always the busiest for crime and anything else, for that matter. Although Riverdale generally enjoyed a comparatively low crime rate and Fieldston, the neighborhood where Cate Caldwell lived, had almost none, it was still part of the Bronx, for one thing, and whatever criminal element did operate near the fringes of the precinct boundaries were hard at work during late afternoon into the evening.

It was a few minutes after seven when they arrived. Two squad cars had arrived first and secured the scene. Onlookers and witnesses were gathered around the yellow tape that the officers had erected in a trapezoid figure around the immediate crime scene. The officers on scene would need to keep it secured until the ME and photographer arrived to record the scene and the ballistics expert would then determine the likely trajectory of the bullet. Fitzgibbons and his partner would get the CCTV footage for the parking lot to sift through the cars and plate numbers in the vicinity and maybe get lucky. But he doubted it would be that easy. Ducking under the tape as the officer lifted it for him, he walked over to the shooting victim to take a closer look. With his gloved hand he gingerly lifted the edge of the coat that someone had used to drape over the body, took stock of the surroundings, and read the notes scribbled by the first responding officer, and it was immediately apparent to him that the homicide was likely a paid hit. It was efficient and detached—there was no passion involved here.

He looked up as his partner approached. "Looks impersonal," he told her.

She nodded and her eyes darted around, taking in the surrounding area. "I'm thinking the killer was probably standing over by those trees." She pointed to her left. "With dusk falling early, he wouldn't be all that noticeable."

Fitzgibbons shook his head and rose, tried to suck in air through his congested nose. "Nah, he stayed in his car, I'm betting. Why take the chance of being on foot? In a crowded parking lot at rush hour who's gonna notice a man—or woman—sitting in a car with the window open?" Looking around, he spotted the patrolman standing guard over the scene and crooked his fingers. The young cop broke into action, rushing over to the two detectives.

"Give me a quick rundown, Officer…" he tilted his head to look at the man's name tag. "…Mendoza."

"Sir, the first call came in at 6:40 p.m. through 911. I have the names and contact info of four witnesses."

"Did they witness the actual shooting?"

"They all said they saw the woman fall and ran over to assist her. It wasn't until they got close that they saw she was gone. Six subsequent calls came in to 911 in less than a minute. One man," he paused to gesture over to his squad car before continuing, "heard a shot but didn't see where it came from."

"So we're assuming only one shot was fired?"

The officer's face flushed. "At this preliminary juncture we don't have enough information or corroborating evidence. We're waiting on forensics."

Fitzgibbons nodded. "Thank you. How soon after the shooting was the scene secured? Did anyone touch her?"

"They claim no. Well, except for a Mr. Johnson…" He checked his notes. "…no, I'm sorry, Jansen, Richard Jansen, said he crouched down next to the victim to assist her but immediately saw she was gone. He touched her wrist only to check for a pulse and realized she was beyond help. He's waiting over there," he said and pointed to a lanky and tired looking man, late 30s, waiting by the crime-scene tape. Fitzgibbons eyed him briefly. "The other people never got as close to the victim," the officer finished.

"And what time did officers arrive on scene?" he prodded.

"My partner and I arrived on scene at 6:51, sir. We immediately set about securing it."

"Do we have an ID?"

His hands gloved, Officer Mendoza handed Detective Kelvin some latex gloves followed by the victim's wallet. She took it by the very edge and flipped through it quickly, stopping on the driver's license. She checked the photo and then, bending down low, she looked at the victim's face. "Catherine Caldwell of Kipling Road, Riverdale."

"Has the medical examiner's office been contacted?"

"Yes, ma'am. Someone's on the way."

"Good." She looked at Fitzgibbons. "I guess we need to notify next of kin." She wagged the wallet held so gingerly. "Let's start with this address."

"You go. I'll wait for the ME."

Chapter 13

A car honked, long and loud, as if someone was leaning on the damn thing.

Jane heard it at the same time her doorbell rang so she grabbed her ballet flats and headed downstairs, bare feet slapping against the ebony-stained hardwood as the bell chimed again. The night before, Mel had gone back to her apartment to run errands but promised to return around late morning since she had the day off. Jane couldn't move too fast, though she felt her energy increasing now that she was healing and dragging around less body weight.

"Hold on, you, I'm coming." She pulled open the heavy front door, sure that behind it was an impatient Mel, tapping her toe and checking the time on her phone. It wasn't Mel, though.

Standing outside her door were a tall broad-shouldered man, early thirties, and a shorter wiry female with dark skin and of similar age. Jane thought they were strangers, but she couldn't be certain since her memory was like Swiss cheese. It was a stupidly strange feeling that she didn't even know who she knew.

"Hello. May I help you?" she asked, just as the thought of whether they were on the up-and-up flashed through her mind.

"Are you Jane Jensen?"

"Yes, I am. Why?"

"Ms. Jensen, I'm Detective Rob Fitzgibbons, and this is my partner, Detective Myla Kelvin. We'd like to ask you a few quick questions if we may."

She stood there holding onto the oak door, leaning all her weight on it to keep it from swinging. "Um... OK."

Gently he prodded, "May we come in for a moment? Here... I'll show you my badge."

From the inside pocket of his suit jacket he produced a black wallet and flipped it open. Her eyes darted between the badge and his face, and then she jerked her chin at the woman with them. "What about her?"

Myla Kelvin, a macho Latina woman—or maybe biracial—with a snarly look on her face, rolled her eyes but nonetheless fished out her badge and held it aloft for Jane to read. Nodding, she stepped aside, allowing them entrance into her home. "So... what's this all about?"

"If you can just be patient with us, we'll explain in a bit," Det. Fitzgibbons said as his eyes scanned the surroundings, flickering all around the hallway and living room.

Jane led them into the living room. "Um... sorry, I just moved in recently and have no furniture yet. But there are folding chairs so, uh... please have a seat."

"Thank you," they chimed in unison.

"May I offer you anything?" Jane directed her question to Fitzgibbons—the woman's demeanor put her back up.

"Thank you. Coffee or a glass of water would be great," said Fitzgibbons.

Myla Kelvin piped in. "Same for me, thanks."

Jane nodded. "I'll be right back."

Mel came in as Jane was pouring spring water into the coffee machine's carafe. "What's going on?" she whispered as she sailed into the kitchen. "Why is that hot cop here? They are cops, right?"

Jane rolled her eyes. "One-track Mel, always on the prowl. Yes, they're detectives, and I have no idea why they're here. They showed up five minutes ago and want to ask me questions. I'm making them coffee. You're not on a tight time schedule today, are you?"

Melanie shook her head. "Uh-uh. Not really. I might have to go to Jersey later tonight to have dinner with my dad but that's not until, like, seven. Should I wait in here… or where?"

"No idea." She chewed her lip—certainly didn't want to piss off the friendly neighborhood cops going into her third month in the house. "You know what, just come in with me. They didn't say it was private or anything..."

"Goodie, so I can ogle him at my leisure."

Mel watched as the coffee dripped through the cone, turning into the rich, dark brew that suffused the air with its aroma. She helped Jane carry it in to the two detectives. Together they placed the steaming cups on a card table that served as Jane's makeshift dining table along with the tray bearing milk, sugar, and spoons. Pathetic yet serviceable. Both detectives looked long at Mel, and Jane sputtered an introduction.

"Oh, uh, sorry, th-this is a friend of mine, Melanie Bartholomew. We have plans today, so as soon as we finish here, we'll be going out. She and I."

As Kelvin sipped her coffee, Fitzgibbons eyed Mel, his gaze lingering longer than was polite. After a minute of gawking, he dragged his eyes away from her to look fixedly at Jane.

"We'll be as brief as possible, Ms. Jensen," he said, slicing into her thoughts. "First, I want to ask you if you happen to know your next-door neighbors, the Caldwells?"

Before Jane could censor herself, her head whipped over to look at Melanie, her eyes going wide.

Kelvin lurched up in her chair, her posture stiff. "Why are you looking at your friend? Is there something you need to tell us?"

"Um..." Jane's heart began to thump as if she'd done something wrong, and she started to perspire. She remembered this whole domino effect from school: get embarrassed or nervous; the insecurity causes you to break out in a cold sweat. Cold sweat makes you wet and shiny, and then you start to wonder if you smell bad. Dread of smelling bad leads to an all-out panic attack, and you start to get itchy. Before you know it, you're scratching all over, leaving angry red welt marks on your skin and looking as crazy as a loon. Crippling social anxiety.

"I... um... Melanie asked me if I knew Mason Caldwell. I told her I went to school with someone by that name."

Melanie interjected, "Detectives, I don't know if you're aware of it, but Jane was in a serious auto accident a few weeks ago, and as a result of a TBI, she's suffered significant memory loss."

"No, we didn't know. I'm sorry to hear that," Detective Kelvin replied. "So, in effect, you're telling us that you may know the Caldwells and just not remember them?"

"Exactly that, yes."

"Where did you go to school, Ms. Jensen?"

"In Pleasantville, ironically... where I grew up."

Neither said anything, not even casting her a questioning glance. Jane concluded that either these two detectives were entirely devoid of a shred of personality, or they simply hated her for unknown reasons. Fifty-fifty call.

"It was ironic," she blurted out unasked, "because it wasn't pleasant. For me anyway."

Detective Kelvin consulted her notepad, flipping back a few pages before snapping it shut and giving her partner an inscrutable look. "Yes. Caldwell grew up in Pleasantville so chances are more than good he's the same one you attended school with. Did you know him then?"

"No," she shook her head. "Not really. I mean, I knew *of* him—he was really popular—but I didn't know him personally. We didn't run in the same circles..." her voice petered out. When the detective continued looking at her, as if waiting for more information, she elaborated. "I was the fat, ugly girl and he was the good-looking, popular jock. I had a crush on him—as did every other girl and probably a few boys—but he didn't know I was alive."

If he was surprised, the detective didn't show it. Fitzgibbons had been sipping his hot coffee, watching Jane over his cup the whole time, his face devoid of expression. She could feel his eyes on her, and it made her squirm in her uncomfortable chair. Now he put the coffee cup down and cleared his throat. "I'm sure that's not true, Ms. Jensen," he said in obligatory fashion. His tone said considerably more than his words. "So... is your memory being recovered at all as time goes on?"

"Yes," she said quickly. "When I first woke up, I couldn't remember much beyond ninth grade. Now I have some memories from a couple of years ago, when I first started at my job. And of college. But it's not linear, you know. It's just a memory here and another one there—it doesn't run in chronological order."

"I see." This time he looked over at Kelvin and she

nodded. "How long have you lived at this address?" he continued.

"According to paperwork, I closed on the house in late June but I didn't move in until mid-August. It's why I have no furniture..." she offered him a rueful smile.

"Where did you live before you moved here?"

"I have no recollection of the last ten years or so but I've been told that I had an apartment in White Plains."

He looked up sharply. "You don't remember living in White Plains?"

"No. I have only spotty memories, here and there, of the last ten years."

"Wouldn't you have furniture from your place in White Plains?"

"Ooh, I could answer that," Mel exclaimed, raising her hand like a schoolgirl. "Pick me, pick me."

Now Fitzgibbons smiled—and it seemed genuine, leading Jane to surmise that he just didn't like her. Mel, he did, watching her with interest and amusement. "OK, tell us."

"The furniture she had was all hand-me-down from her mother, and Jane thought it was the color of puke. She donated it all to the Salvation Army and told me she was going to get new furniture."

"Uh-huh. Makes sense. How long ago was your accident, Ms. Jensen?" Kelvin interjected.

"Just about a month ago. September 2nd. A day that will live in infamy." Again, no reaction from the cops. At least Mel grinned at Jane's remark, but Mel was always grinning like a loon. It was one of the reasons Jane loved her so much. She was a happy girl.

Fitzgibbons put his coffee cup down on the card table and reached for a manila folder he'd placed on the floor adjacent to his feet. Removing an 8x10 glossy, he handed it to Jane. "Do either of these people seem at all familiar to you?"

Jane stared intently at the photo, her expression blank. When she looked up, she shook her head and offered him a slight smile. "No, I'm sorry but I'm getting nothing. Is this couple the Caldwells?"

"Yes. So you don't recognize either one?"

"Not really, no. I mean, he looks different from when I knew him—which was almost ten years ago so…"

"All right then. Ms. Jensen, I'd appreciate it—*we'd* appreciate it—very much if you'd call us if you regain any memories that could possibly pertain to the Caldwells. Oh… before we go: have you seen either of them lately?"

"I didn't even know what they look like," Jane admitted. "I might have seen them when I first moved in, but I honestly don't remember. As far as I can recall, I haven't seen Mason since high school."

"Actually, they moved in right after you, I believe. At the end of August… so just a few weeks ago. And," Kelvin again consulted her notepad, flipping pages and Jane wondered why they didn't have an electronic device. "… you moved in almost two months ago. So about three weeks prior to them."

"Hmmm. Maybe if I see them, I'll remember something. What's going on? Can you tell me now?"

Detective Fitzgibbons lifted his pale green eyes to hers, looking at Jane directly. She felt as if she had his full and undivided attention, and it agitated her for some reason. "Mrs. Caldwell was shot to death last night."

Mel and Jane both audibly gasped, clapping their hands over their mouths. They looked at each other in shock, and Mel pulled her hand off her mouth to say, "When I came to get Jane's clothes for her to wear home from the hospital, I saw the woman's husband. Later when

I looked out the window, I saw him again, this time with who I assumed were his wife and dog.

Fitzgibbons consulted his notepad now. "Afghan hound. Yeah."

"Where's the dog? Is it safe?" Jane quickly asked.

The detective just looked at her with flat eyes without responding until Jane asked again. Looking reluctant to answer her, he finally conceded. "Yeah. Her mother came and got the dog not long after the incident." His eyes shifted to Mel. "When was that, by the way? That you saw them with the dog?"

"Last week. Wednesday, I guess."

Jane turned to her friend. "No, Mel, it was Tuesday. You came and got me on Tuesday."

"Right. Tuesday."

Jane interjected again. "Was it a random crime?"

Fitzgibbons shook his head. "We're in the preliminary stages of our investigation so nothing is ruled out. Of course, we look at everyone until we can rule each one out."

Jane cleared her throat. "Yes, but it's true that generally in any murder investigation the spouse is among the top suspects. Right?"

Neither detective replied to the comment.

"Fuck. Poor mofo." Mel stood up to take the empty coffee cups into the kitchen.

"Mel," Jane chided.

Melanie rolled her eyes.

The detectives also stood. "Why do you say that?" Kelvin asked Mel, sniffling as if she had to blow her nose. "Like you feel sorry for him? He may have hired someone to murder his wife."

"No, I meant, poor guy if he's innocent, of course. I

mean, he seemed like such a nice person when I spoke with him the other day."

Fitzgibbons snorted. "People say that about almost every piece-of-shit murderer—not that I'm saying Mr. Caldwell is one. But for every convicted killer, there's always someone to swear he was a helluva guy."

He turned toward Jane and said, "Ms. Jensen, thank you for your time. As I asked before, please get in touch with us should you remember anything else that might be pertinent."

"Sure. Um… was she killed in her house? I mean, if she was, it would make me feel uncomfortable staying here."

Kelvin took this one. "No, she was gunned down on her way home from work, at the train station parking lot. She drove her car to the station and took Metro-North into Manhattan.

As soon as the detectives walked out the door, Mel turned to Jane. "How fucking creepy is that? You might have a murderer living next door to you, Jane. God."

"It's just supposition at this point. They haven't arrested him for it, so it must mean they have no evidence."

"Yeah, well, it's still creepy. And I'm wondering if I've met that detective before. He looked so familiar."

"Is that why he kept staring at you?"

Mel's head whipped over to look at her friend. "No, he was staring because he probably couldn't quite believe that anyone could be so gorgeous." She paused, giving Jane a chance to laugh at her joke.

"I didn't like him much. He kept shooting me these looks, as if he didn't believe a word that came out of my mouth. He was… ornery."

"An ornery cop? Stop, there's no such thing. So," Mel

said, breaking off a corner of the brownie Jane gave her and popping it into her mouth, "I wonder what Mason does for a living?"

Jane shook her head "No idea. Why don't you ask Officer Fitzgibbons?" She couldn't help the smirk on her face. Mel saw it.

"Wipe that smirk off your face. There's nothing there… yet. If I have anything to say about it, though, I'll have him in bed before the month is out. He's got a great build, don't you think?"

"I guess." Jane's fingers worried a small tear in the fabric of her frayed yoga pants. Cops made her nervous. Maybe she was a lawbreaker?"

"I bet he has a big dick too."

"Mel, for God's sake, did you have to put that image in my head?"

She wore a wicked grin. "What's wrong with having that image? He's hot."

Hard knocks at the door startled them. "Yes?" Jane called out.

A muffled voice barely penetrated the heavy wood door. "Detective Fitzgibbons again."

As Jane cackled, a red-faced Mel jumped to her feet to open it, swinging it wide for the quarterback cop. "Yes, Detective? Did you forget something?"

"Yeah," he replied, staring at her chest. Mel had pulled off her sweater and had on only a slinky camisole underneath. She had fairly big breasts for a slim girl as Fitzgibbons was now learning. "Uh, just wanted to let you ladies know," he hauled his eyes back up to her face as he quickly continued, "not to divulge anything we said about this case."

"Of course not." She looked over her shoulder. "Jane, you know not to do that, right?"

Jane nodded, mustering a token grin in the presence of the cop. "As long as you're here, Detective Fitzgibbons. We were wondering what Mason Caldwell does for a living. Can you tell us?"

"He runs a commercial real estate firm. He and his partner redevelop blighted properties. They do nice work actually."

"Ohhhh. Sounds like a good thing. Environmentally friendly. Don't have to rip out more trees, right?"

Fitzgibbons rolled his eyes at Mel. "Oh boy. One of those, huh? Good day, ladies." He tipped an imaginary hat and took his leave. Mel turned around and bestowed upon Jane the most mischievous smile.

She definitely liked that cop.

Chapter 14

Jane stared down at the nonstick pan, watching the eggs fry, the whites curling crisp and brown at the edges while the center around the yolk bubbled and cratered. After a moment of staring intently, the eggs disappeared, and she was instead seeing chocolate. Bubbling, boiling chocolate in a huge cauldron-like pot at a different stove, a big commercial stainless range, and she was laughing… with someone. Someone else was with her and they were laughing. Someone with a deep voice.

A man. But she couldn't see his face. Could it be the man at the hospital? Ed Jensen? Was he her boyfriend?

It couldn't be. If she had someone, he'd have come forward by now, reminded her of his place in her life. No one had. Maybe Ed Jensen was just someone who'd seen the accident and was concerned about a stranger?

But she'd been taking birth control pills. She found them partially taken and saw the reminders on her calendar. Why? Jane could find out easily enough—she'd schedule an appointment with her gynecologist and ask her the reason for the BC. It could be medical.

But often she had this odd sense of missing someone… or perhaps something. She chalked it up to having huge tracts of her life missing… but maybe it was more specific than that. The not knowing was beyond frustrating.

Her solution to the lonely feelings was that she should get a dog. The more she thought of it, the more she liked the idea. After breakfast, she'd do some research on what kind of dog to adopt.

Mel had gone home for the weekend and wouldn't be back until Tuesday morning so Jane had to amuse herself for the next three days. She thought maybe she'd look into buying some furniture for her new house. Living like a college student waiting for the financial aid check to come was getting old.

She took a bite of the eggs with a piece of buttered toast. What was all that chocolate for, she pondered?

Fudge, came the answer, sliding right into her head as if someone simply answered her question.

Fudge? She knew how to make candy?

"Who was making the candy with me?" she asked aloud, thinking maybe the answer would come just as easily as before.

It didn't, but this time she got a flash of a beautiful smile, with straight white teeth and a dimple on one side. No matter how much she concentrated, she couldn't get anything else. Pushing away the half-eaten breakfast, she folded her arms on the table and slumped her head on top, closing her eyes. She was tired of the disjointed images coming at her in both sleep and consciousness. Trying to make coherent sense of them was taxing all her strength.

Upstairs she grabbed a pair of jeans and a shirt out of the closet. When she pulled on the jeans, she laughed. They were way too big on her. She tried cinching them with a belt but it looked ridiculous. Chewing her lip as she gazed into the mirror, she tried to think of what else to wear.

Mel had promised her they'd be going shopping soon to buy Jane a new wardrobe. Meantime, she'd have to stick to yoga pants with a drawstring and T-shirts. She found the black pair that fit her best, threw on a light pink T-shirt and a thick gray cardigan on top of that, slipped on her Mary Jane ballet flats and went out. She just had to get out of the house for a little while. As she walked, she once again tried to figure out what those memories that came back to her last night were all about. The one today about the chocolate was too fragmented. It was just a snippet.

The earlier one had to have something to do with the car accident since there was an ambulance—of that she was positive. What else? That blond girl. Who was she? Jane thought she might be someone from high school—her face looked so familiar. Just as that thought made its way across her brain, the name Kendra flashed in front of her eyes.

Kendra? *Kendra.*

Kendra Ortalano. One of the girls who made Jane's life a living hell in high school and who Jane loathed with every molecule of her being. Why the hell was Jane remembering her above all others and why was she figuring so prominently in her memories?

Jane hadn't seen Kendra probably since high school graduation. That was seven years now. It was bizarre that her hated face would pop up into Jane's mind now, when she was instead searching for good memories that would help her regain her equilibrium. That horrible bitch. Why, though, was she near the ambulance? There were a lot of other kids around too. It couldn't be the car accident.

Jane scoured her mind for any high school memory where someone got hurt enough for an ambulance to be called, but she couldn't find any. Then again, she barely remembered high school.

After buying a couple of novels at the independent bookstore, Jane headed to Whole Foods to pick up some groceries and stopped in the liquor store to stock up on wine for Mel. Because she couldn't yet carry anything without hurting her ribs, she took them out in a cart until she found a cab outside the market. As she got into the car, she felt a moment of panic seize her but it passed quickly. Odd that she didn't feel any fear when Mel drove her home from the hospital. In fact, Jane had started thinking right then that she should look into buying another car.

Chapter 15

"How long you know Jane Jensen?"

Mel had been sitting outside a coffee bar having a text argument with her sister when who of all people should stroll up to her but the hot detective. Fitzgibbons. How the hell did he know how to find her?

He laughed at her no-doubt-confused expression and repeated his question.

"Um, about two years. Maybe a little longer. How did you find me?"

"I'm a detective, remember. I'm on my lunch break. Wanna join me? My treat."

"Aw, that's so nice of you." She looked at her watch. "As it happens I'm on my lunch break too. We'll go local, right?"

"Nah, we'll fly to Paris for some snails."

Melanie tried really hard not to roll her eyes. Why did he have to say such stupid things? He was handsome and had a totally hot bod, but she wasn't sure she could tolerate his cop-sarcasm and dumbass remarks.

"C'mon," he said more meekly now. "I know a good pizza place two blocks from here. You'll love it."

"If it's pizza and it's within a mile radius of me, it's pretty much guaranteed I've eaten there at least ten times."

"Aha. So you like pizza?

"What the hell? Do I look like a freak to you? Of course, I do. Does that elevate your opinion of me?"

He tossed his head back as he laughed. "Matter of fact, it does. I could never like anyone who didn't like pizza. It's downright un-American."

"All right. Take me to this paragon of pizza parlors. I happen to be starving."

"Let's go."

As they walked, side by side when the crowded sidewalk allowed it and her in front when it didn't, Melanie considered the situation. After a moment, she had to ask, "Are you hoping for some inside dirt on Jane and her neighbors from me? Is that why you're here?"

Detective Fitzgibbons's eyes dropped to his scuffed black boots as he strode alongside of her. "If you have any information you think might help my case, I'd certainly welcome it. But no. I'm here because I happened to be in the area and knew from my investigation that you worked around here. I was planning on going up to MT's floors to find you but then there you were, on the bench outside in the plaza."

"Yeah, my sister was thoroughly pissing me off. Text fights are mad frustrating 'cause you're typing so fast you don't notice the autocorrects till it's too late. You end up sending an incomprehensible message."

They reached the pizza place and he opened the door, holding it wide so she could step in first. "Do you and your sister often argue by text?"

"My sister and I argue by any means available. Why?"

He gave her a lopsided grin. "I just think it's funny is all. Angry typing."

"Yeah, well, if you knew my sister you'd lose all your good humor. She is one toxic female."

"Speaking of which, that takes me back to my original question: you said you know Jane about two years?"

"Are you calling Jane poisonous?"

"Maybe," he said lightly. "At this point, I'm not sure about anything except that a young woman with everything to live for is dead, murdered way before her time."

"When is the right time to get murdered then?" Mel quipped.

The man behind the counter heard what she said and took stock of them. "What can I get for you folks?"

Fitzgibbons looked at Mel, his expression so serious it was comical. Apparently, he didn't take good pizza lightly. "I recommend the plain and the Sicilian. Put too much on top of pizza and it spoils it, in my opinion.

Mel nodded, trying not to laugh at him. "I'll take a plain slice."

"Yeah, we'll take two regular slices and one Sicilian, please." He turned to Mel. "What would you like to drink?"

"Water. Thank you."

He wouldn't let her pay. "My treat, no strings attached to this pizza, except those made of mozzarella."

Mel laughed. Fitzgibbons was sort of fun, in addition to being smoky hot sexiness on two rubber-soled boots. But a cop?

Once they sat across from each other Mel gave him a long look. "So… to what do I owe this visit?"

"I like you, Melanie. And I'm worried about you."

"Worried?"

"Yeah."

"About?"

He just looked at her with a stony expression.

"Worried that my boss is overworking me? That I'm nearing thirty without a marriage prospect in sight? That I drink too much alcohol? Care to elaborate, Detective?"

"Worried that your friend is dangerous." He sighed. "Look, I just don't want anything bad to happen to you."

Mel quickly chewed a bite of pizza. It was so lava-hot that she'd shredded the roof of her mouth with the first taste, but she wasn't about to let third-degree burns stop her from eating it; employing a mammoth effort, she put it down for a minute to cool off. "...Tell me why you think Jane is toxic?"

Rob took a huge bite into his pizza and continued to chew as his narrowed eyes watched her. She waited patiently as he swallowed. "It's not that I've made up my mind that she is... I'm just not sure yet what's what." He put his slice down and placed both of his hands flat on the table. "Let's look at the facts.

"Mason Caldwell's wife is gunned down by a professional hit man. It was clean, quick, and unseen. What do we have? OK, we have a spouse who may or may not have sociopathic tendencies. Caldwell is a friendly enough guy, but judging from surface appearances he seems to be vain, self-centered, and a little shallow. I can't call him a murderer—not yet—but he's not the sincerest widowed husband I've ever met."

"He's also a young guy and no doubt used to getting things easily," Mel interjected before he could continue.

"Maybe. Now, next door we have a woman who went to high school with Caldwell. By her own admission, she mooned over him, but he never noticed her. Then with an entire big city to choose from, she just happens to move next door to him and—"

"Wait," she interrupted. "*He* moved next door to *her*. Remember?"

Fitzgibbons picked up his napkin and wiped grease from his hand. "Possibly, though the Caldwells went into contract before Jane Jensen did. They merely asked for a later closing date."

So... Jane hurried up and bought the house next door and then rushed into contract? Seemed farfetched.

If the detective noticed her skeptical expression, he didn't show it as he continued to lay out his case. "From all accounts so far—and we've interviewed a few people who knew both of them in high school—Jane was sort of a stalker when it came to Mason Caldwell. Everyone we talked to—admittedly not a high number—remembered her following him around like a lost puppy. She didn't hide her obsession much. As for Caldwell, he barely recalled that Jane Jensen went to the same school as he did."

Mel hiked her shoulders, feeling a chill pass through her. "So what? She had a crush on a hot guy in high school who didn't know she existed. There are a lot of people in the world who could say the same—doesn't make them murderers. Not everyone could be popular in high school, you know. All a boy has to do is be athletic and he's in." Her hand sailed through the air.

Fitzgibbons smirked and hiked his left eyebrow. "Is that so? Well, guess I was in since I was a quarterback."

She sniffed and picked at the burnt edge of cheese on her slice. "Not surprised. What's your point?"

Laughing, he shook his head. "No point. Anyway, the thing is—I don't know yet who contracted the hit, Melanie. But I can't rule out your friend yet. I will say, though, that she has to get in line, one that's becoming longer by the day."

"Why are you telling me all of this? Isn't it against the closed-rank cop handbook?"

Fitzgibbons chuckled. "Yeah, as I said before… it's not the brightest thing I've ever done. But I like you for some reason—"

"Smooth. You like me and you want to trash my friend in my presence?"

"Just giving you a warning, that's all. I wanna make sure you're not in any danger."

"Danger from Jane? Come on."

"Don't repeat anything I'm telling you."

"I won't tell a soul, not even my dog. Cross my shriveled-up black heart."

He shook his head, suppressing a grin. "What kind of dog do you have?"

"I don't actually have one. But my parents do, so he's still sort of mine. He's a Bernese mountain dog. Pierre. I love him madly. So… go on."

He'd just taken another big bite and now he used the small rectangular paper napkin to pat the oil shine from his lips. "Turns out," he begins with his mouth full, and then finishes chewing and swallows, "there may have been trouble in the Caldwell marriage, but that's all I'm saying. I've gotta be crazy to be telling you even this much," he said under his breath.

Mel gasped quietly. The Caldwells were basically still newlyweds and besides, Mason was super hot and his wife was beautiful. Why would they stray? If that's what he meant. "I'm actually shocked. So the range of suspects expands?"

He shook his head. "Not necessarily. But we need to look at everyone a little closer. Mostly her husband. Mace. Is it just me or is that nickname annoying?"

Not waiting for an answer, he went on, "In any murder

investigation, the smart thing to do is look at family and friends first. A no-brainer if there's no theft involved."

"Wow," Mel said, taking a sip of water, "the plot, as they say, thickens. Why do people even bother getting married?" When Rob just shook his head in disgusted agreement, she went on, "So who are the new suspects?"

"Not sure yet; we're still digging. But your girl is definitely among that list since from all accounts she stalked him in high school. Every single person we spoke with was aware of it."

"High school was a long time ago, Detective." She finally braved another bite of the hot pizza. "So how long were the Caldwells married?"

"Little over a year. They met a few years ago through Mason's cousin. Apparently, Mrs. Caldwell dated the cousin—Jake Emerson—in college. Jake moved on to another girl, and Mason took up with Cate. Cate Cobb.

"How long were they together exactly?"

"Uh… I guess three years? Why do you ask?"

"They're recently wed. I mean…" she sighed. "Why do people off their spouses… generally?"

"All different reasons. Jealousy. Revenge. Money can be a primary factor—usually insurance money or alimony. All sorts of reasons."

"OK, so is money on the table here?"

He shook his head. "Not so much. Both parties had their own money. There were insurance policies but they weren't very impressive."

"Then… are there any other possible motives?"

He inhaled deeply, blowing out the breath in a huff. "We have a few theories we're bouncing around. I'm not at liberty to discuss them."

Mel took a few minutes to eat her pizza and think about what he said. He was right: the pizza was excellent.

She might even have to get another slice. She craned her neck around to see the counter—a long line had formed. Then again, maybe not. She turned back. "I would think if they truly married for love, it's too soon for any other factor to become strong enough to want to kill each other. You know?"

His face flooded with amusement. "How long do you think a couple needs to want to kill each other enough to take out a hit?"

She pursed her lips in mock concentration. "I'd hazard to guess at least five years."

"So by the time you finish that slice of pizza you may want to kill me?"

Mel looked over at his plate: there was nothing but an elbow of crust left of his two slices. She still had half of her single one. "You eat too fast. It's not good for you."

"Yeah, well, I was hungry. So, Ms. Bartholomew… is there anything you can tell me about your friend that may help us strike her off the suspect list? You know, like maybe she has a boyfriend she really fancies… or she's now a dedicated lesbian?"

"No and no. But neither of those things would necessarily exclude her from your list, now would it?"

"It would help." He flipped his wrist to look at his watch. "I suppose you need to get back to work. Shall I walk you back?"

"Sure." She got up and slung her bag across her chest, then picked up the pizza. "Not leaving without this."

Just before he left her at the front of her building, he grasped her arm. "Do me a favor and watch your six, OK?"

"What?"

"Be careful. Don't be so trusting and so sure that friend

of yours is safe. You can be in danger without even realizing it."

"Danger from Jane?"

"Yes." His tone was obstinate.

"Even if she was involved—which she's definitely not—you said the killer was a hit man, right? That would mean that whoever was responsible paid someone else to do the killing. So is that person really technically a killer and therefore dangerous?"

His eyes held incredulity. "Are you kidding me? If someone is evil enough to contract a hit, that person is a killer. If a killer is cornered, he or she will kill again." He wagged his finger in her face, causing her to pull away. "Make no mistake about it.

"So yes, danger from Jane. Watch your back, Melanie."

Chapter 16

Mel gaped at the detective. "You found Jane's photo where?"

Fitzgibbons had shown up unexpectedly at Jane's house late Friday afternoon. Normally, Mel would be back at her place in Manhattan but when Jane learned that Mel was leaving work early today, she begged her to come to Riverdale. Not at all unhappy to see him, Mel couldn't deny that she liked the detective but it was becoming weird being between him and Jane. He was starting to feel more and more like Jane's adversary and was putting her right in the middle of a tug-of-war between them.

"In Caldwell's dresser drawer," he answered, his voice grim, and handed her the glossy photograph. "Why would he have a photo of her?"

"You're asking me?" she said, staring intently at the photo for a long minute before her breath hitched audibly. "Does this mean he was stalking her... rather than the other way around?"

The big cop heaved a long sigh. "We're not sure what it means at this point. Where is Ms. Jensen?"

"Doctor's appointment." Her eyes tracked down to the photo again. "Hold on a sec, I just realized something. I took this photo."

"You took it?"

"I snapped it, I mean. Jane asked me to take a picture of her house in the morning sun. I took some photos of her at the same time—I thought they came out good."

"Did Jane ever see the photos?"

"Yes, she loved them."

"Do you know if she ever posted this one online anywhere? Maybe that's how Mason got a copy?"

"I'm not sure but I can ask her."

"Actually, I'd prefer to ask her myself. When did you say you expect her? Are you living with her now?"

"Uh, she should be home like really soon, actually. No, I don't live with her. I'm only staying for a couple of weeks until she heals a little more. I help her with laundry and cooking and stuff."

The detective stared at her for a protracted moment, distracting her with his good looks. *But a cop, Melanie? Not your best idea.* Even so, she wouldn't mind seeing those muscled biceps in action…up close and personal. Mel would bet money that he could make her eyes spin in bed with that hunky body.

"Well," he says, intruding into her dirty reverie, "you're a good friend to Ms. Jensen. Would you mind if I wait for her?"

"Tell you what. If you help me cook, I won't mind at all." Mel couldn't believe she just said that to a detective investigating a murder, but he was beginning to feel like a friend. And instead of getting pissy about it, the stony-faced cop cracked a grin, and Mel felt fluttering butterfly wings deep in her belly. Yes, she decided, he was most definitely handsome.

"I doubt I'll be of much help. I can cook two things really ace and that's about it."

"Lemme guess," she said, holding up her hand. "Barbecued anything—"

"Wrong," he interrupted, tsk-tsking. "Such a sexist remark. Actually, bacon is one. The other is marinara sauce, for your information."

"Marinara? Hmmm. I'd like to try some sometime."

"My mother is a paesan—I learned from the best. And bacon is a favorite of mine..."

Her turn to tsk-tsk. "Bacon is deadly on the body, and pigs are incredibly adorable. I can't eat them, frankly."

"Then don't eat them frankly. Eat them well done."

"Uh-uh. No way. I'm a dedicated vegetarian… mostly… I do wear leather," she said, her tone apologetic. "Have a thing for shoes so it's hard to avoid animal skin. Anyway… tonight I'm making chili *con carne* minus the *carne* for dinner, and I bet you'd love it, carnivore and all."

"A vegetarian?" he groaned. The disappointment in his voice was so palpable that Mel had to chuckle. "And here I thought you were perfect."

Whoa. That took Melanie aback for a moment. Even as a figure of speech it was unexpected coming from him. It meant he was thinking about her in that way. So maybe, just maybe, the attraction was a two-way street. "I am perfect," she said lightly. "You'll try it, and you'll love it."

His snicker said otherwise but he dutifully followed Mel into the kitchen and she handed him a paring knife, pointing to some carrots to peel.

JANE GOT HOME ALMOST an hour later. Mel heard the door. "Be right back," she said to Fitzgibbons and grabbing a towel to wipe off her hands, hurried out to her friend. "Hey, how'd it go?"

"Look." Jane lifted her chin, grinning broadly. "Notice anything different?"

"Er… different?" Mel tilted her head. "Oh my God. Your nose. You got the bandage off. Jane, it looks amazing. Are you thrilled?"

Jane's face split into a huge grin. "Yes, I love it. It's my nose only better. That surgeon is phenomenal."

Grasping Jane's chin with her hand, she examined the new nose from various angles. "He truly did a fantastic job. It's a beautiful nose. Listen, Jane," she lowered her voice, "Detective Fitzgibbons is here—he needs to ask you a few more questions."

Jane's smile collapsed. "Why? I don't remember anything more."

"I'm here because of this photo, Ms. Jensen," said Fitzgibbons, striding into the foyer and waving a manila envelope in his hand. He slid the photo from the envelope to hand to Jane, closely watching her reaction.

She studied it for what seemed like a long time before she looked back up at Fitzgibbons. "It's a nice photo, but I don't remember taking it."

"Do you remember posting any photos of yourself online at all?"

Jane's eyes shifted back to the photo. "I don't remember. Why do you want to know?"

He looked at Mel. "Was the photo always digital or did you have hard copies made?"

Mel shook her head. "I only made digital copies but I can't speak for Jane."

His eyes shifted to Jane. "And you don't remember anything about the photo?"

"No, I honestly don't. I may have had some printed but… I have no memory of it."

"Have you recalled any other memory since we last spoke, Ms. Jensen? Maybe something about your next-door neighbor?" His attention was trained on her face with laser-like intensity.

Jane shook her head, her eyes unfocused. "No… I haven't. I mean, I recover a memory here and there pretty much every day but nothing substantive." She peered intently at the detective, trying to glean what was running through his head. "Why?"

Fitzgibbons was in the process of unrolling his shirt-sleeves and refastening the cuffs. "Because, Ms. Jensen, we found this photo in a dresser drawer in Mr. Caldwell's bedroom. He insists—vehemently—that he never placed it there."

Paling, Jane reached for the side table and held onto it but her eyes never left the photo. The room got quiet for a protracted moment before Jane commented softly, "How odd. Why would he want a photo of me? Or my house for that matter?" She chuckled weakly. "He's got one just like it."

She finally glanced up at him though her reluctance to look him in the eye was obvious. "Detective, I apologize but with my memory issues, I don't know what I knew or didn't know."

"Does it surprise you that Caldwell would have a photo of you in his drawer?"

"Yes." She let the sibilant ess trail on her tongue. "I mean, why would he? He's him and I'm me."

The cop frowned and shook his head. "What does that mean, Ms. Jensen?"

"Just that…" She hesitated. "…He's always been miles —universes—out of my league, Detective."

Melanie slapped a hand to her forehead, dissipating the tense environment. "Shit, my chili! Detective, will you join us for dinner?" she asked as she hurried toward the kitchen and tossed over her shoulder, "It's only fair since you helped prepare it."

Fitzgibbons allowed her to distract him and smiled in her direction. "Now how can I decline that offer? Thank you."

A HALF-HOUR LATER, the three of them sat around the long hand-hewn oak table—one of Jane's recent acquisitions—and Mel waited until Fitzgibbons took his first bite, watching him expectantly. He chewed slowly and swallowed; she waited but got nothing. "Well?" she finally asked in exasperation.

He grinned. "It's good. That stuff you put in it actually tastes like meat."

"I know," she said, beaming. "I've made my famous vegetarian chili for many a carnivore, and they all say the same."

"I'm impressed. What is it, by the way?"

"Textured vegetable protein, whatever that might be. I try not to dwell on it too much."

Jane broke into their conversation, changing the subject. "So… Detective Fitzgibbons… getting back to my photo… what do you think it means… and what's the status of your murder investigation? Or aren't you allowed to talk about it?"

"As a matter of fact, that's why I'm here…" he began, putting his fork down. "I need to ask a favor of you, Ms. Jensen."

"Please call me Jane."

He managed a tight smile. "Despite all evidence to the

contrary, I do need to maintain some professional distance. The main reason for my visit this evening is to ask you to come to the station and get fingerprinted." He saw her expression and talked faster. "Since we found your photo at the Caldwell house, we think it's prudent to check your home for prints that don't belong here and we need to be able to discount yours. Would you be so kind…?"

Jane flushed at his direct focus. "Of course, I will. Just tell me where and when, and I'll be there, Detective."

Chapter 17

Kendra Ortalano had finally replaced the burned-out bulbs in her bathroom and the harsh glare from four naked 100-watt bulbs above the mirror caused her to nearly gasp when she flicked on the unforgiving light. She leaned in over the vanity to get a closer look at her many imperfections.

"Shit. I'm supposed to look good and do it in less than an hour," she complained to the sallow image in the mirror.

At twenty-five, Kendra had already clocked a lot of mileage on her face from living hard and fast. Poor complexion and yellowing teeth from smoking and eating sugary junk food, and loss of skin tone from drugs and tobacco smoke all conspired to ruin her looks.

"Ugh," she growled aloud. Her natural hair color was a sort of light brown if she recalled correctly, but she went blond way back in middle school. Hair dye was sort of like narcotics: it had a diminishing-return factor. Soon going four shades lighter was not enough. She kept going lighter and blonder. Not satisfied until she was platinum, she realized that twelve years of bleaching her hair had taken a heavy toll: it had the texture and pliancy of straw. Even was sorta the same color.

It was ten to seven and she was meeting the old bastard at 7:45. She began the cosmetic routine that had become rote. Step one: slather on thick foundation to cover broken capillaries from drinking too much booze and the scars given her by that douche-bag pimp three years ago. Jingo Gonzalez had really done a number on her face that night he beat her. *Hope the maggots are feasting on the piece of shit in a shallow fucking grave somewhere*, she thought. She managed a small smile at the thought as she performed step two and lightly brushed on the mineral powder that filled in the large pores on her nose and cheeks, giving her skin a more even tone.

Step three was the eyes: carefully she applied bronze shadow on the lid with black liner in the corners extending out and added black mascara to lengthen her sparse fringe of light-brown lashes. The final step involved rouge and lipstick, both going on last, after she got dressed.

A half hour and heavy dipping into ninety dollars' worth of cosmetics later, she thought she looked good. Being realistic, good came with a qualifier: she looked good *for her*. She knew that lots of people fool themselves about their looks, somehow convincing themselves they're better looking than they actually are. Expensive mirrors and lighting can help keep the fantasy on life support, but right now Kendra didn't have the coin for such luxuries. She picked up the hairbrush with the puppy-chewed handle and began to aggressively stroke her hair, thinking that maybe a good brushing would restore some of the shine and bounce that all the dyes, bleaches, and ingested drugs had leached out of it. That was asking a lot out of a five-dollar hairbrush.

Rushing into her bedroom, she started yanking things out of drawers to find what she needed. She was running late. In her disorganized closet, she found a navy blue skintight sheath but all her stockings were buried, either in overstuffed dresser drawers or the laundry hamper. She finally found a pair stuffed way in the back of her underwear drawer.

Slipping on the spandex dress, Kendra discovered the dress was not as tight as it should be and used to be. She tried to remember the last time she wore it when it had fit her like a glove. Six or seven months ago? She attempted to smooth out the wrinkles with her bony fingers but ended up having to hike it up to pull on her stockings. Once she had on the nude hose, she searched out her five-inch blue suede heels and slipped her feet into them. Before she left the bedroom, she slipped on her silver bangles and four of her favorite rings then darted back into the bathroom to apply the final makeup touches.

Feeling as if she was forgetting something, she looked around the rundown apartment, finally going into the galley kitchen for a glass of water. Kendra had been pleading with Aaron to help her get a better place but he refused to fork over more money to upgrade, the tightwad. Two years of begging and superior blow jobs had gotten her nowhere. Still, things were looking up now. Maybe soon she'd have a nice place with a pretty stainless-steel dishwasher. It would be so nice to have one again—washing dishes was death on manicures, not to mention the look of the skin.

Not that she did that many dishes—if there were four in the cupboard to choose from it was a good day. But time wasn't being all that considerate to Kendra, and she was going to need to take better care of herself. For a girl whose stock in trade was her looks, it was important, and Kendra used sex as her currency. It was the only thing she was good at. That was why, when her old high school pal called her with his plan, she went all in. Right the fuck away. The money he'd pay her would allow her to start over. The bonus was that she'd be helping a friend—and as far as friends went, he had been the best. She seriously loved him. A lot. Always had. It was just too bad they'd drifted so far apart in the years since high school graduation.

Her life had been descending into an ugly place in recent years and the crumbling apartment mirrored the rest of her existence, a physical manifestation of the deterioration inside her. As he always managed to do in the past, when things were getting tough in Kendra's life, Mason came rushing to the rescue. His phone call last month came out of the blue but Kendra was down for anything he suggested. She never really had a strong moral compass to begin with, and she'd do anything for Mason—she loved him. Always had.

He cared about her too—just not in the way she'd have wanted. They were friends, good friends. Even after the incident in junior year, Mace was one of the few people who stuck by her, and so she stuck by him too, refusing to give him up in any way, no matter how jealous his various girlfriends became.

Then again, all of Mason's friends stuck by him—and to him—forever. He was just that type of charismatic guy. There was Ben Beneke, the giant linebacker who was always hanging onto Mason, following him around like they were attached by a string and basking in Mason's reflected glory. They'd met in first grade or something stupid like that.

And, of course, Jake Emerson, Mason's bestie and cousin—they'd been tight since, like, birth, given that they were related, and they were in business together now as adults. In middle school and even high school, the two of them were so similar that they could totally pass for brothers if not freaking twins, but even so, Jake still couldn't measure up to Mace.

No one could—not even if he had an identical twin or clone. There was just something about Mason, some irresistible force of energy, charm, mojo—whatever.

As for girls, Kendra was certain one of Mace's high school girlfriends would try to keep him, but no one was successful in that pursuit. Tess Gardner tried her best, terrorizing the girl he'd left her for—little-miss-perfect Shannon Graham. Kendra found the whole drama hilarious, especially when Tess went so far as to stick a dead rat in Shannon's locker, a crime for which she never had to answer. She definitely had Shannon running scared, the psycho bitch, but she never managed to get the boy back. He went off to college a single man and met his wife sometime after. Kendra wasn't sure when; she only knew that he'd been married for a year or so.

With regard to his most recent request, Kendra didn't lose a wink of sleep over it. She'd never met the woman, but if Mason said she was a bitch, that was good enough for Kendra. And who cared anyway? No one… well, except Mrs. Caldwell herself.

And the woman they were going to frame for the murder would too.

But when had Kendra ever given a shit about her? She was a fat slob, an unattractive girl who didn't even try to make people like her. How dare she be both ugly and a bitch? Kendra had taken an instant and massive dislike to her from the moment she'd seen the stupid girl in the hall of the high school, freshman year. The last time Kendra had tried to put Jane in her place, the slob had ended up in the hospital for a week, and Kendra had become ostracized at school for her part in it. It's not as if she planned it or anything. It just happened.

But Kendra didn't shed any tears over it, truth to tell. When Mace first called her with the plan and he said they needed a scapegoat, maybe someone from high school, she'd easily come up with Jane. Kendra clearly remembered how much the pathetic girl mooned over Mason when he barely knew she was an inhabitant of the planet. It used to piss off Kendra how the fat, nerdy bitch would follow him around.

It was at the first football game of their freshman year that Kendra started really hating Jane. Mason was the newest star of the team, having been recruited while still at Sandringham Middle School to join the team as soon as he entered high school.

Kendra and her friends had front-row seats, right behind the cheerleaders. Kendra had almost made the cut for cheerleader but when Shannon Graham decided she wanted in, Kendra was out. Shannon was one of the high-gloss girls of their town so of course she dated Mason at one point. They made the perfect couple. That night Kendra had been huddled on the bleacher, bony fingers wrapped around a cup of hot chocolate and zoning out when she zeroed in on a conversation behind her between two females.

"Mason is going to win the game, I'd bet anything. Just look at him: he is perfect."

"I don't know about perfect, but he's definitely hot. I doubt he'll be the deciding factor, though, since he's a new player. Maybe next year… or junior year, but not now."

The first girl practically hissed at her friend, "Don't you

dare dis him. He's going to score more than one touchdown. Just wait. I can feel it in my bones. Watching him play is like seeing poetry in motion."

"Whatever," the other girl had groaned.

Kendra whipped her head around to check out her competition. At that point, she'd still hoped for a romantic alliance with Mace. That hope wasn't doused until the middle of sophomore year when he'd made it crystal clear that he considered her a very good friend but that they'd never go beyond platonic. He said he wouldn't want to ruin their solid friendship. Kendra hoped that was the reason and not that she wasn't pretty enough. All the other boys thought she was hot. Fact was, Kendra blazed through pretty much the entire football team by senior year. The only two she didn't do were Mason and Rick Brando, and Kendra was sure that Rick was a closet case.

When she saw who was swooning over Mason that night, she was torn between two emotions: laughter at the absurdity of it and anger over the audacity of the stupid girl. As if she'd ever have a chance with the hottest guy in the whole school. At that minute Kendra was filled with hatred for the outcast named Jane Jensen.

Just because she had the audacity to think she could have a crush on the most popular boy in the whole school.

Just because she existed.

Just because.

Not that Mason belonged to Kendra—he didn't. She knew that, even accepted it after a while. He would date other girls, but they always had to tolerate Kendra as his friend. If they didn't, they didn't last long as his girlfriend.

They never lasted long anyway: Mason was impatient and easily bored, but those two failings were his only shortcomings, so they could be overlooked—at least as far as Kendra was concerned. So despite wanting Mace beyond anything else, they remained only friends as Kendra worked her way through the roster of high school jocks. There were a few of them that she liked quite a lot. Like Tomas Velez… and Adam Toledo. Yeah, Adam was built like a brick shithouse.

No boyfriend ever lasted, though—but her friendship with Mason did. She was his protector; she ran interference for him. That's why it drove Kendra crazy that stupid, fat Jane Jensen spent her days mooning over Mason as if he'd ever notice her in a million years. She had no right to even think about him.

Kendra decided to make Jane pay for her audacity. That's why whenever any chance presented itself, Kendra snatched it to humiliate the girl who always dressed in brown and tried her best to make herself inconspicuous. Nowadays Kendra would be called a bully but back then… it was a rite of fucking passage. The strong versus the weak. No one could really blame Kendra for her teenage shenanigans any more than anyone can be blamed for stupid shit done in the volatile crucible that is adolescence.

This time, though… this time it was a golden opportunity to get at Jane. And it all worked so beautifully. Mace got pissed when she improvised, but Kendra considered every unexpected opportunity a gift. She still didn't understand his reaction. Yeah, it wasn't planned but it worked out fine. But no, he wanted every last detail planned out to the nth degree—Kendra on the other hand was a spur-of-the-moment kind of girl, the kind of boy that he used to be.

Anyway, she made it up to him when she risked going to Jane's house, passing herself off as a realtor when some scary dude started messing with her, asking her what she was doing there. Kendra went there hoping to leave some more incriminating evidence, a letter ostensibly written by Jane to Mason, professing her love for him. She put it in the slob's underwear drawer, tucking it under her panties, which to Kendra's ever-loving surprise were actually pretty lingerie. Wasted on that woman, for sure.

She was about to get the hell out of Jane's townhouse when she thought better than to leave the letter. What if it made Mason look guilty too? They were treading a fine and dangerous line here—the spouse is always the first suspect. Plus, Mason had warned her not to go anywhere near Jane's house, even though she thought he was being overly cautious. It's not as if the police were going to look at Kendra, after all. While she was deciding whether or not to leave the letter in place, the doorbell rang and she got spooked and took off. Now she was slightly worried that she'd made a mistake, but she had plenty of time to retrieve the damn thing if it came to that.

Her phone buzzing jolted her back to real time—her date tonight with the boss. She called him boss because he essentially owned her—for now, anyway. The most accurate way to describe the old bastard was sugar daddy, though he sure didn't give her all that much sugar, just the bare minimum to keep her afloat and on a leash. He paid her monthly bills in return for favors whenever and wherever he wanted them. A lot of fucking favors. When she took him on a few years ago, she figured he wouldn't be able to do all that much at his age and assumed it would be easy money.

It wasn't.

Pfft. She *would* be the lucky one to get a geezer who could still get it up like a young dude. She'd been screwing this guy for almost three years already, and he showed no sign of letting up. Grabbing the phone, she ignored the call, instead texting him to say she'd be down in five minutes, but that wasn't good enough for him. A minute later, her phone rang again.

"I'm almost ready, sir." The fucker insisted she call him that. He was going to be sixty next year, and he said he deserved the respect and deference of his years.

"Kendra, how many times and ways do I have to tell you that I expect punctuality? My arm hurts from beating your skinny ass last week, so don't make me do it again."

Her face burned, remembering the belting the sadistic bastard gave her to punish her for forgetting to take her birth control pills. She'd had vicious welts on her thighs and ass that were just now disappearing. "No, sir. I'm just trying to look good for you."

"Well, that might take a small miracle," he said under his breath but loud enough for her to hear the snide remark. "Just get your ass down here. I'm outside your building already."

"Yes, sir," she said and disconnected the call. "Oh my God," she screamed to the wall, "I cannot wait to tell the old goat to go take a flying fuck. A million dollars will buy me the ability to burn all my bridges.

"And who knows? Maybe I could even buy some fucking furniture while I'm at it." She stormed out of the apartment, her heels pounding the bare wood floor.

Aaron Rinder sat in his white Lexus, the engine idling. He had the look of a man who'd been handsome when he was young but those same features that had made him attractive—almond eyes, pointed nose, angular cheekbones—now served to give his face a cruel bent. Or maybe it was just his rancid disposition that petrified his bad moods into a permanent scowl.

Whatever the case, Kendra was forced to look at it and him for the moment. She stepped closer to the curb and opened the passenger door.

"Good evening, sir," she said as sweetly as she could stand as she folded herself into the car.

Anemic blue eyes scanned her up and down before he frowned, put the car into gear, and smoothly pulled away from the curb. Once they were moving onto the FDR he lit into her. "You do realize that I'm paying a fair amount of money every month for a hole on the side—and this is the best you can offer?" He jerked his chin at her. "You look like a street hooker, Kendra. Honestly, I can probably do better picking up a slut at a strip joint. At least I wouldn't have the monthly outlay I do now to maintain you."

Kendra nearly bit off her tongue to keep silent. The old bastard had been insulting her since they'd met years ago at a party, but this time his biting words crossed even Kendra's almost nonexistent line. To be called a body part —and a fucking crude one at that—as if her entire worth was tied up in only that piece of her anatomy was almost more than even she could bear. The idea of jamming her small yet effective switchblade into his pale belly crossed her mind seriously.

His eyes once again left the road to glance at her. "The late nights and all the drugs you do are taking their toll, my dear. If you lose your looks entirely… then what?"

She leaned back on the headrest and rolled her neck to confront him. "What do you care? You're just buying a product, right? A hole, I think you said?"

He didn't acknowledge her comment. Instead, keeping his eyes on the road, his hand slid down to unzip the fly of his suit trousers, and then he reached his arm over to her, his hand curling around the nape of her neck, and forced her head down into his lap.

Kendra had to use every bit of willpower not to bite down with fury. She hated this motherfucker with every molecule of her being. She could barely wait for the day to come when she wouldn't need him anymore.

Soon.

Who knows? Maybe he'd meet the same fate that Mason's wife did?

Chapter 18

The car engine idled as Detective Fitzgibbons waited for his partner to emerge from the deli. It was a gray morning and the humid air was thick and cloying, hanging low like fog. Too warm for October, he thought, as he loosened his collar, jerking it down with two fingers. He thought maybe he should get off his ass and go see what was taking so long when he spotted her coming out behind a throng of other customers. He leaned across to reach through the open window to take the coffees from her.

"Thanks. I got you a buttered roll, too. Here."

"What, no egg and bacon sandwich today?"

She opened the door and climbed in. "You have to cut down on your cholesterol, Fitz."

He snorted. "Bread and butter doesn't seem much better."

She tsked. "Gimme a break, will you? I didn't know what else to get. It's a fucking bodega, not a full-service restaurant."

Unwrapping the wax paper, he bit into the roll. It was still warm and the butter had melted into the pores of the bread. The way it slid down his throat instantly improved his mood. Grunting, he licked his lips. "We should talk to some of Mrs. Caldwell's colleagues today—get that out of the way. Try to prove or disprove the adultery allegation." Fitzgibbons held his paper cup of coffee to his lips, waiting for her acknowledgment.

Myla darted him a look out of the corner of her eye. "I suppose so. After hearing from her mother, you'd think she was competition for Mother-fucking-Teresa."

He took the first sip of his coffee and almost spit it out as it shredded the roof of his mouth. Gulping it down, he shook his head, "Shit. Usually the coffee is tepid. I wasn't expecting liquid lava."

His partner rolled her eyes and sighed. "You always find something to complain about, Fitz.

"Pfft. C'mon. Let's see what all the PR people have to say about Madam Caldwell."

Myla fastened her seatbelt and slammed her door closed. "Let's go."

As they drove, Fitzgibbons ruminated over the investigation thus far. His reptile sense was tingling over Jane Jensen though he knew intellectually that she wasn't a likely candidate for doing the murder. Wonder what his partner thought?

"So… Myla," he began.

She was busy eating her roll. Hers had a slice of Canadian bacon, he noticed. Maybe he'd get that tomorrow. Finally, she cast her eyes up at him, her mouth stuffed with food. "What?"

"Tell me what you think of our investigation so far."

She swallowed and took a swig of her coffee. "Ow, you're right. It is hot. Um… I haven't formed any opinions yet, to be honest."

"Mmm," is all he said, his mind turning over all the information, flipping through it like a Rolodex.

"WHAT EXACTLY DOES this company do anyway?" Rob asked, looking around the high-end lobby of the office building.

Myla Kelvin laughed. "It's called a boutique agency—means small as shit. They handle things like press releases and trying to keep their clients in the public eye. Plus, if someone is involved in a scandal, they use this kind of agency to try to scrub them clean again. That kind of thing. Nice building, right?"

Rob Fitzgibbons eyed the luxurious furnishings. "Yeah, nice. PR must pay a lot. What floor are they on?"

Myla was checking the directory. "Seventeen. Suite 1711. Let's go."

They rode up in the stainless-steel elevator with six other people, all of them wooden as they watched the floors tick by.

At the seventeenth floor, four of them, including the two detectives, got out. Rob slid his pad from his pocket and checked the name: a guy named Rafael Bono was the head of the small firm.

The two people who got off the elevator with them also turned toward suite 1711. Myla murmured something under her breath, but he didn't catch it.

They followed the faster two people into the double doors of the suite and were stopped by a long, low-slung glass desk. A redheaded young woman sat behind it. She wore a black-on-white print dress, black leggings, ballet slippers, and neon orange on her nails. She nodded to the two who walked right past her, obviously employees, and then turned her attention to the detectives, her clear green eyes curious.

"May I help you?"

He held open his badge. "Detective Fitzgibbons and this is Detective Kelvin. We're here to see Rafael Bono." He pronounced it like the Irish singer.

"It's Bono," she replied, smiling, "like Sonny Bono." She dropped her voice to a loud whisper and said, "If you know who that is because I do not. But that's what Rafe says to people all the time."

Rob grinned crookedly, never hesitating to use his Irish charm on any female, regardless of age. Even his four-year-old niece wasn't safe from it. "Is Rafe old?"

She answered his grin with a smirk. "Older than me, for sure. Hang on and I'll see if he's available."

Rob almost retorted with a "he better be, 'cause he doesn't have a choice," but decided he'd play nice at least until he didn't. She shortly returned, and the detectives were ushered right into Bono's office.

Rafael Bono was not all that old. He was probably inching close to forty but he still had some time left before that milestone. Fitzgibbons eyed him intently. The guy was probably less than 5'8" but his confident posture said otherwise. He was dressed so impeccably in a tailored pearl-gray suit and crisp white shirt that his diminutive height didn't detract too much from his impression. He was also very cordial to them. When Rob led the way, following the receptionist to the palatial corner office, Bono came out to greet them, extending his hand and sporting a welcoming smile.

"Good day, Detectives. Please come into my office."

Rob's eyes bounced around the room before he took a seat where Bono indicated on a leather bench opposite his desk. He went around to the other side and placed his hands, fingers spread, on the desktop. "Tell me what you need to know. I want to help in any way I can to solve Cate's terrible murder." He clapped his manicured hand against his chest. "It was such a personal loss to us—she was superb at her job and an all-around great human being.

As soon as Bono opened his mouth, Rob already knew two things: one, that Raphael Bono was gay and two, that most likely he despised Cate Caldwell but kept her on because she was good at her job. Call it a cop's intuition.

"We'll start with the basics," Myla began. "How long did she work here?"

Bono's eyes shot up to the ceiling. Rob noted that they tracked to the right. It was important to note that since in all likelihood, he'd be telling the truth to this question.

"Oh, it has to be more than two years at this point. I can pull her employee record if you'd like and tell you for certain."

"For now, don't bother, but on our way out, if someone could look it up, it may prove helpful. Did you hire her yourself or did someone else?"

"I did."

"Do you remember what struck you about her at the time?"

His eyes went to the right again—honest answer. "Her roster of clients that she'd built up as a freelancer was impressive. That alone would have sold me, but she also had a lot of personal style—she was actually a perfect fit for our agency."

Another question for an honest answer. "How long has your agency been in existence?"

Up to the ceiling and to the right. "We'll be celebrating our fifth year in March."

"What was her reputation here? Was she well liked?"

"Hmm," he said and this time when he thought about it, his eyes went to the left. Rob decided he wasn't going to be truthful here. "I would say… that some people liked her quite a lot."

"Can you be more specific?"

He snickered. "OK, the men in particular liked Cate—she was very beautiful. The women…" He seesawed his hand. "…not so much. To be frank, Cate could be a bitch at times. She was also very direct, a quality not everyone appreciates."

"Anyone hate her enough to do her harm, in your opinion?"

His hands fluttered. "God, no, not like that. I was referring to petty things, nothing that would involve murder, for God's sake. One thing everyone did appreciate about Cate was her knack for PR. She was so good that she made everyone else look good too. Our agency is not the same without her.

"In fact," he said, sitting up straighter, "I was pleading with her to come on board full time. She started working here only a couple of days a week and I kept asking her to stay later or come in on her days off. By the time she died, she was nearly at full time."

"Did she have any kind of affair going with any of the male employees?"

A strange look passed over his face, and his eyes again went to the left. Another potential lie. "It's not impossible, but I didn't know of any. She had a pretty amazing husband."

Rob almost laughed at his comment. Was Bono attracted to Caldwell? "How many employees in your firm, sir?"

"Currently, we have six reps and two full-time administrative people. We also employ three part-time temps."

Myla looked up from her notepad. "Does that number include Cate Caldwell?"

"Yes. So I guess we have five now."

"Who else should we talk to?"

Bono shook his head. "I don't know that anyone could shed any more light than I have, but her closest female ally here was Bettina Ross."

"And male? Ally?" Rob prodded.

"Male?" He laughed. "Well, there are three men and counting Cate, three women, excluding the admin staff—of the admins, Cate really only dealt with Emma on a regular basis. You might try all three guys, but I cannot promise results."

"All three in two years, huh?" Rob snapped his pad closed and turned his head to try to see outside the frosted glass wall. "Are they all here now?"

Bono picked up his phone and pressed a button. "Tess, who's in the office right now? Uh-huh. Kai is due back when? OK, thanks." He looked at the detectives. "Of the three men, we have one here now, and one should be back in the office within the hour."

"And the third?"

"Is in LA. He'll be back Tuesday."

The two stood up and Bono followed suit. "Point us to the first victim, please—oh, and is there an office we can use?"

Bono nodded as the three filed out the door. "You can use our conference room."

FITZGIBBONS FOLDED his large body into the black mesh chair directly across from Alex *Yoyo* Arroyo, studying him closely before uttering a word. His black hair was slicked back and his fingernails buffed. His most noticeable accessory, though, was his overconfidence. They guy had an air about him that Rob didn't much care for. Arroyo was about thirty, a good-looking guy but spent way too much time on his appearance.

"Rafe said you wanted to see me, Detectives?"

These hipster types annoyed the fuck out of Rob, and he couldn't understand why women would be drawn to a moron like this guy, but out of the corner of his eye, he could see his partner's interest perk up as soon as the asshole sailed into the conference room. Rob couldn't stop his smirk because he'd have sworn on a stack of Bibles that Kelvin batted for the other team.

Maybe he should let her take the lead? He made a split-second decision to do just that and waited for her to pick up on it and begin. When she looked over toward him a minute later, he jerked his head.

"Yoyo. Unusual name," she started by commenting. "Is the nickname derived from your surname or because you play with the toy?"

The man smiled thinly. "My name."

Rob watched his facial expressions as well as his body language. Right off the bat, he didn't trust him—but then he'd probably say the same about everyone in this office. They were all fake to some degree. This guy looked as if he religiously worked out at the gym and spent all his discretionary income on clothes.

"OK, Mr. Arroyo, we're here to ask about Cate Caldwell. How well did you know her?"

Yoyo shrugged and flattened his lips. "I knew her enough. Enough to know she was a cutthroat when it came to business."

"How long did you know her?"

His eyes went up and to the left. "Mmm, I'd say about

as long as she'd been here. Cate was the kind of woman who attracted attention."

"Did you date her?" Myla probed.

"Not really."

The detective huffed a chuckle. "I think my question warranted a yes or no answer. Yes, you did date her, or no, you did not? Can't be both ways."

He sighed in annoyance. "Yes, I did date her but very briefly and at least a year ago."

"Was she married at the time?"

"Not yet but she was getting ready to walk the plank."

"Is that supposed to be funny?"

He shrugged. "I'm not a fan of marriage. Anyway, I suppose Cate saw it as a last fling—or at least I thought so at the time."

"What changed your mind?"

"She fooled around after she was married. Cate wasn't the faithful type, I guess."

"No? Why do you think she bothered to get married?"

"I dunno. I think in her way she loved Mason. And I doubt she'd leave him over a quick thing. But Cate lived her life at ninety miles an hour, you know? She was a force of nature."

"Really? Do you know who else she may have had an intimate relationship with?"

"I can't say for sure, but she seemed very tight with Jared. It's possible it was innocent, though. I'm not sure."

"What ended your fling with her?"

"Nothing ended it. It just ran its course."

"How long was its course?"

He pursed his lips. "I guess about two months, give or take a week or two."

"Who walked away first?"

There was an expression that flitted across his face too fast to read. "She did."

"Were you upset?"

"Not really. I mean, I was taken by surprise that it was over so quickly, but I didn't expect much more either. You know?"

"No, I don't know. Are you saying you expected it to last longer?"

"Maybe." His fingers tugged at his lower lip. "Maybe a little longer. Whatever, I guess I knew it was coming since she was getting married."

"All right, Mr. Arroyo, if you think of anything that might help us in our investigation, we'd appreciate hearing it. Meantime, if you were me, who would you question next?"

A sly smile. "Jared Exton. Definitely Jared Exton."

THE TWO DETECTIVES shared a look when Jared Exton swaggered through the door. He wore skintight jeans, a blue gingham Oxford shirt hanging out and Italian loafers with no socks. What Fitzgibbons really couldn't forgive was the man bun on the top of the guy's head, holding his long sandy-blond hair in a messy knot—he thought they were ridiculous and emasculating. Just looking at Exton made the cop squirm in his chair. Total waste of oxygen and knowing that Cate had anything to do with him made her slip more than a few notches in his estimation—even further down than when he learned she was a cheater.

About the only positive thing the detective could say about this guy was that he was attractive in a very specific way: blond, big green eyes, and lean, girlish body.

He seemed nervous in their presence. His eyes shifted rapidly between the detectives.

"You need to talk to me about Cate?"

"Have a seat please, Mr. Exton." Myla gestured.

He took the chair she pointed to and crossed his foot over his knee. Neither detective spoke right away, unnerving him. It was a time-honored technique that never failed to yield quick results.

He uncrossed his leg and leaned forward. "How can I help you?" he asked, wiping his right hand on his pants.

Sweating.

Fitzgibbons cleared his throat and jumped right in. "How long were you and Cate Caldwell having a thing?"

"A thing?" The spineless guy almost smiled.

Fitzgibbons waved his hand in the air. "An affair, whatever. How long?"

Exton shrugged. "Only a couple of months—if that. It was too intense, so it burned out quickly."

"Tell us about it."

Licking his lips, he appeared to choose his words carefully. "I knew Cate was married when I started here, but I was physically attracted to her nonetheless. She was beautiful, and I think every heterosexual man who ever met her was attracted to her."

"And?"

"And I learned a few weeks later that she liked me too. We went out for drinks after work one night… her husband was out of town… one thing led to another."

"When did the two of you stop seeing each other?"

He pressed his lips together and stared at Rob before he answered. "We hadn't actually stopped. But Cate had told me that night—the night she was killed—that it had run its course."

"How did you take that?"

His voice raised. "How do you think I took it?"

"I have no clue. Why don't you enlighten me?"

"I was upset, for God's sake. I was falling in love with her—and to her I was just a side lay."

"All right. So how expressly did it end between you?"

"It was ugly, I guess. When I didn't agree right away to stop seeing one another, she got mad and started flinging insults at me and she… whatever. She left the office soon after."

"She what? You were starting to say something?"

"She was just Cate being Cate—she could be a ruthless bitch if she wanted to, and she said really mean things."

"Did you insult her back? Yell at her? How did you react?"

"I was upset, OK? I said things I didn't mean." He looked around the room and threw his hands up in the air. "This is ridiculous. I didn't kill her, for God's sake."

"Do you know who did?"

He shot up out of his chair, the volume of his voice rising with his anger. "No, I don't know who killed her, but I'd hazard to say that Cate got what she fucking deserved the way she walked all over people. Serves the bitch right."

THREE HOURS LATER, they'd interviewed everyone who was available. There was only one admin and one temp in today, so they conducted those interviews as well. When the last one walked out of the conference room and closed the door, Fitzgibbons swung his tired eyeballs over to his partner.

He arched his brows. "What are you thinking?"

"Not sure. Exton is a possibility—it's not difficult to get him riled up. We need to check his background carefully. The rest? Not so much."

"Yeah, but that Vanessa woman seemed awful peeved

that Cate bought the same shoes she had—as if Cate saw them on her feet and then ran out to buy them."

"Hey," said Myla, "she might have. Imagine the horrors of owning the same shoes and possibly wearing them on the same day." She shuddered dramatically.

Rob laughed and uncrossed his leg. Eying the room done in purplish gray and ivory with pewter accents, he felt twitchy just sitting here for a few hours. "Yeah, well, we needed to conduct these interviews, but I have to be honest —I can't wait to get out of this place. It's making me itchy."

"It's all the negative karma floating around here," she retorted. "You must be allergic to it."

"Yeah, maybe. Allergic or not, we have a killer to find."

Chapter 19

Two days after Jane got the last of her medical paraphernalia off—the neck brace was the last to go—was a Saturday, and her doorbell rang at eleven a.m. while she was still in her pajamas: loose yoga pants and an oversized T-shirt. All her clothes were loose on her except for the few things she'd added to her wardrobe since she got out of the hospital. Granted, they weren't as baggy as she'd expected, given what everyone had commented about her former size, but that was a good thing since many of her clothes were still somewhat wearable. She headed downstairs.

It rang again as she was on the last step. "Coming," she sang out. Hurrying to the door and nearly tripping over the area rug, she caught herself just in time. *That would be my stinking luck*, she thought. *I'd go right back into some kind of cast or brace*. "Who is it?"

The voice was muffled but audible. "Not a gorgeous man come to plow you, unfortunately for you."

Jane rolled her eyes. Pulling open the heavy door, she greeted her friend with a frown. "Seriously, you need to get your mind out of the gutter. And what the hell are you doing here so early?"

Mel was grinning like a loon. "You're officially recovered, and we're going shopping to celebrate. When you come back to work, you're going to be a smokin' hot babe, and everyone's going to fall all over you in appreciation."

"They already do 'cause I always trip them when they pass my desk," Jane retorted. "It's my only fun in life."

Mel's brows pulled together. "I always wondered why everyone was always so clumsy around you. Well, you're not going to have to trip people for them to fall all over themselves when they see you now, bella. You're gonna be a hot mofo. C'mon, we'll hit a few stores and then have brunch before finishing up."

STOPPED AT A RED LIGHT, Mel's eyes shifted to her. "So how are you doing lately? I haven't been able to see you as much."

Jane nodded, her face somber. "OK… not great, to be honest. No new memories, my head's still throbbing a lot, and I've been having nightmares. I think it's because of this whole murder thing."

"Do you think you know more than you remember?"

A long sigh escaped Jane. "I simply don't know. I've racked my brain trying to remember, but I just don't. I can't imagine, though, in the short time I've been living here that I would have had any interaction with them—the Caldwells. I don't even know if I knew that Mason was living next door. And that detective seems to think I know more than I'm letting on. I don't like him—sorry, I know you do."

Mel's face looked troubled. "Do you think you're a suspect?"

Jane's head whipped toward Mel. "Am I, do you know?"

"It just seems… the cops keep coming to ask you questions. I don't know."

"Mel, it would be horrible if I am. I mean, how can I even help myself when I have no memory of any of it?"

"Don't get mad but let me just ask you this: have you ever had any violent tendencies?"

Her eyes flew wide open. "Mel, please tell me you don't think I could've been involved in the murder?"

"Of course not. I'm just trying to help you feel better. Hey, you know what? We're going shopping, and we're going to have fun, damn it. No more talk about worries or memory or murders. We're here today to make you look even more gorgeous than you already are—and maybe to get a little drunk."

Jane tried to smile in response… but it wasn't a happy smile.

SIX HOURS later Jane collapsed on the one comfortable chair she had downstairs, exhausted from Mel's speed shopping. They had to have gone to at least ten shops before they were done. Brunch was the only relaxing time of the day. Mel wanted to get in a quick cocktail before they parted ways, but Jane was too tired. In any case, she wasn't supposed to drink any alcohol until she was entirely off the pain meds. She'd just about made it home, stumbled through the door, dropping her packages, and heaved herself down on the brown velvet chair, currently the only comfortable chair in the house. She sat frozen in place, not even willing to move to look at her pretty new clothes.

"Ugh, why can't I just sit here forever," she groaned and dragged herself off the chair, summoning the energy to gather up her shopping bags and slog her way upstairs. She opened each one, gently laying out the garment on the bed, until her queen-sized mattress was covered with clothes. Jane smiled.

"That Mel is a shopping goddess," she said to the empty room. "She finds the best prices and locates amazing diamonds among rocks on the sale racks. It's too bad that she's also insane, making me walk all over the freaking city all freaking day."

She dragged off her right shoe and then her left and tossed them toward the open closet while admiring her booty. For a little over nine hundred dollars, Jane now had a decent new wardrobe. She got a suit, a pair of matching navy-blue pumps, two pairs of trousers, three silk shirts, two cotton, a fitted black cardigan, a wool blazer, and a pair of jeans. Mel had checked her closet beforehand and seen an adequate collection of boots, running shoes, sandals, and clogs. Jane's feet hadn't changed sizes luckily.

Mel had then lectured her on the need to get new lingerie and sleepwear but Jane had two drawers full of the former and if the various items were a little big, so what? It's not as if anyone would see her in them. As for PJs, she liked to sleep in her yoga pants, the more worn, the better, and she told Mel the same.

"Uh-uh," Mel had answered, shaking her head vigorously. "Silk for bed."

Jane had grimaced at the thought. "Why? I'm alone. No need to dress up."

"For now, you might be alone. For the moment. But it's for you, anyway, to make you feel sexy and good about yourself." Mel tugged lightly on Jane's hair. "Speaking of sexy and good, can I borrow those Louboutin shoes in your closet?"

"Which ones are those again?"

"Which ones are those?" she mimicked. "Surely you jest. They might as well be made of neon the way they flash their utter beauty in your dim closet. I shouldn't have to tell you this, Jane, but they're the come-fuck-me black heels with the red soles. I don't even care that they're not my size. I want to wear them just once—they're just so freaking gorgeous. Toes can be mended pretty cheaply, right?"

Shaking her head, Jane laughed at the memory. It was so Mel. She should just give her the shoes—or better yet, buy her an identical pair in her own size. Jane made a mental note to do just that. Mel deserved that and much more for being such a true blue.

Refusing to budge off the mattress, Jane spied her journal on the bedside table. She should write a few lines in it. For a while now there was something niggling at the back of her mind. She felt as if it was something big but try as she might, she couldn't tease it out from her damaged brain. Maybe writing would help her remember?

Reluctantly she picked it up, feeling trepidation at what the memory might contain. She knew there were some horrible ones yet to come.

Especially the accident.

Chapter 20

Janey's Journal, November 3rd

DOES Mel think I'm a murderer?

Today we went shopping—Mel and I—and I bought a new wardrobe. On the way there, Mel was asking me some weird questions. Then when she saw me getting upset, she dropped the subject so fast it made my head spin. Honestly, I can't even think about it anymore. I've been making myself sick over the whole thing.

I've been depressed and God, I am just so grateful to have a friend like Mel. I can't imagine how bleak my life would be without her. I definitely don't want her to think I'm a bad person.

Mel is so great and we had fun today. She'd told me last week that I needed new clothes, and she was going to help me get some. First, she went through my closet with me last week and selected the pieces that she deemed acceptable to remain with the rest going into the goodwill box. That was exhausting since I had to fight with her to keep just about anything. Then I tried each one on, and only a few blouses fit me well enough to go into the keep pile. Essentially, we were starting from scratch—except for ultra-casual clothes like my numerous pairs of yoga pants and a pair of jeans that worked with a belt.

Today we hit three or four clothing boutiques, a shoe store, a jewelry shop—where I got nothing but Mel bought herself a sterling silver bracelet—and two department stores, before collapsing at the café table. With less than a thousand dollars, I got quite a lot, so I treated Mel to lunch for lending me her retail expertise. Mostly, I got business attire but I have a drawer full of sweats and Mel said they don't have to fit well since I'm only allowed to wear them at home. *Alone.* She promised next shopping trip we'd buy more comfortable clothes like sexy yoga pants and T-shirts.

I like shopping and I love spending time with Mel, but these pounding headaches are plaguing me, and my memory recovery has all but halted. I keep having dreams about train rides. Slender fragments of memories for which I have no context are more than frustrating, and that's all I've been getting lately. It feels as if my mental recovery has stalled.

The good news is that my doctor has given me clearance to return to work on a modified schedule. MT has been so incredibly accommodating; I feel really lucky to be working for such a great company. Initially, I'll be working three days a week, six hours a day, and if I feel up to it, I'll be working from home the other two days for a total of thirty hours.

First thing, I called Mel.

"Talk to me. What's going on?"

"I got medical clearance to return to work—at least part time. Yay."

"Yay? Seriously, you need counseling. Most people

would be crying in their beer at the thought of going back to work after a nice, long vacay."

"I don't drink beer generally," I quipped, laughing. "Great vacay in the hospital—everyone should try it. Personally, I think a Caribbean island is a tad better. So listen, I was going through my checkbook register and there's a really large check that I'd written out to UNICEF. I'm assuming it must have been a donation, right?"

"Unless you're purchasing children on the black market from some corrupt humanitarian, I'd say it's a good guess. Why?"

She delayed answering for half a minute. "I don't know. It's nice to know that I care about children."

"I actually remember your telling me how two days before last New Year's you sat down and for a few hours, you wrote out a bunch of checks to charities. Not only UNICEF but Greenpeace too. And Doctors Without Borders, I think.

"I'm happy that I made charitable donations. It means that I care about others."

"Of course, you care about others. Jane, you're a kind and decent person. I wouldn't be your friend otherwise." She stopped and then added, "You know, there are other fun things you can do in bed besides reading and watching a screen." She cleared her throat exaggeratedly.

"Uh-huh. I just need to find someone to do them with."

"Not necessarily…"

I laughed but speaking of which… "Mel, did that guy Ed Jensen ever call you back after you left that voicemail for him?"

"No, he didn't."

"Hmm." I tried to hide my disappointment. The idea that he might have been a boyfriend was exciting…

comforting even. What about men in my life? Were there any?

I know I'm not a virgin… well, first because I'm twenty-five. But also because I have wisps of memories of being with a man… or maybe different men. I can't see their faces but there's some muscle memory. I just don't know if there's currently someone or had been recently.

And then there's the birth control pills in my medicine cabinet. I can make an appointment with the doctor on the label and get more information from her.

If there were men in my life currently… well, I would know it by now. It was odd that the guy asked about me the day of my accident. He'd left his number and Mel tried to call him back but no one answered, and the voicemail didn't go anywhere. Mel was never sure if the woman at the hospital got the number wrong or what. He said his name was Ed Jensen. No relation.

The name doesn't ring any bells with me. Besides, if he'd been involved with me, why hasn't he contacted me since?

The only obvious conclusion is that I'm single.

The twinge in my chest tells me how much I wish there were someone.

And who was Ed anyway?

I woke up thirsty. Tried to open my eyes wide enough to see the clock on the other side of the bed. Middle of the night. Lately I wake up needing water, so I keep a filled carafe on my night table. I was sitting up in bed sipping my water when a memory came roaring back out of nowhere. One minute I was thinking about the coolness of the water, and the next I was immersed in a high school memory. The experience was so intense it left me shaking.

It was during the summer between sophomore and junior year that I decided to get my shit together. I was never grossly overweight—only about thirty or forty pounds. In late spring, I began to diet and by the time summer rolled around I was in full swing, stubbornly sticking to a strict diet and exercising like a mad person. By August I'd lost forty-six pounds and was down to 122 on my then five-foot-seven frame—since then I've grown an inch. I wanted a whole new me, so I cut my hair into a different style and started wearing a little makeup. My mother was so elated I thought she'd stroke out from the joy of it, but when school started in September I was terrified to debut the new me.

So I didn't.

I wore baggy clothes to disguise my weight loss and cut out the makeup, returning to the relative comfort of being invisible. Anyway, there was really no such thing as a new Jane Jensen. Mom gave me the stink-eye when she saw me come down the stairs the first day of school but said nothing. Ever. Could it be that she possibly understood me for once in her life?

The week before Halloween I started hearing hallway buzz about a party someone was having. Joe Torres lived in a big house with its own small lake, and his parents were going away for a week, leaving Joe and his older sister at home alone. What could go wrong? Their parents might as well have sent out invitations themselves to every nearby high school. Though it was close to Halloween, the word was that costumes were optional. Everyone who heard about it was invited.

I can still remember how nervous I was getting ready that night. I didn't tell anyone I knew that I was going, not even Sulu, because I planned to go in costume. I was going as the new Jane and half hoping that no one would even recognize me.

From the back of my dresser drawer, I dug out the tight

jeans I'd purchased during the summer as my prize for attaining my weight goal, and I shimmied into them. They were a perfect fit. Reaching under the bed, I pulled out a shopping bag from the favorite teen store in the mall. Inside was a Ramones T-shirt, with a low scoop neck, short cap sleeves, and a handkerchief hemline—long in the center and short on the sides. It was tight-fitting and showed off my new waistline.

Next, I slipped my feet into high-heeled black leather ankle boots.

I wasn't used to wearing heels so I sort of stumbled to the bathroom to do my makeup. Once the war paint was on, I knew I had to be able to get out of the house without my parents seeing me. I had to be ready to go.

Doing the makeup wasn't easy for me. One time in high school, I worked up the nerve to ask Makenna Carter, a beautiful blond girl who was in my English and French classes, about applying makeup. Her face was made up to China-doll perfection and it was seriously hard not to stare at her. When I asked her how she knew how to do it, she looked at me as if I were a bizarre science experiment. Her internal struggle was fun to watch. It was clear that she didn't want to get caught talking to a girl with no name, such as I was, but the opportunity to talk about herself was irresistible. I had, of course, anticipated that weakness on her part and exploited it for my own entertainment.

"I watched my mom, for one thing," she'd finally said. "But usually I follow magazines and online how-to videos."

"Oh," I'd responded.

She'd turned those eerily black-lined eyes on me. "Doesn't your mother wear makeup?"

"Oh, tons of it, but I can't learn much because she slathers it on with a trowel." I wasn't entirely sure that

Makenna even knew what a trowel was, but she got the general idea.

"Well then, go online and find a tutorial. It's easy as long as you have the right kinds of makeup."

"OK, thanks."

I had one of my mother's issues of Cosmopolitan propped up on the vanity to give me pointers. I only owned two tubes of lipstick and some mascara that had dried up, so I had to raid my mom's cosmetic cabinet. I smudged charcoal gray and bronze on my eyelids, then used gray eye pencil to darken around my lashes and piled on the mascara. I smeared on a little foundation but it was too light for my skin so I blotted most of it off as I had seen my mom do countless times and then I applied my dark red lipstick, coating it with petroleum jelly for shine. When I stepped back from the mirror, I couldn't believe it was me in the reflection. Makeup is some amazing stuff. It had transformed me into an attractive hooker.

I couldn't wear my hair in one of my two Jane fashions —long and parted on the side or pulled back in a loose ponytail. So I dabbed some product into it and then combed it over to the other side of my face—almost over one eye and pulled it into a messy bun. I figured I'd wear big earrings to draw attention away from it.

Now I was ready, only needing a jacket from my mother's closet so no part of me would be recognizable as Jane Jensen. I slipped into the master bedroom and tiptoed to her walk-in closet. Flipping the switch, the closet filled with a bright light, and I quickly found a navy cardigan with silver buttons. My dad had a much cooler military jacket, but when I tried it on it was way too big. I stuck to the sweater, wishing I had a leather biker jacket.

Both my parents were in the living room watching television as I silently sidled by, shuffling my feet so as not to let my heels click on the tiled floor. I'd almost passed the double archway and was thinking I'd gotten away with it when I heard her shrill voice.

"Jane? Where are you going?"

Rolling my eyes, I groaned as she got up and walked to the hall. Her eyes nearly popped out of her skull when she took me in, so at least it was good for a laugh. "A party."

Such pure joy radiated from her eyes that I almost laughed right in her face. My mother was a popular girl in school so it was to her everlasting disappointment that her only daughter was one of the untouchables.

"Wonderful." She placed her clasped hands against her lips. "You look absolutely beautiful. Go have fun but be home before midnight."

I checked the clock. It was barely seven-thirty. Yeah, I doubted I'd be much later than nine but no need to burst her bubble. "Right. I will."

It was only about a quarter mile to the Torres house, but I made the most of it. The closer I got, the more paralyzed with fear I became, and my steps got slower and smaller until I was barely moving. Could I do it?

Yes. The answer was yes. I could do it and I would do it. Period.

I REMEMBER THE MUSIC. Nirvana. Cobain was the patron saint of all angsty teenagers. I started hearing it as soon as I got near his property. As I got closer I saw the front door was ajar, and blaring music and voices flowed out with the stench of weed. The two girls who'd been ten steps ahead of me had just walked right in, so I did the same. Scanning the crowded room, I searched for any familiar faces. Here and there I saw people I recognized from high school, but none were in my grade, none were any I knew. They were spilling over from another room and packed into the wide, double-height foyer. I weaved through the coalescing bodies, trying to move farther into the house. When I made it to the living room, there were coolers lining the hardwood floor, filled to the brim with beer and wine coolers. I bent down and grabbed a Corona before I kept going.

Just up ahead was a knot of people. I sauntered over casually, noticing a tall guy in the center who looked vaguely familiar. When I reached the circle, I looked at them all up close and not a one was from my class.

But before I could breathe a sigh of relief, I caught a glimpse of the face of the guy in the center as he turned to answer someone: Mason Caldwell.

Holding court as always.

When he finished the story, everyone laughed boisterously. I slugged my beer too enthusiastically, and some dribbled out of both sides of my mouth. I wiped the back of my hand across my lips, forgetting I was wearing lipstick. A slash of red now decorated my skin but I didn't really care. I was too transfixed on Mason. When I looked back at him, I caught him staring at me.

Me. Mason Caldwell was staring at me. Mason Caldwell was checking me out.

"Hey," he said as he made his way through the group to come closer. "I'm Mason," he added with a slight slur and held out his hand.

He doesn't recognize me. And he's drunk. I reached out to take it, my heart slamming against the wall of my chest. This boy… I'd been crushing on this boy for years now. "Hi. I'm… Janine."

"Pretty name. You live around here, Janine?"

"Um, I used to. Now I'm visiting my cousin. How 'bout you?" I quickly flipped it back to him. The less I had to lie, the better. Even though he totally didn't recognize me for the moment, the less said the better.

"Yeah, I do." He staggered back but quickly regained his footing. His eyes, though dilated, never lost focus and made me squirm. "You look familiar. When did you move away?"

I took another pull at my beer to buy some time. How did he not recognize me? Did I look that different? "Um, about four years ago, we moved."

"Oh, did you go to Sandringham?"

Shaking my head, I tipped the bottle back. If I was drinking, I couldn't talk. Plus, I needed to get drunk soon. "Nah, private school. Did you? Go to Sandringham?"

"Yep, I did. So… are you here with anyone?" His eyes scanned all around me.

"No. I came by myself."

"Do you wanna get another beer and maybe sit outside to talk? It's so loud and smoky in here."

"It is. Yeah, sure."

THAT'S where the memory dissolves into the fog of amnesia. I knew, I just knew there was more to the story, a lot more, but the details refused to budge from their hiding place. Something happened afterward, I know it, and it had something to do with an accident I had in high school, but I just couldn't loosen the ensnarled memories. I had an accident—wait, no, I got hit by a car—but I'm pretty sure it happened around Valentine's Day so it couldn't have anything to do with the Halloween party… but my brain was telling me it somehow did. I just couldn't connect the dots.

The accident was traumatic and ruined my whole junior year of high school.

Sulu and I had gone to a movie. A lot of high school kids were there—it was the opening of a Star Wars marathon. Something bad happened… I can't remember what… but something… and I ran. I ran right into the road. I saw the SUV only a second before it slammed into me. It was huge, a Suburban, and the white-hot pain upon impact was immersive. And then… then something else followed.

Something terrible.

This memory has a passenger: I can sense some kind of disabling depression. I feel it, this annihilating sadness… it encompasses me in a psychic darkness…

I think someone died. I think someone was murdered.

Chapter 21

At seven p.m. Mel was getting dressed for her date with Detective Fitzgibbons. For such a rugged alpha male-type—and he was, at 6'1 with shoulders as wide as a semi—he was kind of shy when he asked her out. He'd gotten her phone number the afternoon they made the chili together. His phone had begun vibrating, and he'd put down the knife and wiped his hands on a dishtowel.

"Fitzgibbons. Yes. Understood. Nine tomorrow morning. I'll be there. Thank you."

Mel tried to act as if she somehow didn't hear a word of his conversation. When the room went quiet, she sneaked a hurried glance at him. He was sitting there, knees spread wide, just studying her as she glided around the kitchen.

"What?" she'd asked.

"Nothing. I just figured as long as I have my phone out, I should take your number. You know..." He grinned. "...in case I think of any questions you could answer that may assist us on some aspect of the case."

She played along with his bogus explanation: both of

them knew she had no further information to give him, but if he needed the cover to ask her for her number, so be it. He'd called her the very next night. Tonight was their second date in a week, the first one being a jazz performance in a little dive bar on Ludlow Street. That bar must have been the last holdout of gentrification on the Lower East Side. She was impressed that he liked jazz—didn't fit the stereotype. Country, yes but jazz was a happy surprise. Good on him.

As far as the performance went, Mel thought the music was probably good, but she'd been too focused on trying not to die of hypothermia to pay it too much attention. The place felt like it had no heat, and the door kept being opened by latecomers, allowing the cold air to rush in continuously.

Tonight, they'd be inside a warm restaurant and then movie theatre. Much better since it was a bitch of a cold November.

Rob had told her to wear whatever made her comfortable, so she pulled on a pair of tight jeans, a new imitation-mohair sweater, and chunky-heeled ankle boots. Applying her mascara, her mind wandered to Jane and she thought about the whole grisly thing with the next-door neighbors. Meticulously staining her lips between the liner lines, Mel decided Jane should list her house and move. Brushing on some bronzer, she concluded that it had to be bad *feng shui* to have a murderer living next door.

The closer the clock inched to 7:45—the time Rob was picking her up—the more excited Mel became. When she thought of him, her heartbeat galloped. Who knew? Maybe this one would work out... She wasn't thrilled that he was a cop—for multiple reasons. Still, Rob had more in the plus column than the minus. For a change.

If not for the specter of the murder investigation, Mel

would really be savoring this exploration, but she was getting the uncomfortable impression that Rob didn't like or trust Jane. Mainly because he said so. And when he was telling them about the photo found in Caldwell's dresser, it had felt more like an interrogation of Jane.

To banish the dour thought, Mel decided she had time for a glass of wine. She was on her way to the kitchen when the bell rang twice, right on time too. Veering toward the door, she flung it open ready to launch herself at him in a sneak attack, but one look at Rob's grim face and Mel's good mood evaporated. He looked… angry. Or maybe troubled. She didn't know him well enough to be able to discern subtle differences.

"Everything all right with you?"

He nodded, tight-lipped. "Yeah, sure. Hungry?"

"Starving. Where are we going?"

"Like Thai food?"

Her eyes widened. "Love it."

"Figured as much," he said, huffing out a sardonic little laugh. "I have reservations at a tiny place in Chelsea. Food's supposed to be really good. You ready?"

"Uh-huh. Let me just grab my peacoat."

"SO… are you going to tell me what's up with you?" Mel finally asked him about an hour into their uncomfortable dinner.

She hadn't endured a meal with such awkward silences since the family dinner three years before when her Uncle Eddie announced over the salad course that he identified as a woman and going forward, wanted everyone to call him Alicia. His announcement was a real conversation killer, Mel remembered. There were a few attempts to get it going again, but after each remark a squirming silence reclaimed the table.

As dessert was being served Uncle Eddie popped up, went into a bedroom, and Aunt Alicia came out in a royal-blue empire dress and five-inch stilettos. Dessert became riveting to everyone around the table. Eyes glued on their dishes, they all sucked down the pie and ice cream as if their lives depended on it and then scattered like broken glass. Mel stayed at the table, noticing that Alicia's eyeliner was uneven and gave her some tips on how to avoid that. Her aunt appreciated the advice and blew her a kiss across the blueberry pie.

"Forget it, Melanie," Rob's voice jerked her back to this dismal dinner. "It's about the case, and you know I can't discuss it with you. Conflict of interest."

"Don't you think you should recuse yourself from it since we're seeing each other now?"

"I would," he said, stabbing a broccoli floret with his fork, "but I just did that recently." He looked at his fork glumly. "What made people think to eat these things anyway? Broccoli does not look like something I would've put in my mouth if I were a Neanderthal looking for food."

"You are a Neanderthal, Rob. Would you finish what you were saying, please?"

He snorted a laugh. "Tree-hugging commie. What I was saying was that my younger brother was peripherally involved in some trouble and I got myself yanked from the case just to be on the safe side. I can't do it again… not so soon after… or it will look odd."

Whatever, but she still needed to know what was stuck up his ass. He'd shown up at her house moody, and his disposition was not improving at all with beer and food. What was going on? She was worried for Jane. She pressed her lips together, trying to think of a way around the impasse. "What would happen if you told me and I kept my mouth shut? Nothing, right?"

His eyes shot up from his plate and they looked mean. "The problem stems from the fact that you might not keep your mouth shut and I—"

"I would keep it shut to protect you," she interrupted. "Why would I intentionally jeopardize your job?"

"Not my job, Melanie, but my case. Do you really have to ask me why?"

"Yeah, as a fucking matter of fact, I really do, *Rob*," she spat out his name.

He scowled, shaking his head, before snapping, "To help your friend. Why else?"

"My friend? Jane?"

He just looked at her with hostile eyes.

"Why would Jane need my help? Is she in trouble?"

He put down his fork, and his lips pulled tight into a straight line. "She might be. Look, that's all I can say. Can we just have a nice dinner and evening?"

"Dude, pretty sure you're the one ruining it. Lighten up and maybe we can. This is only our second date, for God's sake. It doesn't bode well for any future," she added in a jokey way, but the truth of her words hit her sideways. She liked Rob and was enormously attracted to him. Last night all she could think about was getting him into bed tonight and hanging onto those shoulders while he pounded into her. It would be good. She knew he was packing a lot more than his gun, too, because when they kissed goodnight on their last date, she could feel his hardware through his jeans.

Felt pretty substantial.

She wanted him and wanted this thing between them to progress. Maybe she needed to get him drunk? Although drunk and cop might not be the smartest mix. But a nice little buzz…

"Let's go back to my place instead of going to the movies. I'll make us a couple of Irish coffees, and we can watch an old flick. How's that sound?"

Ah, where there's a will… she finally wrangled a grin out of the man. "Sounds good, Mel. Let's do it."

THEY SAT, thighs grazing, on her overstuffed sectional that took up the entire cramped living room, sipping the strong Irish coffee. Melanie went heavy on the whiskey, adding it to decaf so they wouldn't be up all night. Whipped cream and cinnamon topped it. Then she searched through her saved recordings for a lighthearted film. *It Happened One Night* was the winner. She had a feeling that Rob was a black-and-white-old-movie kind of guy.

Mel picked up the mug and tipped it to her mouth. Heat slid down her throat, both from the temperature of the coffee and the burn of the whiskey. Mmm, she'd balanced the two perfectly. Two years as mixologist at a high-volume Williamsburg bar did right by her even now, years after. Braced with liquid courage, she put down the drink and sidled closer to Rob, curling into his side and easing her hand onto his crotch. The slight touch triggered an instant reaction, his body jerking to attention and his eyes swooping to hers. In them she saw the flare of surprise.

"What?" she asked innocently.

"Nothing… just seriously not expecting you to go there." His brows arched. "We pretty much just met."

"Well, I wouldn't want to sully your virtue, Detective Fitzgibbons; however, I beg to differ about just meeting. We've had two dinners and a show together. Plus, a black-

and-white vintage comedy. But if you think it's too soon..."

She waited for him to jump in and refute her last comment, but he didn't. He didn't want to sleep with her?

An ugly thing sparked to life in her belly and began to spread its tentacles of poison. Needing to move, she pulled away from him and leaned forward toward the coffee table, again reaching for her drink as rejection merged with paranoia. Was he just using her to get information to build his case? Seemed like a dead end since she didn't know the Caldwells. But he certainly wasn't acting like a man who was interested, and Mel had never before been rebuffed for sex. That was—

His voice punched through her emotional scatter, interrupting the chaos. "Mel, this is a confusing situation for me. I'm a little worried, you know? About how all of this is gonna shake out?"

"Uh-huh." Her tone was robotic and she said nothing else, just stopping the film and waiting for him to talk, to say something to end this toxic waste of an evening and get up and leave. But he made no move to go anywhere, so instead she rose from the sofa and took the still mostly full glasses into the kitchen, taking her time in the hope he'd be gone when she got back.

But he wasn't. He was still on the couch, elbows on knees, expression inscrutable. She just stood there, six feet away and unwilling to get any closer to him. For Mel, rejection was a kind of infection to be avoided at all costs. She didn't feel its rot often, but she'd felt it enough to know to keep her distance whenever it so much as bleeped on her radar. There were only two feelings that were worse—a loss to death or a lover's betrayal.

Right now, her gut felt torqued. The only cure for it

was righteous anger to burn through the bend, but that took a little time to rouse.

She chewed her lip, wondering what to say to him. Did he really want to watch the rest of the movie? She finally plopped back down, keeping her distance from him but didn't turn the movie back on.

He remained stock-still, only raising his eyes to scour hers, looking for… she didn't know what. After an hour-long minute, he asked, "Can we just finish watching the movie? I want to know what happens," he added with a weak laugh but got nothing back. "I was still drinking the coffee before you snatched it away."

"It's still on the kitchen counter if you want it. I just thought maybe we were kind of done here. We've been on a fast decline since you first got here."

"Why? I thought we were relaxing, enjoying each other's company. I know I was." Sighing, he patted the empty space next to him. "C'mere."

When she didn't move, he grabbed and tugged on her hand. She allowed herself to be pulled over.

"Look at me, please."

He was using his cop voice on her, the commanding tone that civilians ignored at their own peril. Despite her intentions, her eyes tracked over to him but her lips stayed closed—the portal holding everything in. If she kept them sealed, nothing could spill out of her that she didn't want to reveal.

Large hands reached over to cradle her face, and she immediately grasped his wrists, tried to lift them away, but he was ten times stronger, and he wouldn't allow her to budge them. "Listen to me. I like you and find you immensely attractive. I think you've felt how much I'm attracted to you, Melanie. The problem is that I don't want to begin a physical relationship with you right before I have to stop seeing you. That wouldn't be fair, to you or to me. And it's starting to look as if I'll have to cut off all contact with you for a long while… until this case is over and done."

"Why?

"In the main because you are close friends with a woman whom I may have to arrest for murder."

Melanie sucked in a breath, her eyes dark saucers. "What? Why? Jane didn't do anything."

Rob said nothing at first as Mel watched a tic in his cheek and he dropped his hands. His lips flattened into a thin line, and he exhaled through his nose, the expulsion amplified. Frustration or judgment? She wasn't anxious to hear what he had to say next, but he said it anyway.

"Things are starting to point her way, Mel. That's all I can say right now. Thing is, if I'm the lead detective on the case and I'm dating the suspect's best friend… well, I can't straddle that fence. It will hurt my case or it will hurt you… or more likely both. It's no-win, Mel. Unless you're willing to cut off contact with Jane, I can't find a way to keep this thing between us going.

"You know, you don't even know this lady that long, Melanie. I'm concerned about your safety around her until we can definitively rule her out—and that's not looking so good lately."

"Do you honestly think Jane would try to hurt me?" Mel was incredulous.

His thick eyebrows hiked up, and the light in his eyes ignited. "Yeah, I kind of do. Why not?" He flounced back into the couch and crossed his leg at the knee.

"What do you mean, why not?"

Sucking his teeth, he gave her a disgusted look. "It's not impossible if she's guilty of orchestrating someone's murder… and she thinks you have any evidence or might have seen something." He wagged his finger in her face. "You want to know what evil looks like? Let me tell you what was waiting for Cate Caldwell's mother at the morgue, Melanie. Her daughter was a beautiful young woman. She could have landed on the cover of any magazine. The quintessential girl-next-door blond beauty.

"What was left on the steel gurney for her mother to identify was a body with pasty gray skin and scrambled brains. The brain injuries bulged out her forehead and eyes, giving her a strange look that really upset her mother."

Mel's mouth fell open at the graphic description, but it didn't stop him. Her reaction might even have egged him on.

"The hollow-point mushroomed inside her brain, maximizing tissue damage. That kind of bullet never exits—or rarely does—so the havoc is all internal because of hydrostatic shock. Can you imagine all that energy unleashed but contained within someone's skull?

"Oh, yeah, and her perfect straight nose was broken pretty badly from her death fall. It was twisted to one side and packed tight with blood. Apparently, her heart was still pumping for a bit after her brain was pulverized.

"Her poor mother—she was distraught to begin with, naturally. But seeing her daughter look like someone else… someone horribly deformed… it provided that extra kick in the gut for her. Just think about that for a second. When you're up close and personal with the consequences of these crimes, it makes it real hard to sympathize with the person responsible. Real fucking hard."

"But Jane's not responsible, Rob. I mean, she can't be. She's a good person." Though she tried for ardent instead of defensive, even Mel could hear the discordant tone in her voice. It felt like a fight… Rob felt like an adversary.

His green eyes blazed as he moved his face closer to her. Too close. "You do not know that, not for sure. The fact is your friend is under investigation as the possible instigator of a vicious crime. If she's guilty then she's not all that good, now is she?"

Mel emptied the air in her lungs in one weighted whoosh, already exhausted by the conversation and effectively ending it by refusing to utter another syllable. Rob finally moved back into his own space, sitting on the edge of his seat, his knee bouncing. She could see the spark in his eyes awaiting re-ignition, challenging her to keep fighting him on this. Mel refused to give him the pleasure. Instead, she threw her hands in the air. "Whatever. I'm done talking about it. Let's just watch the rest of the movie."

Sitting next to him but a million miles away, Mel stewed in her own pissed-off juices. Although the option of abandoning Jane when she needed her most was not one she would consider—and he had to know it—they continued with their shitty evening. She brought back the coffees—actually made fresh ones—and they silently watched the rest of the film.

By the time the credits rolled, Mel had a pleasant whiskey buzz, but it wasn't enough to stop her from being just as vexed as the big guy sitting next to her. When Rob stood up and stretched, Melanie rose from the sofa to see him out, anxious now to be alone. Instead of heading toward the door, his arm snaked around her waist and jerked her closer to him. His other hand palmed her ass, pressing her against his erection and grinding it against her.

"If you want this to happen under these fucked-up circumstances, I guess I'm willing."

"Pfft. How noble… and romantic," she breathed as she looked up at him.

But he wasn't waiting for approval; his lips began trailing up and down her neck, her throat, and behind her ear, sending shivers skipping along her spine. "You want me to stop," he murmured against her skin, "tell me now."

The word go was crouched on her tongue, ready to pounce, and Mel so wanted to let it rip, tell him to leave—she was pissed off and hurt and wanted to pay him back for the earlier rebuff and for accusing Jane of something so horrendous. But she'd been wanting him for days, daydreaming of making love with him…exploring his muscled body and licking every tattoo inked on his golden skin.

So… matter over mind, she gulped down her pride for just this one night, hoping any resulting gag wouldn't be too violent, and allowed him to lead her into the bedroom.

Chapter 22

A thwacking noise, followed by some kind of rolling against a hard surface in the apartment above hers, unceremoniously yanked Melanie from sleep the next morning. She sat up, rubbing her eyes, and as the fog of Morpheus lifted, she remembered details of the night before. Glancing down at the bed, she saw her hunky cop in all his naked glory, sound asleep next to her, the sheet only partially covering him. How could he sleep through that racket? She looked up at the ceiling. Were they roller blading up there?

She watched him snooze for a few minutes, studying his features. Rob had a pronounced brow ridge above a near perfect nose, high cheekbones and full lips. But it was his jaw more than anything else that made him undeniably masculine. It was as square as they make 'em.

"Damn," she muttered. "He is gorgeous." The thought of taking dirty photos of him flitted through her mind but she'd left her phone in the living room… plus, he might not appreciate it. *But damn*, she thought, gingerly lifting a corner of the sheet to again check out the goods. So tempting to snap a few shots for posterity.

Rob kept himself in primo shape, making him an effective cop as well as undoubtedly popular with females. He probably could intimidate criminals just by standing up to his full height and shoulder girth. As far as women were concerned, Mel didn't even want to think about how many interesting propositions he must accumulate in an average day. Fortunately, as a detective, he wasn't in uniform or else it would be a total lost cause. Mel knew that slutty women and hot men in uniforms were like peanut butter and jelly.

While she was busy starting the Detective Fitzgibbons fan club, the memory of their conversation last night itched at her conscience. Why would he think Jane was guilty of murder? She didn't even know the Caldwells—not recently anyway. What would her motive be? That she'd been pining after him since high school and decided to take out his wife?

That must be it... but the thought was just ridiculous. Jane had a lot going for her—a great job, money in the bank, youth, and, now that she lost all that weight, even beauty. Why would she risk it all to do something so wacko for a man who didn't even know her? She'd have to be a complete psycho.

And Jane wasn't insane. Mel would have seen evidence of it if she'd been. Wouldn't she? In the two years Mel had known Jane Jensen about the most critical thing she could say about her had to do with her fashion sense and her introvert tendencies. Nothing set off alarm bells.

Yet there had to be a reason the police were starting to suspect her. Mel so wanted to know what it was, but she couldn't compromise Rob's position. She glanced down at him again. Her chest tightened at the thought of not seeing him anymore. It was, as he pointed out, a no-win situation. He must have been analyzing it from every angle long before he ever mentioned it to her.

Fuck.

She couldn't even warn Jane because that would be doing exactly what Rob was afraid she'd do. In reality, he put her in a crappy position by divulging the little that he did. But he couldn't think Jane killed Cate Caldwell because of a high school crush? The idea was patently absurd.

The cops had to know something bad, something much more that she didn't, but Mel had a sinking feeling that whatever it was, she just might be better off not knowing.

Glancing at the bedside alarm clock she saw it was four minutes before Rob's alarm would go off. That was so freaking annoying… didn't even pay to go back to sleep.

She closed her eyes anyway and was about to slip under again when a booming voice cracked like a whip in the upstairs apartment. What the fuck? Was a dominatrix living up there?

And yet, the cop slept on, right through the loud and belittling discipline. Poor chump, Mel thought. Why would he take that… want that? It took all kinds…

Maybe she should send Rob up there? The woman could beat some sense into him for Mel. Other than that, shopping was the only thing that would make her feel better.

Retail therapy always did. It helped right many of the wrongs of the world, and alcohol took care of the rest.

She couldn't help it, though. Rob's accusations against Jane were having some effect: she was starting to worry about Jane being dangerous, and she hated herself for it.

Chapter 23

In his still-dark bedroom, Mason awoke disoriented and sweaty. He'd been dreaming about Cate again. Wiping the perspiration off his brow with the back of his hand, he finally acknowledged the fact that he missed her. He even missed that stupid dog of hers. If someone had told him a few months ago that he'd feel this way, he would have laughed in the idiot's face. But not now. Cate had been invading his dreams almost every night—haunting him, no doubt.

He reached over to angle the clock toward him. Five thirty. He didn't have to get up until eight. Really, he didn't have to get up at all since his cousin was his boss. He could roll in whenever he felt like it. Besides, no one wanted to be unkind to a man whose wife had very recently been murdered in cold blood.

His eyes were burning, allergies, no doubt, and he rubbed them with the heels of his hands and finally sat up in bed, flipping the 800-thread-count Italian duvet off his body. Cate had a penchant for fine bed linens and the bed was layered with multiple reminders of her indulgences. Maybe he should just get up and shower. Or hit the gym?

Jake wouldn't mind even if he didn't go in to work at all—he'd always had his back, always helped him out whenever he needed a leg up. There wasn't too much Jake or anyone for that matter could do about Cate, though. She was gone, so gone, and it was inevitable that suspicion would rain down on him. Staying out of prison was Mason's primary objective now. He had his fingers crossed that the police didn't find out about his extracurricular activities.

He remembered the last time he saw his wife, just before he left for his business trip. Coming home early that day, he'd walked in on Cate, who'd been in the study on the phone with someone, her voice raised. When he strolled in, she'd whipped her head around, and her expression was a blend of alarm and guilt. She'd looked… caught.

"What's up?" he asked her. "Who you talking to?"

She shook her head and said into the phone, "I've got to go. We'll have to do this some other time. Yes. Right. Goodbye."

He could hear the other person—a male—protesting as she disconnected the phone. Was Cate cheating on him? Because that would be rich.

Wiping her face clean of any concern, Cate popped up from the sofa and strode over to him. "Hey, what are you doing home so early?"

Before he could answer her, she'd wrapped her long arms around his neck and kissed him. Disarmed him. His hands on her narrow hips, he pulled back and eyed his wife. Cate was gorgeous in any situation but that day she was dressed to kill— in all-black formfitting clothes. Pants, shirt—both silk—and high heels. Stilettos.

"Why? Did I interrupt something?"

Color bloomed in her cheeks. "No, just a business call. By the way," she said, taking a step back from him, "some woman named Tess Gardner called earlier. Twice. Said you'd know who she was." Her blue eyes were unwavering, fixed on his. Challenging him even.

Mason smiled at her finesse. She'd neatly flipped the heat of suspicion right back onto him. Did she know about his never-ending affair with Tess? Keeping his voice casual, he answered her. "Of course, I know who Tess is. She was my favorite high school girlfriend until she went complete psycho on me. Left a dead rat in my new girlfriend's locker."

"Ew." She reared back a little farther away. "Very comforting to know you have a crazed stalker, Mason. Is she going to come after me now?"

"I seriously doubt it, Cate. That was a very long time ago. She's since been married and divorced."

Her eyes narrowed into that patented Cate squint—her expression that says you're full of crap and she absolutely knows it. Using her head, she flicked her golden hair back over her shoulder where it obediently stayed. "Why is she contacting you now if that's the case?"

Mason had his own patented expressions, and he pulled one out now from his arsenal—his sincere face: arched brows, furrowed forehead, lips pressed together. He held it for a beat as he gently shook his head. "We're friendly. I ran into her recently, and she told me about a property Jake and I might be interested in. Nothing more than that, babes."

"Hmm," she trilled, signaling the end of the conversation, but with her sarcastic tone it was more an indictment than a musing. "So," she came closer again and adjusted his tie as she asked, "to what do I owe the pleasure of your unexpected company?"

"I had a light day. Thought I'd come home and chill. I'm meeting my dad for a drink later."

"Oh, that's nice. What about dinner?"

"Let's go out. What time is good for you?"

"I'm not working today; I had an appointment earlier, and now I'm just making a few phone calls. When you're done with your dad, call me, and I'll meet you wherever."

"Sounds good."

"By the way," she said, running a contoured fingernail down his face in a sharp caress, "don't forget we have the ballet day after tomorrow."

"I won't. I'll be back from my trip by late afternoon, early evening at the latest. Curtain's at eight, right?"

"Yes. What will you wear?"

Cate always worried that he'd embarrass her with his imperfect sartorial choices. "I brought my navy suit to the cleaners. It'll be ready tomorrow. If you can pick it up, I'll wear that. You like that suit."

"The navy Armani? Yes," she'd said, smiling as her eyes flashed. "I do."

That was followed by some pretty fantastic sex that afternoon. She'd pulled him up the stairs by his tie and shoved him down on the bed. Cate was always dominant in the bedroom, which is why they often clashed—Mason liked to take the lead in bed too. Two alphas do not a peaceful love life make, though the sex is always sizzling hot.

He'd left for the airport the next morning and never seen her alive again. Actually, because he begged off due to a weak stomach, he'd never seen her again at all. Her mother had accepted the burden of identifying her body at the morgue, saving Mason from that image that would surely have been indelibly etched into his brain.

At least in his dreams she was still a perfect ten.

Chapter 24

Stuck in creeping rush-hour traffic, Rob let his mind wander over the last twenty-four hours. Yesterday started out crappy, but he'd consoled himself by looking forward to his date with Mel. Then even that went bust. But he managed to salvage it in the end, didn't he? And what a nice end it was.

The reason the date went south was because he liked Mel so damn much that he didn't want to stop seeing her. It was dumb, he had to admit, to get involved with someone so close to the center of his homicide investigation, but there it was. And he knew going in that he wouldn't be able to convince her to abandon her friend—Mel was too good a person to do that. But damn, Rob's gut told him that Jane Jensen was involved in this murder. And… not only did he want to continue seeing Mel, but he was also looking out for her safety. If Ms. Jensen was capable of hiring a hit man to kill someone, what else was she capable of doing?

A loud honk sounded behind him and he snapped out of his reverie to see traffic was moving again. Yeah, he should have been paying attention, but that didn't mean he didn't want to get out of the car and harass the idiot who honked. He forced down the impulse and drove. He was already late to meet his partner.

When he'd been assigned to Kelvin, he hadn't been happy. Not even a little bit. It wasn't that she was female, he told himself. She seemed tough enough despite her relatively compact size. It was more that she was so butch that he felt uncomfortable around her. You coulda knocked him over with a feather when she had eyes for that pretty boy at Cate Caldwell's office. Now Rob didn't have a clue as to what her sexuality was, but he was fast realizing that it didn't matter. She was a damn good partner, a great detective, and she had his back. That's all that mattered.

Almost an hour later, he pulled into the spot next to Kelvin's muscle car. She was outside the vehicle, leaning back on the driver's door, arms crossed. Pissed off, no doubt. He slid his car window open and she rested her hands on the roof and leaned in.

"What the hell, Fitzgibbons? You're fucking late."

He snorted. "Thank you, Captain Obvious. I got stuck in traffic, so what else is new? Where we going today?"

She shrugged as she locked her car with the key fob and got into his. "I figure we need to talk to more of Mason's friends."

"Pleasantville?"

She nodded. "Yeah, coffee first."

"You got it." He turned his attention to the road, trying to figure out the best route possible for this time of day. Once on the Sawmill, he glanced at her. "Think we'll wrap this case up soon?"

"Hope so. I've got a caseload on my desk taller than I am. We've been devoting too many hours to it."

"No shit. I'm sick of it already. I thought it would be open and shut."

"Yeah, no such luck."

He felt the heat of her focused gaze. "What?"

"You still seeing the friend?"

"Yeah. I told her last night… gave her an ultimatum. Either shut down her friendship or stop seeing me. I've got a nasty feeling she's going to dump me instead of Jensen."

"Hmm. Probably. Oh well, easy come, easy go."

He gave her a sidelong glance. "Not so easy, Kelvin."

"No?"

"No. I like her."

They stopped talking for a while and the driving soothed the agitation he'd been feeling since yesterday morning. He was almost sorry when he reached his exit. He steered onto the exit ramp and turned toward the village, not looking forward to the next few hours.

"Oh, swing into this place, Fitz. I like the coffee here."

The first sip of strong, hot coffee began restoring his equilibrium almost instantly. Amazing how medicinal that first cup can be. "So how many on the agenda for today?"

"Three, maybe four. I want to speak to Jensen's friends too, if we could find any. Maybe Caldwell's parents again? We'll see how the day shakes out."

Rob narrowed his eyes. "Who exactly are you liking for it at this point?"

"I don't know, Rob. I share your suspicions about Jensen, but I'm honing in on Caldwell. If it's him, I doubt he'd be in collusion with Jensen. Just doesn't fit that he'd drop his wife over her. Just doesn't fit."

"Yeah, I hear you. I suppose it could be just one person planning it, though. No reason it had to be more."

"You're right. Then again, there could be three accomplices. Who knows? If we get one, we're more likely to find the others, assuming there are any. I'm gunning for the husband."

Rob laughed. "Why doesn't that surprise me? It's always the husband for you, Kelvin."

Now she chuckled too. "Wonder why that is." She pointed toward the right. "Turn down this street. It's a shortcut to our first interview."

"And who might that be?"

"We'll start with a guy named…" She looked down at her notebook. "…Todd Tennant, an old football buddy of Mason's. Tomorrow we have appointments with his cousin Jake Emerson and his parents. So today, maybe Mason's old girlfriends? I talked to one of them yesterday. Tess Gardner. If we strike out there, let's see if we can dredge up any friends of Jane Jensen's. We'll play it by ear." Her head swiveled toward him in query. "Good by you?"

"Yep, let's do it, sweetcheeks."

He didn't even have to check to know she was giving him a filthy look. "Say that again and lose your balls."

Rob's laugh came from his belly. He loved to poke at her. "You're not gonna file a sexual harassment charge against me, right?"

Kelvin grimaced. "No way, I'll handle it myself, so watch your six, buddy."

"Will do. Now let's go catch us a scummy murderer."

"OK. First Tennant. Then Tess Gardner. Let's go."

TESS GARDNER WAS NOT what Rob was expecting in the least. He figured all of Mason's exes would be blonde Barbie-doll types. Tess was very different. Thin, pale, redheaded with giant tits that made her look like she'd tip over at any minute. In high school, before she sprouted into her curves, she probably looked coltish—all legs and lanky frame. Lots of freckles. Not the kind of girl a guy like Mason would notice. Then again, she may have been an early bloomer—and she knew how to make the most of her assets. She'd dragged up the front zipper on her skintight green dress, stopping well short of decent. Looked like she had nothing on underneath but a skimpy shelf bra—that poor frail bra had to hold what looked like God-given double Ds.

It was close to dusk by the time they'd knocked on the door of the big white Colonial with black shutters and a tired looking young woman in blue jeans and a faded black Pearl Jam T-shirt had answered the door.

"Is Tess Gardner available?" Kelvin had inquired of her.

She angled her face to the side and raised her voice. "Tess? People here for you."

Kelvin stepped closer to the threshold so that the door couldn't close, an old cop trick. "Are you related to her?"

"She's my sister."

"Be right down," they heard a voice call.

Rob flashed his badge at her. "Can we come in please?"

She took her time looking at it and then turned blood-shot eyes toward Kelvin and waited. Annoyed, Kelvin fished out her own badge and showed it to the woman. Only then did she back up and allow them entrance.

She led them into a living room. "Have a seat. My sister will be down soon. She's getting ready for a date."

Rob gave her a long look. "OK, thank you." Before taking the proffered seat, he took stock of his surroundings.

The room was nice, kept well, but the furnishings looked worn. There were a few good antique pieces mixed in with more modern stuff, but it all worked to make a comfortable room. A lived-in room. Rob approved and chose a wingback chair perpendicular to the sofa.

"Tess," the woman yelled up again, her shrill voice making both Rob and Kelvin jolt. "Would you get your ass down here. People are waiting."

"Joe?"

"No. Police officers."

"Police officers?"

"Yeah. That's what I said."

A minute later they heard what sounded like high heels on the wood steps. Click, click, click. A minute later, there she was.

She strode gracefully into the room, extending her hand, first to Kelvin and then Rob. They stood and shook her hand. "Hello, I'm Tess Gardner. I'm sorry to keep you waiting."

"No problem, Ms. Gardner," Rob began, "we won't take up too much of your time. We just need to ask you a few questions."

"About?"

"Mason Caldwell."

She nodded and gingerly took a seat at the edge of the sofa. "Please sit."

Rob assessed her while Kelvin started asking questions. She had swept up her glossy red hair into a bun just above the nape of her slender neck. A black-lacquered hair-stick held it in place. The dress she wore was a vivid emerald, which played off her fiery red hair. Her shoes were black leather with stiletto heels. She looked like hot sex on high heels.

Apparently, she was going out and Rob was eager to see who her date was—if they could stretch out the questions long enough. He refocused his attention on the interview just as Kelvin was asking her about Cate Caldwell.

"Had you ever met his wife?"

"No, I just knew the little bit that Mason told me about her."

"So you were in contact with him recently?"

"Oh yes. Mason and I remained friends all throughout college and afterward."

"Just friends?"

She licked her lips. "Good friends, yes."

"Let me be clear. Did you have an intimate relationship with Mason Caldwell in recent years?"

She hesitated only slightly. "Yes."

"When exactly?"

Brushing invisible lint off the skirt of her dress, she murmured, her voice so soft it was nearly inaudible. "On and off. Forever."

"So after he was married too?"

She wrinkled her nose as if trying hard to remember, but Rob wasn't buying it. "I think we may have spent one evening together after he married, but we talked on the phone quite a bit. We had some mutual business interests. I was married before he was, so we didn't really have an opportunity where both of us were free agents at the same time. But we managed to keep our relationship going."

"Do you know if Mrs. Caldwell knew about your relationship with her husband?"

"I don't think she did. Mason wouldn't have wanted the hassle."

"I see. What are your present feelings about Mason Caldwell?"

The doorbell rang at that moment. "Cam," she called out to the other room, "can you get it? It's probably Joe."

The sister muttered something and went to get the door, and Tess turned her piercing green eyes straight at

Rob when she answered. "I love Mason, and I always will. He's a good friend."

The sister ushered her date into the living room. Dressed sharply in a charcoal suit with a black sweater under the jacket, he stood there for a moment, stupefied.

"Hi, Joe. These nice police officers were just leaving. They were here to talk about Mason Caldwell's wife."

"Oh, yeah, I heard about that. Tsk. Terrible thing."

"Yes, it is," Rob answered and stood up. He fished out his card from his wallet and handed it to Tess Gardner. "Here's my card. If you think of anything that might be of assistance to us, please give me a call. For now, this interview is over. We may have need to speak to you again."

She plucked the card from his hand. "Fine. We'll walk you to the door, Officers, since we're leaving too."

Rob and Myla sat in their car and watched the couple get into a sleek black Mercedes sedan. "What did you think of Ms. Gardner?" Rob asked his partner.

She shrugged and looked at him. "I think she's a filthy liar."

Rob laughed. "I got that impression too. I think she not only knew a lot more about Cate Caldwell, I also think she was screwing Mason all along."

Kelvin twisted her face as she tended to do when she was thinking. A moment later, she nodded her head. "Agreed. I say we take a closer look at big-titty Tess."

Shifting the car into first, Rob neatly pulled out of the tight parking spot as he chuckled at the nickname. The girl did have some impressive ta-tas.

Chapter 25

Janey's Journal, late November

MY PHOTO?

Oh my God. I cannot believe he had a photo of me in his dresser drawer.

Me.

Plain Jane Jensen.

Who is this guy, Mason Caldwell? Did he really have his wife killed? If so, why? Mel tells me in the fast glimpse she had of the woman she looked young, blond, and pretty —all the requisites for a happy female life. And excellent wife material for a hottie like her husband.

To me, Mason Caldwell represented all that was right with America and its culture. Popular, athletic, kind, friendly, smart, and liked by everyone. He just had it all...

Ergo, he didn't know that I—or people like me —existed.

. . .

ALL OF THESE thoughts and questions shuttling back and forth through my head have begun to peck at my peace of mind, and I desperately want the answers but my fickle brain is not cooperating. Sometimes I'm seriously tempted to bash my head against the wall in the hopes of jarring things back into place. The urge is strong and crazy, I know. Plus, with my luck, I'll just get a huge hematoma and land myself right back into the hospital—that or drop dead on my way to work or something. Earn a one-line story in the news, maybe a funny epitaph. Here lies plain Jane, a head-banger, it turns out.

The memory I'm most afraid of recovering is of the car accident itself. It must have been unbearable, traumatic, a catalyst of nightmares, and I don't want to ever remember it. Having giant gaps in my memory, however, is uncomfortable. Walking around, seeing people and wondering if I know them is bizarre and difficult. If someone's eyes are on me too long, my cheeks burn, thinking I must know them and they're waiting for me to say hello or acknowledge them in some way. Sometimes, I start to imagine they're looking at me strangely, suspiciously even, and I think maybe I had some kind of… I don't know… nefarious relationship with them. We robbed a bank together? Belonged to a sordid sex club? Were fellow inmates in a Turkish jail?

And those whom I know I know, still I wonder what the extent of our relationship was. Were they trustworthy or backstabbers?

I returned to work today, the first time in the persona of the new me. *Janey.* Everyone was kind but I could spot the stares, could feel the heat of them, especially from the men. One thing I'm sure of is that I never got this kind of attention before, and it feels weird. Good but weird. Somehow, I thought it would be more rewarding. In my better moments, though, I try to be grateful for this gift I've been given—liberation from my failed life. A rebirth. I feel beautiful for the first time in my wretched existence.

The mirror confirms it too. I'm as thin as Mel, and with my new and more perfect nose I'm pretty, truly pretty. Not pretty with a caveat—she's pretty for a *fill in the blank*. Fat girl. Smart girl. Dull girl. Young, old, annoying, the potential qualifiers are many. My hair is past my shoulders, which Mel says is the longest she's ever seen it —Mel's stylist cut in long layers and left my bangs overgrown. He also gave me blond lowlights so my light brown hair—usually as drab as a dead mouse—has depth.

Watch out, world, here I come. Seriously. I know looks aren't everything, but they definitely do smooth out life's little bumps, the cellulite of the mind. I've suspected it for a long time, and now it's my turn to prove it.

My clothes are different, too. I know my colleagues could probably easily attest to my regular type of business attire. It's so consistent it might even be called a uniform—dark trousers, a light-colored silk or cotton shirt with either long or short sleeves, depending on the weather, a pair of sensible pumps, and if I'm feeling really festive, a strand of pearls. I don't need to remember that—my closet told me all about it.

Not today.

Today I took a risk—it's important to take risks every now and then. Borrowing it from Mel's closet over the weekend, today I donned a tight-fitting electric-blue sweater with a white camisole underneath to tame the sweater's plunging neckline, and with it I wore a short, flouncy, multi-colored skirt—pink, yellow, and blue on a black background, the blue perfectly matching the sweater. It's something I would never have dared to wear ever before—not even long enough to try it on in a clothing store.

Just as that thought flutters through my mind, there's a memory taunting me, just out of reach. The more I try to pin down the fugitive memory, the farther away it flees. And then the moment I give up trying, it slides right into the assembly line of my thoughts: I'm wearing a brown skirt and brushing crumbs off it… on the train to work, I think… sitting behind a man. Staring at him. I'm behind him but diagonally so I can watch him without being noticed. When he turns to speak to the person sitting across the aisle from him, I can see his face. He catches me staring, smiles at me. Winks. He was so handsome.

I wonder when this happened… or even if it ever did. Memory is elusive, and my memories are slipperier than most. False memory is insidious and can hijack the real thing and become as entrenched and as real as the genuine memory. The psychologist I visited cautioned me about that possibility.

Still, I didn't invoke the memory in any way, so I'll consider it authentic. I've taken to listing my recaptured memories on a separate sheet from my journal. As the number rises, it gives me hope of a full recovery. Hope is a good thing.

It could be a soul-sucking thing as well.

So, yeah, I needed some air and decided to take a walk to Whole Foods when I got home from my half day of work today. The afternoon light was fading into dusk and it was not too chilly. I planned to start walking daily in an attempt to build up stamina to eventually take up running. My doctor advised me that physical exercise in moderation is important to the healing process.

As I walked home from the store, I'd just gotten to the house adjacent to mine when the front door opened and a man emerged. I sucked in my breath, instantly knowing two facts: one, that it was Mason Caldwell, and two, that he was the man on the train in my recovered memory. How could I not have known? He looked like an older version of the boy I knew in high school. Our eyes connected and he waved to me. "Hey."

I raised my arm in a halfhearted gesture but kept walking. It felt odd to be friendly with him. The cops believe, after all, that he contracted a hit on his wife. But as I strode closer to my house, he broke into a sprint to catch up with me.

"Jane?" He waited for my acknowledgment, looking at me earnestly.

As he got closer and I caught a really good look at him, I almost choked—no exaggeration. Coughing to stall, I allowed myself the luxury of admiring the man up close and personal. He'd been a beautiful boy, and now he was an incredibly handsome man. So handsome, in fact, that merely looking at him caused my body to have an instant all-systems go: my pulse roared in my ears, ovaries contracted, mouth dried, respiration sped up… All from a single close-up of my next-door neighbor.

"Um… hi. Mason, right?" My voice sounded high-pitched and tinny. I recognized the anxiety domino-effect thing again happening—beginning with drenching perspiration—and tried to curtail it. Not giving in to panic was the key to managing it.

"I'd heard you had amnesia from your car accident," he continued as if he were an ordinary mortal. "I hope you're feeling better. Are you?" Picasso-blue eyes peered intently at me.

I pushed away the shyness I felt around him. "Much better, thanks. I don't have all of my memory yet, but it's coming back, slowly but surely."

"That's good. You look great, if you don't mind my saying so. Uh… I saw you with packages and thought you might need a hand."

Did I need a hand? *His* hand? Here I was trying to carry on a coherent conversation with him while questions were roiling inside my brain. What is the etiquette? Should I mention his murdered wife or is that taboo since he's the prime suspect? Can I have sex with him right now or would that be in poor taste? How well do I actually know him? All I can remember is how I swooned over him in school. I find comfort in his voice, smooth and deep. I also remember how kind he always was to me—and to everyone for that matter.

Just as that thought flitted through my head, it's countered by an instant image, front and center. He and I are sitting in a car. It's what we're doing that catches me off guard. I'm leaning back against the car window and he's nearly on top of me… and we're kissing.

Like crazy.

I swooned a bit… and not in a good way.

"Are you OK?" he was asking me. "You look pale."

"Oh…I-I…uh," I stammered, hot blood rushing to my face, now surely no longer pale. "I'm fine."

"I hope you're not afraid of me, Jane. I'm assuming the police told you that I'm a suspect in my wife's murder?"

I couldn't entirely prevent the smirk in response to his nonchalant comment about *murdering his wife.* In fact, I almost laughed. Which was crazy. I mean, wasn't my reaction… unexpected? How would most people respond? Maybe it's the shock? I collected myself quickly and nodded, a little bit ashamed of myself even though I didn't do anything wrong. "I'm sorry. May I offer you my condolences?"

"Yes. Thank you. It's hard enough…" his voice choked

up, "...without being considered the main suspect. But I suppose the police are only doing their jobs—they even told me it's nothing personal. We do need to find my poor Cate's killer."

Making sympathetic sounds of support didn't seem adequate, so I asked, "Are they making any progress?"

"The only thing they're fairly certain of is that it wasn't random, which is even creepier to think that someone targeted her."

"It does seem odd."

"What does?"

"Well, from what I've read in news articles... it's just that your wife comes from an upper middle-class background and she was a dog trainer. Not much there for making mortal enemies unless another dog was hell-bent to win."

He chuckled feebly. "You've no idea how cutthroat those dog-show peeps are. But Cate did the circuit only in her spare time. She was a publicist."

"Oh. Would she make enemies doing that sort of thing?"

"Jane," he said, and I loved the way my name sounded on his lips, "anyone can make enemies anywhere. Some people are just kooks, you know? And Cate was beautiful and inspired jealousy quite a lot, I think."

After that conversation I felt wobbly, as if I'd taken a three-mile run. It was Mason Caldwell. He affected me. Radically. Dramatically. I kept getting the feeling we hadn't just met again, that we'd spent time together ... but then why wouldn't he say? Why would he allow me to believe we were strangers?

It had to be wishful thinking.

Chapter 26

Janey's Journal

SO I'VE DECIDED.

I don't believe Mason's guilty of the crime. He's much too nice to commit such a calculated, evil undertaking. Divorce isn't the end of the world if the marriage was really a mistake. Why have someone snuffed? Killing someone is too big a sin for most people to tolerate and it alters the universe permanently—there's no coming back from it. It must be a very heavy psychic burden to carry… as Lady Macbeth learned the hard way.

So the question becomes why do it if it's not completely necessary?

I doubt he needs the insurance money. He co-owns a successful commercial real estate company. And his parents are more than comfortable as far as I know.

So money was not a motivator for him.

His wife was thin and beautiful. So no reason there.

I just can't come up with a good reason for him to do

it, and ever since I remembered how kind he used to be, how much I loved him as a teenager, I felt more than ever inclined to give him the benefit of the doubt.

EIGHT P.M. Boom. I jolted awake up from a nap with my heart pounding a mile a minute. As soon as I opened my eyes the memories came flying at me, like a reel-to-reel on warp speed. It's a terrifying experience to see a slew of scenes from your own life unfurl before your eyes while you try to make some kind of coherent sense out of them. This time it was even worse.

This time I had blood on my hands.

Lots of blood. Literally on my hands. Dark night, bright lights. A horrible sound. Ugh, no, it must be the accident. What else did I see that night that I'm going to remember? Squeezing my temples, I try to stop remembering. It's too scary.

Or was it the previous accident?

Dr. Lavelle asked me if I'd been in an auto accident before, based on my prior injuries. I need to call my parents and ask them. I suppose I could call Sulu instead. I'd rather call Sulu but truth to tell, I really didn't want to talk to any of them. Still, I should find out more about what I'm missing. When I woke up in the hospital thinking it was ninth grade, I'd thought my memory was intact at least till that point but I seem to have gaps peppered throughout. The accident was later, though. Why do I remember some but not all of it? And what does it have to do with a Halloween party?

I could be mixing it up with my recent accident as well. But I don't think so. There are kids all around me, teenagers, and some bleached blonde leering at me. I feel such profound sadness all around me, cloaking me in thick despair.

What happened to me? Do I even want to know?

I FELL ASLEEP AGAIN WATCHING old movies. Something, some kind of noise, woke me up at half past midnight. More memories began to bombard me: trips I took with my parents, one to California, the other a Caribbean cruise—torture because I couldn't lose my parents for ten whole days. Both trips took place in the same year, probably why they both came to me at once. I know it happened during my senior year of high school because I had to order my cap and gown before I left for one of the trips—I can't remember which one. So now I'd reclaimed some memories of that year but my whole sophomore and junior years were still blank.

MIDDLE OF THE NIGHT. I can't sleep so I get up, make a cup of tea, try reading. I pick an anthology of short fiction—it was the only one lying around. Read a story by Tobias Wolff. Great writer so still wide awake. If only I had Henry James handy. I drink a small shot of brandy. Nothing seems to help me get back to sleep so I pick up my journal. I have the pen nib poised on the paper to start writing about my day when I begin thinking about the flashback I'd had while speaking with Mason—kissing him in a car. Then without warning, bam. Disjointed images begin streaming through my brain. As I work to piece them together, I start to remember.

It was after the party; I left the Halloween party with Mason. We went outside to talk, and before I knew it we were in his car. He leaned over and kissed me. *I was kissing*

Mason Caldwell. We were making out in his car and his hand began wandering. I was ready to do anything with him, and he knew it. But he didn't know it was me. He thought I was someone else. Someone pretty. Someone normal. Someone named Janine.

"Will you come with me, Janine?" he'd asked, his voice hoarse, his breath liquored.

"Where?" I could barely get the word out.

"My basement. There's a separate entrance so no one will know we're there." He hovered over me and kissed me again. "I want you."

My throat was so tight that I couldn't squeeze out any sound, coherent or otherwise, so I nodded. He shifted back in his seat to turn on the car. I drank in his every detail: the way his masculine hands held the steering wheel with casual confidence, how his hair fell over his right cheekbone, the satisfaction that glowed in his eyes as his car picked up speed. Everything about him was thrilling to me. I loved him so much.

That's where the memory ends. It's so frustrating I could rip out my hair.

I desperately want to know what happened. Did we make it to Mason's basement? Did we have sex? What happened afterward? Did he ever find out that Janine was me?

Grrrr. I just don't remember any of it. I will admit, though, that just the fact that I kissed Mason Caldwell is shock enough for me. After all, he's him and I'm me, yet somehow, I tricked him into believing I was a girl who was pretty and popular, a girl who knew how to dress and have fun, a girl who went to parties and met cute guys.

A normal girl named Janine.

Not Jane. Never Jane.

Chapter 27

Late December

THE DOORBELL RANG at 6:47 a.m. as Jane was stepping out of the shower. She threw on her robe and dashed down to answer the door. Her peephole was stuck in place by a sloppy paint job so she called out, "Who is it?"

"The police, ma'am. Please open up."

Jane opened the door to reveal two young officers in uniform. She stepped aside and held the door open. "Please come in. Um, I was just getting ready for work. Will you excuse me while I put on some clothes?"

"Yes, miss. Please be quick about it. We need to speak to you."

Jane nodded and sprinted up the stairs. There was a time not long ago when she couldn't race up any steps but in the nearly three months since the accident, she'd healed almost fully—physically at least—and the weight loss gave her more energy. No more bulletproof coffees for her.

In her room, she'd laid out her outfit for work the night

before. She'd never before had so much fun planning her daily wardrobe—thanks to Mel and the weight loss, of course. Tight black dress with white geometric shapes, black tights, mid-calf biker boots. Over that she put on a charcoal cardigan that fell just to her hip. It was perfect for the chill of December.

Like a speed demon she zipped into the bathroom and grabbed her blow dryer, aiming at the back of her head and angling it back and forth rapidly. Her hair was only semi-dry when she put it down to do her makeup. Over the last few months she'd actually gotten good at it, having been shown how to expertly apply it by the very sweet woman with the too-strong perfume at the counter at Bloomingdale's where Jane dropped four hundred on the products.

One of the officers called up to her, asking her to come down.

She checked her watch: eight minutes all told. The police officers were getting pissy about the wait. Grabbing her handbag and coat, she made her way downstairs where they stood at the foot of the stairs.

"I'm so sorry for the delay," she said as she took the last two stairs. "What can I do for you, Officers?"

"Miss Jensen, it is my duty to inform you that you are under arrest for the murder of Catherine Caldwell. I must further inform you that anything you say can and will be used against you in a court of law. You have the right to an attorney..."

THE JENSEN WOMAN was shaking so much that Officer Perrine could barely snap the cuffs closed. He was generally a hard-hearted bastard, which served him well as a cop, but he actually felt sorry for the woman. She was obviously terrified, trembling so violently he expected her bladder to let loose at any moment. Now that would piss him off, no pun intended.

He led her to the back of the car and Theo, his partner, opened the door. He knew, despite the fact that they moved quickly, that neighbors would see. They had radar for this kind of thing. It would be all over the neighborhood well before dinnertime. The poor lady—he hoped she was guilty 'cause if she weren't, it would really suck what they were doing to her rep. Especially in an area like this one where reputation was everything. Rich people have sharp eyes and long memories.

ROB FITZGIBBONS LEANED one shoulder against the refrigerator, his flat gaze squarely on Mel. "Jane's fingerprints were all over the photo."

They were in Mel's galley kitchen. She was measuring scoops of Colombian roast into the gold cone filter, trying to remember if she'd already put in four or five. Rob had shown up ten minutes earlier in an apparent effort to ruin her day. "I guess I'd rather have strong coffee than weak so I'll count from four," she muttered to herself.

"Did you hear me, Melanie? I said Jane's fingerprints were all over the photo."

"I heard you, and that's only natural since it was her photograph." She wiped wayward grounds off the cream-colored granite counter that her contractor brother had installed the week before, dropping the handful into the stainless garbage can.

He came closer, putting his face in hers and grasping

her elbow. "Yes, but they were also all over the dresser drawer where we found the photo."

"Mason's drawer? Maybe they were having an affair?"

Rob scowled, shaking his head. "Come on. Jane is an attractive woman but you saw Caldwell's wife. She was fucking gorgeous."

Mel wrenched her elbow out of his grasp and turned back to the coffee machine. "Combine blond hair and a pair of tits and most men are so dazzled they call it beauty. Anyway, looks aren't everything. His wife may have been a bitch on steroids."

"Maybe." He paused. "Even if that were true… that would only support her guilt. Easier to have a bitch whacked than a nice lady."

Mel didn't respond—she felt anger bubbling hot in her gut and she wasn't exactly sure why. Maybe it was his attitude toward Jane that was just so unfair… She grabbed the carafe to fill with spring water, glad for the distraction.

He followed her to the other side of the counter where he could again see her face, leaning his slim hip against it. She tried not to focus on his good looks—she needed the anger to get her through what she knew was coming between them: a total break.

"Mel, think about this rationally. Why would he have an affair with his neighbor? If he wanted to cheat, there are smarter options with less chance to get caught at it. And you yourself said that before the accident Jane was overweight and wore frumpy clothes. A guy like Mason Caldwell wouldn't give her a second glance back then. Now maybe, but not then."

"That's your only evidence? Her fingerprints and some convoluted logic? Because it's pretty damn skimpy."

"No. We're on solid ground. We've identified the hit man. Caught some luck for a change. Vice received an anonymous tip about underage prostitution, possibly trafficking. There was enough to get a warrant to search the premises but they found only one girl there and she was of consenting age. They did find a cache of weapons in the guy's apartment. Ballistics matched one of them to the Cald—"

"What?" she prompted when he abruptly cut off.

Rob's face had drained of blood. "You cannot repeat any of this, do you understand? You could really fuck me over."

"I won't. I promise. Where did you find the killer? I mean, was he local?"

Grim satisfaction spiked his tone when he answered her. "Just over the Putnam border, in Dutchess County."

Mel gasped so hard she nearly choked. "The site of the accident," Mel sputtered. "We always wondered why she was there."

"Jane's bank account had a huge cash withdrawal. The hit man had ten in cash—we checked his account and what he had stashed under his mattress. Not a very imaginative guy. Jane had no explanation for the withdrawal, claimed she didn't remember anything about it."

"She did lose her memory, you know." Sliding the carafe under the filter, she flipped on the coffee machine.

"So she claims." He crossed his arms. "I don't believe a word she says."

Mel took note of his combative stance—it spoke volumes about his intractability. A shiver slithered up her spine and she wrapped her arms around her body, feeling chilled despite the cardigan she wore over her white knit shirt. "Did the withdrawal amount match what was paid to the hit man?"

Rob focused a heated gaze on Mel before he turned to the sink to pour himself a glass of water, chugging most of it. Some dribbled down his chin; he wiped his mouth with the back of his hand before shifting his eyes back to her. "Minus about three grand."

"Where do you think that came from?"

Shrugging, he took another gulp of his water, draining the glass, and putting it in the stainless sink. "We figure she had it somewhere in her house. In cash."

"Ten seems low for a hit. I mean, it's a lot of risk to take."

"Probably the final payment."

Shit. A deep breath helped to center her from this onslaught of bad news. "I can't accept any of this. Do you really believe it?"

Chin up, hands now on hips, he was making his closing argument, confident in his win. Well, she had news… "Yeah. I do, Mel. And I'm sorry to have to tell you this, but we arrested Jane this morning. She's being charged with premeditated murder."

"So now you've stopped looking at anyone else? You're just going to work to pin it on Jane and forget about further investigation?"

He scoffed. "We investigated a lot of people. We interviewed all of Mrs. Caldwell's coworkers, clients, former boyfriends. We interviewed her husband's old girlfriends too. There was one in particular I took a long look at—I think there was something going on there. No proof, though. And I did look. Anyway, regardless of extramarital activity, the Caldwells' marriage seemed to work for them, and while I'm not a hundred percent convinced Mason had nothing to do with the murder, I'm at ninety-three or thereabouts."

He held out his hand and ticked off each finger as he enumerated. "We looked at Mason's cousin who used to date Cate Caldwell before she met Mason. In fact, he introduced the two of them. We checked out all of Mason's friends and of course, Cate's friends off the job. Family members, anyone who had the remotest chance of holding a grudge. Nothing. Just nothing. Jane Jensen had motive and opportunity, and there's sufficient physical evidence for us to prove it in court."

Melanie slapped her hand to her forehead as she turned to pace. "Oh my God. I find it impossible to believe she'd do that. Completely, entirely impossible."

"How well do you really know her? Think about it, Mel. Have you even ever known someone who was off the rails?"

"You mean apart from my whole family?"

He narrowed his eyes. "You have sociopaths and psychopaths in your family?"

"Definitely."

"All kidding aside, Jane can easily be someone she doesn't resemble precisely because she's putting on a show, a façade, to lure others into thinking she's a normal person with empathy and morality—when she's not. You might even be in mortal danger."

"Oh, come on, Rob. That's ridiculous."

"Is it? Is it ridiculous? What if she thinks you're aligning yourself with me—and she knows I believe she's guilty. Maybe she told you something inadvertently that could incriminate her? If she's a killer, do you think she would hesitate to kill again if she's feeling threatened? You're the one who has to come on. You don't know the woman all that well, certainly not as well as you think you do."

The insult whirled her back around. "How well do I know you? I mean, how well does anyone know anyone? I can tell you that Jane's just not that stupid either—quite the contrary. She's got a very high IQ. Why would she leave such obvious incriminating evidence like a huge cash withdrawal? And fingerprints all over the Caldwell bedroom? Come the fuck on. That's just a little too sloppy. It very obviously points to Jane being framed."

He twitched his shoulder. "Just means she never thought she'd become a suspect. Plain and simple.

"I want you to think hard, Mel. Is there anything about Jane that doesn't add up? Maybe you learned something that was out of character for her? Because sociopaths hide behind a normal disguise, but usually they mess up here and there and reveal a hint of their true identity."

"Grrr." Mel raked both her hands through her hair. It was just no use arguing with him. Detective Fitzgibbons was not about to be talked out of his conviction about Jane. He had his cop's intuition about people, and he obviously put a lot of stock in it. Not wasting any more of her breath, she left it at a glower. He obviously felt no such limitation.

He was leaning against the counter, staring into space, but he kept his mouth running. "Since I met Jane, I always felt something was off about her. My cop sense told me so, and I always listen to it. It's never let me down, good or bad."

OK, Mel was so done with the discussion. She knew that her friend—knew with not only her heart but also her logical mind—wasn't a coldblooded killer. Mel rarely fell back on her emotions for important decisions—she was a left-brainer, a person who relied on facts and figures. And in this case, those facts and figures just didn't add up. Or added up too well.

For Detective Fitzgibbons with his cop's suspicious brain it was a slam dunk, but Mel was two steps ahead of every conclusion he drew. She knew that the so-called evidence had to be manufactured, but she didn't know how to convince the big lug—or anyone else for that matter. For God's sake, why the hell couldn't the stubborn bastard see it the way she did? She was frustrated by his complete unwillingness to consider Jane being innocent. She felt insulted too. "Plain and simple, you said?" she huffed. "Nothing about this is plain and simple."

The coffee had finished its drip. He dragged his gaze to her, breaking out of his hypnotic stare into space. "Yes, Melanie, it is simple. Think horse, not zebra. Ever hear that?"

"No, it isn't." She crossed her arms and glared at him. "Simple."

Rob threw up his hands, his voice growing in volume. "For fuck's sake, sometimes you don't have to look for complicated webs of intrigue; sometimes the truth *is* simple and staring you right in the face. Trust me, Jane's guilty as sin. Wrap your head around that."

"Is there any other evidence?" Mel knew she was pushing him since he shouldn't divulge details of the case to anyone, least of all to someone so close to the suspect. And he'd already given her a lot, way more than he should have. But she and Rob had gotten close, and she hoped he would trust her that far.

"Yes, there is," Rob said. A trace of apology crept into his tone. "I can't divulge any more, though. Not right now. Most of what I told you is already a matter of public record and Ms. Jensen has been made aware of it. But some is still being withheld pending trial. You understand, right?"

"You said you don't believe a word she says. Do you think she engineered her own near-fatal car accident?"

His temper seemed to be winding down, his green eyes dulling, but Mel couldn't allow herself to care. He was the one on the warpath; he was the one making demands on her. "No," he began as he reached for the coffee pot. "Do you mind?"

She gestured for him to go ahead and help himself.

Pouring his coffee, he picked up the thread of the answer. "I think that was unexpected. Two eyewitnesses say another car cut her off."

Mel got the milk and half-and-half out of the refrigerator and placed them on the counter near his cup. She watched as he fixed his coffee—meticulously pouring the cream and sugar, stirring it for long seconds. Mel was far too impatient to spend that much time preparing her coffee. But that was Rob: plodding and methodical. Meticulous even. Hunching her shoulders, she chafed her hands up and down her arms as another shudder swept through her. But the cold was filtering more through her soul than her body. Jane was in jail, for God's sake, and Mel felt entirely helpless. She needed to get rid of him and try to help her poor friend.

She rubbed her eyes and only afterward realized she'd already put on her makeup. Fuck. Probably looked like a raccoon now. "Look, Rob… I'm having a really hard time with this whole thing. Jane's essentially a very sweet person, and I cannot see her doing harm to anyone. As far as I can tell, she's never even met Cate Caldwell."

His callused hand landed heavily on her shoulder and instantly annoyed her—it felt patronizing. "People become obsessed. She had a miserable time of it in high school and pinned her focus on this guy. Obsession isn't rational, you know?

Plucking his hand from her shoulder, she went to put away the milk. While he drank his coffee both of them were silent. There wasn't much left to say really. After taking a few gulps, he drained the rest of it, then stepped over to the sink to rinse out the cup. He was almost out the door when he made his final remarks.

"For argument's sake, let's say she is this delusional psycho stalker who kills the wife of her object of obsession. That makes her a dangerous person, and you could be in her sights next if you piss her off. I'm actually worried about your safety spending too much time with her. Think about it.

"And do me a favor, Melanie. While you're thinking, take twenty-four hours to also think on giving up contact with her for the sake of our relationship if not your own safety. I think we could be really good together—long-term. I know it. If you do too, maybe you should change your mind about Jane Jensen."

He wanted her to take twenty-four hours?

She didn't need that much time. Or any time at all. Mel wouldn't be deserting her friend when she most needed her. Not even for a hot cop she had already fallen hard for.

Not even for him.

Chapter 28

He steered the Porsche neatly into the parking space in front of the office. Just as he turned off the ignition, his phone chimed. He looked at the caller: Kurt Redding. Must've heard something on the police scanner. He tapped the button to answer the call.

"What's going on, Kurt?"

"Doing as you asked, bud. The only big thing that came across today was that the cops picked up Jane Jensen, arrested for premeditated murder. She's being processed now at the big R."

"OK. Thanks, Kurt. I owe you a steak dinner."

His amused snort came through the line, loud and clear. "Dude, you owe me a helluva lot more than that, but I guess I'll settle for it. As long as it's someplace pricey."

"You got it. Take care."

He disconnected the phone and leaned back, letting the soft leather bucket seat surround him in comfort. Things were working, finally going according to plan. For a little while there he didn't think they would. They'd spent so much time meticulously planning out every last aspect, only to have the whole damn thing almost get fucked by an off-the-cuff improv. Fortunately, though, it was back on track.

He closed his eyes and visualized this upcoming business deal going through as planned. It would be a giant coup and would put the company firmly in the black. Everything would all fall into place just as he wanted and planned. He straightened his spine and inhaled from his diaphragm.

Regardless of the confident image he projected, he felt a drop of sweat trickle down between his shoulder blades. Every deal was the same: until the ink was dry on the contract, it could all go south. He'd learned his lessons well and knew that hubris was nearly always tailgated by a fall. Humility and preparation were the tools to achieving success.

He opened the door and got out of the car. Today's appointment was with a new banker to discuss a huge mortgage application. If this deal went through their company stood to make some serious coin and a blighted downtown area would get a major facelift. Big win for everyone, and it would make the company even more valuable if and when they sold it. He strode across the lot with crossed fingers and a winning smile.

Chapter 29

Jane's Journal, December

I'M A KILLER.

I'm not a nice person at all. I'm the extreme opposite of nice. I'm a killer.

That's what the police are saying. I don't remember being a killer. I don't remember paying someone to kill his wife. I don't even remember his wife.

But that's what the police say I did, that's what the evidence points to. The fact that I have no memory of it is irrelevant, they say. I'm still a killer.

When I woke up after the accident I was an unknown entity. I won't lie—it was traumatic to have no idea of my past or present, but… it was also an opportunity to live a brand-new life, to literally reinvent myself. I was operating under the assumption that I was inherently a decent person, capable of doing kindness, and aspiring to bigger and better. Wouldn't everyone think that?

Now I'm being told that I'm evil, the worst of the

worst, a cold and calculating murderer. That I withdrew money from my bank account to pay a hired killer to murder the wife of a man I was stalking.

They say I hired a hit man to shoot Cate Caldwell dead. Assuming I did that, how did I even know how to find a hit man, I wonder? Why would I think to do that anyway? It's not like Mason Caldwell would be interested in me if his wife died. The whole thing made no sense.

They have me in a holding area with four other women. We're all attempting to ignore one another and a guard was kind enough to give me a pen and paper to further that end. The room is cold, the walls are a putrid green, and the smell of urine poorly masked by the harsh scent of bleach permeates every corner of the place. On my lap is the gift of a torn-out piece of notebook paper—I don't have my journal with me. I can barely see what I'm writing—tears are spilling on the page and the ink is running. Would a killer cry at being called one? Maybe I'm not that good a killer and that's why I'm at Rikers right now.

The week before I had my accident, I apparently made a large withdrawal from my savings account. Seven thousand dollars. The police have surmised it was part of the payment for the hit. They were looking for more cash—maybe stashed somewhere in my house or maybe in a different account they hadn't yet tracked down. I just wish I could remember what happened even if it's bad. To not know whether I'm being falsely accused is a horrible turn of events.

Maybe I'm being punished for trying to be a new person, a beautiful girl named Janey, instead of fat, ugly, acid-tongued Jane. Maybe the stars had misaligned because for once I felt happy. I know it wasn't a usual thing for me because it felt so alien, like walking in stiff new shoes.

Maybe my audacity to think I could lead a happy and successful life was too great an insult to the cosmos.

I'm starting to think it would have been better if I'd just died in the car accident—me instead of that poor man. He probably had a much better life, was a much better person. Sometimes fate just plays a colossal prank on pathetic humans and we can only laugh while we cry. Me, I'm sick of being the butt of these cosmic practical jokes. But what the hell can I do about it, short of offing myself? I'm too much of a coward to seriously consider that as an option. At least I think I am.

Then again, we never know what we're capable of doing until we try.

I'M deathly afraid to sleep. Not only because I'm in Rikers, though that's reason enough for anyone. My greater fear, though, is that I'll dream about killing Cate Caldwell… or worse, remember it. If I have a flashback of paying a killer off like the charges say I did, I don't know what I'll do. The idea is right out of scenes from a nightmare.

I'm also worried. What if I'm not a killer? That means someone targeted me to get the blame, which means that someone is out to get me. If I'm not a killer, it means I have enemies, serious enemies. Maybe they'll try to kill me, make it look like suicide. Who would question a killer at Rikers facing a life sentence offing herself?

If I am a killer, maybe I had an accomplice. Maybe that accomplice wants me to get the full blame. Maybe my accomplice will try to kill me. Dead men tell no tales.

I'm exhausted, mentally, emotionally, and physically… but I cannot close my eyes. I try to stay distracted, listening to other people, sounds, whatever. When there is nothing to focus on, I try to remember lyrics to songs I like.

Or the lines to poems I remember.

It usually leads me back to my present reality. Death.

Do not go gentle into that good night… Dylan Thomas.

Because I could not stop for Death; he kindly stopped for me… Emily Dickinson.

Out, out brief candle… Macbeth. Or pretty much anything by Shakespeare—his tragedies, at least.

This is the end, beautiful friend, the end… The Doors

Any distraction, no matter how morbid, is better than none. I search my brain for any and all of them so I don't have to dwell on my current personal crisis.

Chapter 30

Mel sat up and punched the pillow as if she meant it before flopping back down onto it. It didn't help that her small bedroom was stifling from the overactive radiator and light from the street lamps seeped in through stuck-open slats in the shutters covering the casement windows—she had to get her brother to fix them soon. The later it got, the more panicked she became to fall asleep and the more elusive sleep became. It was a vicious cycle. The clock now read 2:58 a.m. and she had to be up at seven to get ready for work. Getting less than seven hours of sleep made her physically ill.

She'd been at war with the duvet and pillows since eleven last night, maybe dozing off for a few minutes here and there but deep sleep continued to elude her. Her mind was just too busy, crowded with Rob's ultimatum and Jane's impossible situation. Poor Jane. Mel couldn't bear to think about where Jane was sleeping tonight, and there wasn't a damn thing she could do about it until tomorrow.

Mel's plan was to go to work in the morning—get there an hour early—and leave at lunchtime to go see Jane.

Meantime, she looked online for the names and numbers for a few criminal attorneys in case Jane needed them. Mel also planned to bring five hundred in cash on the chance that it would be needed for something. She wished she could head over to Rikers first thing, but they had a big job scheduled for the morning, and Mel couldn't be absent, especially with Jane being gone too.

At 3:13 Mel got up and stomped to the kitchen, swallowing a Benadryl with half a glass of water. She knew she'd be drowsy all day tomorrow, but at least she'd get a few hours of sleep. Finally, about twenty minutes later she went out.

It felt like she had just fully closed her eyes when the monotone beep of her alarm went off. "Ugh." She slapped down the snooze button.

Then she slapped it down two more times. The fourth alarm finally got her out of bed. She dragged herself into the tiny bathroom and turned on the shower. There were plenty of negative things to say about Mel's West Side apartment but the water pressure wasn't one of them. Standing under the shower nozzle, the force of the spray nearly pinned her to the back wall of the stall and the hot water massaged her into a much better frame of mind. Though she was operating on about four hours of sleep, she felt decent after the shower.

Mulling her choices, she stood in the closet for a couple of minutes before selecting a navy skirt and a white sweater. Over her skirt she wore a tartan-plaid fabric cummerbund, navy tights, and her knee-high black boots. She stood in front of her giant mirror and chewed her cheek. Was this a proper outfit for visiting a prison? Mel thought it said professional but not haughty, female but not looking for action. Nodding her approval, she went in search of coffee.

At a little past noon, Rob showed up at the office to take her out to lunch. He wasn't aware of her afternoon plans and she wasn't in the mood to share. When Susan buzzed her to tell her she had a visitor, Mel didn't expect it to be the detective.

"Pizza for lunch?" he asked when she strode into reception. He was wearing blue jeans and a black leather jacket, and she hated him for looking scrumptious.

She gave Susan a pointed look. "Remember what I told you this morning? I'll do that right after lunch."

Susan smiled and bobbed her head, and Mel winked. She was a smartie.

So Rob wanted her answer now, and he wasn't going to like it. It wasn't a conversation she ever wanted to have. But Rob had forewarned her—it was the reason he hadn't wanted to start a sexual relationship with her. Regardless of this outcome, though, Mel was glad they did start it. Having that experience was worth whatever pain was headed her way.

They ate their pizza in virtual silence but as soon as he finished his second slice, he launched into his spiel. "I hate to put you in this position, Melanie," he said, licking grease off his thumb, "I do, but it's where we stand right now."

She put her pizza down, her appetite going flat. "What am I supposed to do, Rob? Just say, 'See ya, Jane. I'm dropping out of your life now. Oh, and by the way, good luck in that murder trial coming up on you.' I can't do that to her… she has nobody in her corner, not even family."

He picked up his soda and guzzled it. His eyes were on the three people at the table next to them who were loud talkers. Mel glared at him, but he didn't see it.

She let the silence hang between them, waiting to see how long he could hold out. Picking up his phone, he slid it in his jacket pocket, then plucked his keys from the table.

His skin was stretched taut across his face. "Then we stop seeing each other," he snapped, "at least for the duration of the trial."

Now it was Mel who looked away—away from his piercing eyes—leaning back in her seat and hoping he would leave her soon. His presence was oppressive, and it was sucking all the energy from her.

"I already spoke with the prosecutor," he went on, using his car key to scratch his eyebrow. "To say she wasn't pleased about our relationship… yeah, like saying hell is mildly tropical. She said it wouldn't be ideal in any circumstances but the better scenario would be for you to put distance between you and the defendant, stat. For us to continue as we are? The defense attorney would shred me. Though I'm not the arresting officer, I'm the lead detective on the case."

"Seems to me since you're on the side prosecuting Jane and not defending her, your credibility shouldn't be hurt by dating me. But whatever. *Que sera sera.*"

"That's not how it works, Melanie. If there's a whisper of impropriety of any kind—and that would include a conflict of interest—it can hurt the case one way or another. We try not to provide any reason whatsoever that might lead to a mistrial. It has to be clean all the way…"

Rob paused when another patron got too close to their table, waiting until the guy passed by. As he did, he took a long look at Mel. The stranger's appreciation didn't escape Rob's notice. "I guess I have to hope you don't meet some tall, dark, and handsome stranger in the interim while the trial works its way through the court."

"Stranger than you?" She grimaced. "Not likely. And ditto, by the way. How do I know you won't be swept off your rubber soles by some big-breasted blond paralegal tilting over the keyboard in the prosecutor's office?"

His laugh emerged as something between a snort and a bark. "We'll just have to have faith, I suppose," he said lightly but then sniped, "just remember that I'm not the one choosing Jane over you."

"No, because Jane isn't your friend… and you're not the only person that she has on her side in the whole entire world. And it's really unfair of you to say that, Rob, and you know it. I'm in no way putting Jane over you. I'm refusing to abandon my friend. I would like very much to keep you. You're the one insisting that we can't see each other."

He filled his cheeks with air and blew the breath out noisily. "What can I do? Jeopardize the entire case? I can't do that, Melanie—you know I can't."

"I get your circumstances, Rob. It's just that I happen to believe that Jane is innocent and to abandon her in her hour of extreme and dire need would be just…" She searched for the right word. "… unconscionable. Not to mention this all coming on the heels of a nightmarish car accident in which she almost died. It's unimaginable."

"Yeah, well she should've thought of that before she took out a hit on the guy next door's wife."

Seemed like his petulance was giving way to anger again. Mel narrowed her eyes—fuck this, she thought. "She didn't… and I'd wager a year's salary on that conviction."

"Well, I'm wagering my salary on the conviction the prosecutor will be getting in court." Abruptly, he stood up, scooped up his paper plate made transparent with grease, and plopped his napkin on top. "See you around, Mel. Hope she's worth it."

Melanie watched him toss his garbage and stalk out of the pizza joint and let her face drop into her hands. She was going to miss the stupid ass.

But she knew she was right, and Rob was wrong to ask that of her. And Jane's reality was so much worse, it wasn't even funny.

How could she not help her? For fuck's sake, why bother having friends if you're not going to be there for each other when desperately needed? Melanie knew she had to support Jane, but she wasn't sure of the best way. Visiting hours were from one until nine so she had plenty of time to see her, but she wanted to get there as soon as possible so Jane didn't feel all alone. Once she spoke with Jane, she'd figure out where she could do the most to help.

Mel unhooked her handbag from the chair back and slipped into her coat. The dank gray day matched her mood as she leaned her shoulder on the heavy glass door and headed out into the misty afternoon.

SHE SAT on the worn plastic chair, her eyes darting around the room. As soon as she caught anyone's eye, she'd avert hers immediately. Mel had never been inside a prison before and Rikers was a notorious one. Though she wasn't up on prison etiquette, common sense told her it probably wasn't a good idea to stare at anyone or even to get caught looking.

She'd been instructed about the dress code for visitors when she called, so she'd been careful to wear a conservative outfit. She wore her navy peacoat over it. Some of the women on line with her to enter were pulled off and not allowed in because of their attire. Mel watched one woman sob because she'd come so far to visit her son and then wasn't allowed in.

Waiting for Jane to be brought to the visitor's room, Mel tried to occupy her mind with details. The cinderblock walls were two-tone: a very pale snot-green on top and a clashing hunter green on the bottom. The chairs were plastic and the tables were low, like coffee-table height. There were a few items for babies and children in the corner—booster seats and the like. Overall, the environment was depressing as hell.

Four minutes later, Jane appeared in the doorway, escorted by a female guard a head taller than she was. She looked so pale and tiny that Melanie almost didn't recognize her. Her heart jolted in her chest at seeing her friend faring so poorly after she'd already had so much grief in her life of late.

"Hi, honey. How are you?" she asked as Jane approached the table where Mel sat.

She seated herself across from Mel and lifted her swollen eyes, welling with fresh tears. "Mel, they think I'm a killer. I can't even defend myself because I can't remember a thing about any of it."

"I know, Jane. It's a lousy situation. Have you had any memory recall lately?"

The younger woman shook her head. "Old stuff, yeah, lots of it. But not recent… and not for the lack of trying. But nothing much. Just minor details… but who knows? Maybe they might help the investigation since one involves driving—maybe on that day? I'm not sure and I don't even have my journal to write them down as they come back to me. Do you think you might be able to get it and overnight it to me, or something? I don't want you to have to come all the way back here. I don't even know how long I'll have to stay in this pit. My father is arranging for an attorney. Hopefully, I can get out tonight, but I don't want to go home. Not right away. I'm scared to."

"Of course, I'll get it for you. I can get it tomorrow after work but I probably can't come back until Monday. You won't have to stay that long, will you?"

Jane tried to smile but it fell short into a grimace. "I don't know how long I'll be here or even if they'll give me bail. I don't know anything. But there are no visitors allowed on Mondays and Tuesdays. Can you overnight it to me here possibly? I'm so sorry I've been such a burden on you recently, Mel, what with the car accident and now this."

"Stop it. None of it is your fault, Jane. It's fine."

"Did Fitzgibbons give you any details?"

Mel shook her head—she didn't know what would be all right to repeat. "You need a good lawyer. Have you phoned your parents?"

"Yes. My mother is mortified that my reputation is shredded." She choked on a sob. "She doesn't give a damn that I'm here in this rank jail, terrified out of my wits, and surrounded by scary criminals." She whispered the last part, peering around anxiously.

"Are they coming, your parents?"

Jane looked up at her, her eyes bloodshot. "I really don't know. She said she'd cover some of my legal fees. Whoopee. What a great mother, right? I don't even need her damn money, but that's all that's on offer, apparently." She wiped tears from the corners of her eyes with the heel of her hand. "God, I really hit the jackpot when it came to parents," she said, sniffling and looking around for a tissue but finding none.

"Have you talked to any lawyer yet?"

Her face twisted. "No. My father has. The attorney he called is coming to see me this evening. I'm hoping whoever it is will get me bail so at least I can go home. I've been here almost two days."

"Is he a good attorney?"

"He's my father's friend. They—his firm—normally don't handle criminal law but he said if he couldn't take the case, he'd recommend someone who could. He should be here by six, he said. I'm hoping I can leave with him." She wiped her nose with her hand. "But I don't think that's possible. I think I have to wait to be arraigned. The arraignment is supposed to be tomorrow morning. So maybe then."

Melanie nodded, hitching her shoulders. The room felt so cold despite it being filled with people. "Jane, listen to me. You need a top criminal attorney—these charges are serious. You need one of the best." She leaned in a little closer. "Do not settle, do you hear me?" She waited until Jane looked her in the eye and nodded in assent. "God, I wish you could remember more about the time around your accident. I mean, you must have told someone where you were going that day."

"If I did, I don't remember. God, it's so frustrating, Mel. I just want to jump up and down and scream."

"I know it is, Jane. I wish I could do more to help…" She tapped her foot as she searched her brain for ideas. "Hey, what about a hypnotist?"

Jane looked skeptical. "I suppose I could try it—it might help jog my memory. I don't know… Mel, you have to get Fitzgibbons in here to speak with me. Maybe he could make sense of these little details that I've been recalling. They might be important."

Mel tried to steer the conversation away from Rob. "What details? Tell me some of them."

"They make no sense. Making fudge with some man, car keys on a sterling Tiffany key ring, driving to meet up with a scary suicide blonde with mirror sunglasses…"

"Suicide blonde?"

The question elicited the tiniest of grins from Jane. "Dyed by her own hand. Never heard that one?"

"No," she said, chuckling.

"Detective Fitzgibbons might help piece them together. Maybe he has information that neither of us have, you know?"

Mel nodded miserably, knowing that he would never do it. But she couldn't deny Jane that hope she saw spring to her eyes. "I'll try, Jane. But if not, tell your attorney."

"But my attorney won't be a detective, Melanie. Detectives are supposed to solve crimes and yours is the lead one on this case."

Mel's eyes were glued to the table, her fingers making invisible swirls and figure eights on the beige surface. "He's not mine, but yeah, OK. I'll try to talk to him as soon as I leave here. But he probably can't meet with you anymore because of conflict of interest…" She dragged her gaze up to Jane and saw the feeble light fade from her friend's eyes and hurriedly said, "We'll see. Meantime, how are you?"

"How do you think?" Her bottom lip began to quiver. "I'm in prison, Mel. Rikers. For a crime that I'm pretty sure I didn't commit."

ENTIRELY INEFFECTUAL IS how Melanie felt before leaving Jane. The poor girl desperately needed a strong advocate and had none. Only her very inadequate friend from work stood between her and ruin. Jane desperately needed someone on her side who could actually make things happen. Mel's mind went immediately to Detective Rob Fitzgibbons who had refused to help. Mel knew he was in a difficult position but she wanted him to do the right thing and that was to keep an open mind.

Mel had almost no doubts about Jane. But when someone like a cop tells you with authority and near-absolute certainty that another person is guilty of a crime, you can't help but pay some attention. Mel felt as if she knew

Jane pretty well and with ninety-five percent of her brain and all of her heart knew Jane wasn't a killer. Knew it.

Still there was a tiny itch at her peace of mind. That niggling five percent of doubt, sowed with determination by one hottie cop. Could it be true? Those expensive Louboutins in Jane's closet were so out of character for her. Mel should just ask Jane about them. For all she knew, they didn't even belong to Jane. Maybe someone gave them to her.

Jane also owned a lot of expensive and erotic lingerie. Those point to sex, ergo, a man being in the picture regularly. Yet no man had come forth. If he wasn't Mason Caldwell, why not?

And the fact that there was a huge cash withdrawal from Jane's bank account. What did she do with all that money? If it was a purchase… why cash?

According to Rob, there was even more damning evidence that he couldn't share with her. But from what he did confide, it almost seemed to Mel that someone was trying to set up Jane. It was all too pat for Mel's comfort—the high school crush, the real estate purchase, the cash withdrawal, the photo found with Jane's fingerprints. If Jane was guilty as charged, she was the worst criminal ever, leaving a sticky trail of crumbs following her.

The thing was—Jane wasn't dumb; she was smart. Why would a smart woman be such a dumb murderer?

Friday was slow and Melanie felt like she was clawing her way around in a thick fog. Instead of leaving at four, as was her plan, she told her colleagues that she was feeling off—the truth actually—and she got out of there at one, heading straight to Jane's house in Riverdale to get the journal. The train ride was uneventful and in less than thirty minutes she was walking the two blocks to the townhome. On the way, she passed the tiny café where Jane had taken her for brunch all those weeks—and a lifetime—ago. In their little kiosk, Mel saw the local paper.

On the front page, the headline screamed *Revenge of the Nerd* and featured an awful photo of Jane right next to it. The publication painted Jane as the fat, ugly girl who pined after the popular handsome jock for years until finally snapping and having his glamorous wife killed. Mel leaned in and read the first few lines. Ugh. It said that in her deranged mind, he'd become interested in her once he was single again and they'd live happily ever after.

Mel fervently hoped that Jane hadn't seen it. The newspaper had printed two photos of Jane, probably from the high school yearbook. Neither was very flattering—naturally. The one published of Mason Caldwell was of him in his football jersey, holding the football and grinning at the camera, looking like a million bucks.

Life just wasn't fair.

"WHAT THE FUCK?" she muttered aloud when she approached Jane's house. A makeshift memorial had been created at the foot of the Caldwell driveway, filled with plush dog toys and flowers. Immediately adjacent to it was Jane's property, and her driveway was smeared with broken eggs, shaving cream, and shards of glass from broken bottles. Worse, there was neon pink paint sprayed in words going across the asphalt, up her walk, and on the white door.

Murderer. Slut. Killer.

Must have just happened, Mel reasoned, since this wasn't the type of neighborhood where they'd tolerate this kind of thing. Riverdale was well tended and moneyed—sidewalk memorials and vandalism didn't quite fit in with the climbing ivy and bluestone.

Only three days since her arrest and Jane was already tried and convicted in the court of public opinion. As Mel walked up to the door, someone shouted to her. "If you know what's good for you, you'll steer clear from that house. People not so happy it belongs to a killer."

Melanie turned slowly toward the voice, her pulse accelerating. The man was large and formidable, full-sleeve tattoos running up both his forearms—as much as she could see with the sleeves of his leather jacket pushed up. "I'm a realtor, sir. We'll be listing this home in coming weeks. Do you live around here?" She knew he didn't.

He trained beady gray eyes on her. "No, I don't live around here, matter of fact. I don't know any of these people either," he admitted, gesturing up and down the block, "but a little old lady that I do work for lives right up the street and she's been real upset since this poor lady was gunned down, ya know? So I'm lookin' out for her interests, you might say." His shiny bald head, attached to rolls of neck fat, swiveled around as he scanned the immediate area before returning his attention to her.

Mel nodded in a sympathetic manner, she hoped. "Understood. I just need to have a look around, maybe take a few quick shots of the interior. Thanks for keeping an eye out, though."

After studying her for a long minute, he said in a warning tone, "You take care now."

As she started to leave, he piped up again. "Why two real estate agents in one day anyway?"

Mel's back went stiff. "Another realtor was here?"

He grinned, revealing crooked, stained teeth. "Yep, but not as pretty as you. That one was a little rough looking. You know, been around the block a few times."

"Older you mean?"

He spit on the ground to the right of his feet. "Nah, just used up. Anyway, I'll let you get back to your business."

Once the door was closed behind her, Mel leaned back and took a deep breath. What the hell was that all about outside? This area was exclusive and people who looked like Slash out there didn't belong. And who was that other person pretending to be a realtor? As far as Melanie knew, Jane had no plans to list the place and besides, if that sleazeball out there thought the woman was rough looking, Mel was guessing she wasn't a realtor of high-end homes. Maybe she was a reporter looking for a scoop? Unfortunately, Jane would probably have to list the house at some point soon if she was going to be demonized as it appeared was happening.

But why did Jane warrant all of this attention? People get arrested all the time, and some are even innocent. Poor girl just couldn't catch a break.

Pushing off the door, Melanie went in search of the journal in question. Jane wasn't sure where it would be but thought the bedroom a good place to start, so that's where Mel headed.

Creaking the door open slowly, she peered inside. It was just as Jane left it—as if she'd stepped into the shower a moment ago. Her pajamas were strewn across the bed and a towel was hooked on one of the iron posts of the old-fashioned-style four-poster. Clearly, Jane hadn't known what was coming to get her.

While searching for the journal, she came upon a box of books and papers and couldn't resist. She could justify her snooping by saying it was within the realm of possibility that Jane tossed her journal in with the books. Mixed in with some papers was a class photo from either middle or high school. Mel scrutinized the picture, looking for Jane. She finally found her in the top row looking entirely pissed off. The photo was not flattering in any way and it looked like Jane went to zero trouble to look good for it. Mel understood why.

She continued to rummage through the paperwork. Near the bottom she found a photo of a slender woman, nearly nude, in high heels and a skimpy camisole and panties. It looked like a Victoria's Secret photo. The woman's face was turned away from the camera. Mel stared at it for a long time. Could it be Jane? It looked like it could be… but no, Jane had only just recently lost the weight. Before that she'd been heavy. Besides, Jane was not the type to dress in skimpy lingerie and allow someone to take photos of her. Mel just couldn't see it.

Unless she'd been pretending all along? A little chill curled up the nape of her neck.

No. That's ridiculous, Mel decided, dismissing the track of her thoughts. Rob's suspicions about Jane were really infecting her now. After searching the bedroom and not finding the journal, she headed back downstairs. It wasn't in the living room, still devoid of furniture. Mel stood in the middle of the big, empty room, hands on hips, and questioned the room, "Where would I put the journal if I were Jane?"

"OK, if I had to write down my thoughts and emotions for contemplation, I'd want either a cup of coffee or a glass of red wine to help smooth the way." She headed into the kitchen.

Bingo. She spotted it as soon as she crossed the threshold. The brown leather-bound book was lying casually on the granite counter, next to the cutting board. Mel flipped through it and then closed it with a snap. It was private and no matter how much she wanted to read it, she shouldn't.

Should she? As she hugged the book to her chest, she considered the situation and her thoughts began to drift.

Her reverie was breached by the clear peals of the doorbell. She bolted off the stool where she'd perched, her heartbeat accelerating like a Maserati. Who was it and should she answer it? Why did she feel as if she was doing something wrong? She sidled up to the front door, wary in case it was someone out to do Jane harm.

"Who is it?" she called through the heavy wooden door. Nothing. She yelled louder. "Who is it?"

"Delivery, ma'am."

Mel peered out of the sidelight. Sure enough, there was a furniture truck outside. She opened the door to an older man wearing a navy-blue uniform with the name of the furniture company emblazoned in yellow thread across his breast. "What are you delivering today?"

He consulted his clipboard. "Everything except the console, which is still on backorder."

"Everything meaning…?"

"All the furniture you purchased, ma'am."

The man looked discomfited and Mel remembered the graffiti. "This is my friend's home. I just came by to pick something up for her. Can you tell me exactly what you're delivering?"

"Sure. Here's the invoice. Have a look." He handed her a sheet off his clipboard.

Mel looked at it. There was a list of ten pieces. A sofa, $2479; a chair, $899; a coffee table, $499; two table lamps and one apothecary floor lamp, $469; a dining room table and two chairs (already delivered), $2500; dining bench (already delivered), $280. The total bill was $7126, tax included, paid in full, in cash.

In cash.

Ten grand minus three equals seven.

Seven thousand dollars in cash.

Heart pounding like a jackhammer, Mel could barely find her voice. "Do customers often pay in cash?"

The man grinned. "The owner of the store likes cash. He gives customers a fifteen-percent discount if they pay in cash. In this case, the discount was taken in the form of an extra piece—the console table that's on backorder. Mr. Jamison—the owner—is also throwing in a 5x7 hand-knotted wool rug… because of the size of the sale. Your friend furnished most of her house at his shop. He appreciates her business."

Mel nodded, giving up all pretense of smiling and trying to act normally. She opened the door and stepped aside, allowing the deliveryman and his workers access to the house.

Just about stumbling to the kitchen, she perched on a stool, dropped her phone on the counter, and attempted to make a phone call with her shaking hands. She had proof, concrete evidence that could potentially spring Jane right out of jail. Melanie just needed to know how to play it right. She wished she could speak with Rob but…

Chapter 31

It was way past dark by the time Rhett Harmon locked her office downtown near the courts, her sensible courtroom heels clicking hollowly in the empty tiled corridor as she exited the building. The epitome of an ambitious young prosecutor, she was salivating at the gift she'd been given: she'd been assigned the stalking murder case that had so transfixed the city. It was a classic tale of obsession, jealousy, and murder, and had all the makings of a crowd pleaser: a handsome young man, his beautiful wife whose family is rooted in New York society, and the loser girl next door who has stalked the man since middle school and plotted to kill poor wifey. Richening the soup is that fat-loser-girl has a car accident, drops a ton of weight, gets a new nose, and emerges from her blubbery cocoon as a beauty just in time for her murder trial. How could it get any better?

It was pure tabloid fodder.

In first chair, Rhett was going to be the prosecuting attorney who sent Jane Jensen to jail for life with no possibility of parole. Everyone would know the ADA's name by trial's end.

And nothing was going to get in Rhett Harmon's way.

The DA told her to fast-track the trial. He didn't want any of the Caldwell or Cobb family connections breathing down his neck during an election year. Rhett would work as many hours as was necessary to win this case. Hard work never scared her. Losing scared her. Mediocrity scared her. Always feeling insecure about her social standing—her parents were working class—and lackluster education that her less-than-stellar background afforded her, from an early age Rhett promised herself that she'd work hard and excel so greatly that she'd ascend in social standing before she was thirty.

She was twenty-eight now.

Going to work for the district attorney in New York City wasn't the most glamorous or lucrative job she could have gotten out of law school, but it was a means to an end: a prestigious first step toward a political career. She was in her fourth year now and winning this case would be enough to propel her to the next phase of her career.

Rhett wanted more than money: she craved power. What better way to get it than through political office? Accordingly, she needed to pay her civic dues, put in time at the bottom rung before chinning up to the next. She planned to have experience in multiple aspects of the law before dipping her toe into the waters of elective office. Soon she'd be ready to move into the next job.

Winning a conviction in a case that would be under heavy media scrutiny would be the perfect swan song to end her days as an ADA. She'd go to work for the private sector next and then after that maybe move to DC and get to know the players and their recreational landscape. Either that or run for local office, maybe city councilperson, and use that as a springboard. Her ultimate goal was either the Senate or the DOJ.

She planned to get to the top by the time she was forty. Jane Jensen was going to give her a big leg up. Maybe even a catapult.

As far as she could see, the case was a slam dunk. There was motive; there was evidence—both circumstantial and eyewitness. There was a clear money trail. Unless some major exculpatory evidence arose at the eleventh hour, Rhett couldn't see how she'd lose. She sincerely doubted that Jane would prove an effective advocate for herself. Though Rhett hadn't personally met the woman, she'd been told by those who had that Jane was meek and mild-mannered. Not exactly a star witness for the defense.

Jane Jensen was also without strong advocates—people who would support her, take her case to social media, make lots of noise. She had no family in the area, not many friends even, in the vicinity. No boyfriend or husband, few social activities, no one except work colleagues to testify on her behalf. If Rhett couldn't win this case, it would be shame on her.

As she walked toward her tiny Financial-District condo, Rhett finally allowed herself to relax and switch mental gears, trying to decide what to have for dinner tonight and what movie she'd take in on Netflix. She'd allow herself an hour and a half to enjoy it and then back to work on the filings she had to do this week.

The key to success was meticulous preparation. An attorney should never get caught with her pants down. Good advice both literally and figuratively and the kind Rhett took to heart. She was always ready for any contingency.

After sprinting up the two flights of marble steps—her daily exercise for today—she let herself into the sleekly modern studio apartment. Buying this apartment had been a smart move because in the year and a half she'd owned the place, it had already increased over fifty percent in value. One by one, she pulled the hairpins out of her low chignon, letting her sleek black hair slide down, and began undressing as she shuffled over to her small dressing alcove in the corner of the apartment. A few minutes later, clad in yoga pants and T-shirt, she heated up some leftover Basmati rice and mixed vegetables while perusing her movie options. Nothing appealed, probably because she couldn't get her mind off the case. The State of New York versus Jane Jensen.

Forgoing the movie, she sat at her dining table, her dinner on her left, the manila folder on the right and began reading.

MELANIE WAITED until after dinnertime to call Rob about Jane's request and to tell him about the furniture. She felt as if it were her eureka moment and couldn't help feeling smug, but she squashed it quickly. Rob would sense it, and it would put him on the defensive. As for waiting for after dinnertime? Like most men, he was always more malleable on a full stomach.

As soon as he answered the phone, she blurted it all out. Without waiting for him to respond, she went on. "So you have to reconsider the charges in light of this new information."

"Absolutely not, Melanie. It's not gonna happen."

"Wha—are you kidding me? But if there's new evidence? Isn't it your ethical, moral, and professional obligation to investigate?"

"No, because I remain convinced that Jane Jensen

hired the killer to murder Cate Caldwell. There's no new evidence. She's full of shit and desperate to save her own skin."

Melanie now organically understood where the word breathtaking came from. It had never happened to her before but Rob's words were so shocking, so insulting to her, that her lungs just emptied of air in one big whoosh, leaving her gasping. She swallowed hard and then forced herself to breathe, inhaling through her nose from the diaphragm, finding her footing again. Thank God for yoga. Clearing her throat, she was calm as she terminated the conversation. "I see. Sorry I bothered you, Detective. Have a good evening."

Mel jabbed her finger at the red button, obtaining a modicum of satisfaction from hanging up on the d-bag. She raked her teeth over her upper lip. Now what? She'd been so certain that when she told him of her discovery, he'd immediately re-evaluate the case and Jane's guilt. Instead, he said it didn't make a single whit of difference. What the very fuck?

ROB STARED at his phone as the call disappeared from the screen. Stared at it long after, in fact. After the abrupt conversation with Melanie, he experienced a crisis of indecision—foreign for him. Rob prided himself on being resolute by nature, never hesitating to make decisions and never second-guessing his judgment afterward. But now… first off, he regretted the way he'd handled the call—he'd let his temper get the best of him. When he saw Mel's name on his phone, he'd thought that she was calling him to say she'd give up contact with Jane to be able to continue seeing him. It's not as if he asked her to fucking

testify against the damn woman. For
wanted her to cut off contact with her
the case.

OK, so they hadn't known one a
true. Despite that lack, he was seriou
their sexual chemistry was galvanic. He'd instinctively
known going in that it would be, right from the moment he met her, and it was why he'd initially tried to keep her at a remove. Once he gave in… well, that night had been pretty unforgettable. He'd done a fast reload for her after the first time, and he'd never enjoyed just being inside a woman and taking his time kissing her more than that night. He wanted it again, goddamn it. More than again.

As for waffling over a decision made, well, he was doing that too. Melanie had provided him with information that shook their case against Jane Jensen, and he had to go to the DA with it. The decision he grappled with right now was whether he should notify Rhett Harmon directly or let it go up the chain of command. He had no desire to let her rip off his balls when he yanked away her prey. Rhett Harmon was a hungry leopard and she smelled raw, bloody meat in Jane Jensen.

However, the sooner she was apprised of the new information, the better she could retool her case. Rob believed they still had plenty enough on Jane Jensen to go ahead with the trial. New York's blindfold law definitely worked in their favor. Although she provided the defense with some information on their evidence, Harmon didn't release Pernod's affidavit to the defense attorney and wasn't required to. Pernod was their ace in the hole, and though as a killer he was not the most desirable of witnesses, he seemed as if he'd be pretty credible on the stand. He didn't get rattled at all when they helped prep him.

.e jury wouldn't hate him either. As far as lowlife .derous scum goes, Pernod was relatively charismatic. ıe was decent looking and was one of those bizarro criminals who believed in honor among thieves. At his deposition, he insisted on ensuring all the details were recorded correctly. He said he'd never want to be responsible for sending the wrong person upstate.

This from a cold-blooded killer.

When asked about it, he claimed it was a business like any other, and it's something he happened to be good at. He knows he's looking at most of the rest of his life inside but he's yet unrepentant. When Rob asked him how he felt about cutting short the life of a beautiful and promising young woman, Pernod shrugged and said, "It was her time. There are many different cancers in the world."

What the hell did that mean? It made Rob want to bash his head in.

Still, he would help them win the case and put the real killer behind bars for life. In Rob's opinion, the contract killer was bad but the person who hired him was worse. That person has thought about it, premeditated the killing, and went about putting together the resources to make it happen. That takes time, careful thought, and the most impervious of hearts. The hit man merely pulls the trigger on a stranger and walks away without ever knowing the person cut down. Big difference.

Chapter 32

Jane's Journal, December

I CAN'T BELIEVE IT. I can't fucking believe it. Every time my life seems to be getting better, something happens to land me in deeper shit. It makes me want to just give up, go to sleep, and never wake up. It makes me regret surviving the car accident, working so hard on my recovery only to end up here.

In jail.

I'm in jail.

On Rikers Island.

In a holding cell that smells like vomit.

Arrested for murder.

Mel came to visit me. Insisted I get in touch with Sulu to see if she could fill in some gaps in my memory, specifically as it relates to Mason Caldwell. I resisted at first, but my life is pretty much swinging in the balance. So I called.

She took her time answering the phone. I'll write down the conversation as best as I can remember it.

"I guess it's you, Jane, since I don't know anyone else in Rikers."

"Yes, it's me. I'm sorry it took my needing a favor to call you."

"Yeah, what's the favor? I mean, you're charged with murder, Jane. It's not like I can help you out there."

"Sulu, can you come visit me?" The dense silence that followed prompted me to check to see if the call dropped, then remembering a landline didn't drop calls. "Su?"

"Yeah, I'm here."

"I know it's an imposition but I really need to see you."

"Why?"

"Did you read about my car accident?"

"The article I read about your arrest mentioned it. So what?"

"Sulu, my memories are full of gaps. My doctor says he's never seen a case quite like mine where huge chunks of my life are missing. I'm hoping that you can fill me in on some of what I'm missing—at least from our school days—and something in there might help my case."

"I seriously doubt it, Jane."

"Doubt what? That you can visit or help?"

"Help. What can your memories from high school do for you now?"

"Sulu, I think I'm almost out of phone time. Please come visit me. Tomorrow, visiting hours are from one till nine. Please, Sulu, please do this for me."

"I'll try, Jane. Goodnight."

THE OVERNIGHT I spent at Rikers, I was trying to sleep in this miserable cell. It was noisy and there was a constant buzzing noise coming from somewhere—where I couldn't tell. I was trying to clear my mind in a futile attempt to sleep when I saw a bright flash, followed by tires screeching. I saw a man's face looking at me—was it the poor guy in the pickup? Deshaun Cleveland?

Yes, I know his name; now I'll never forget his name. He didn't deserve to die. In fact, now I think it would have been far better if he'd been the one to survive instead of me.

But with this memory there are kids, teenagers, all around me. Why? I must be confusing two different memories. A choking sense of doom accompanies these flashbacks, and I don't have a freaking clue why. I just feel desperately sad when I think about it, the crash, the ambulance ride, the doctor at the hospital. But it's not Dr. Lavelle; it's someone else. A balding man with droopy eyes.

It's all so confusing… and so sad.

It was Valentine's Day, I think. I was wearing a baggy pink sweater, pink for Valentine's, baggy as usual. I… I was running away from something… someone. It had something to do with the Halloween party, the kissing in the car. Afterward, he drove us to his house. Oh my God, we went to his house. I remember that.

Once we were there, in his parents' finished basement, he'd taken a condom out of his wallet and led me to a small room with a couch. It was there that I lost my virginity—happily. To Mason Caldwell. I couldn't believe my good luck.

He was gentle. He looked just slightly surprised when he pushed into me and I gasped in pain. He had to have felt the hymen tearing since he had to work hard to get in. He never said anything, though, and neither did I. I was so happy to be with him, to be touching him, to have him inside me. The sex itself didn't feel so great to me to be honest, but Mason looked pleased afterward. That was all that mattered to me.

Later I wondered how long he'd been carrying around that condom because it failed. It took me more than two months before I realized I was pregnant.

Oh. My. God. I was pregnant with Mason's baby.

Now so much makes more sense where before it didn't. That's why I kept getting the feeling there was more to my relationship with him. That's what was connecting the Halloween party with the Valentine's Day accident. That's what the annihilating sadness was all about.

My pregnancy.

My miscarriage.

The accident caused me to miscarry. I'd been almost fifteen weeks pregnant. No one knew except the ER doctor, and then naturally he told my parents. I wish I could have been a fly on the wall during that conversation. But I was too broken to have enjoyed it. My beautiful little baby gone in the turn of an hour. The heartache was unbearable and unrelenting. I almost wish I didn't remember it… but it's important that I do. I want to always remember. I begged the doctor to tell me the gender. He didn't want to… but he finally did.

It was a boy.

Chapter 33

At precisely one o'clock the next day, Sulu was waiting at the prison to see her. When Jane was led out and saw her old high school pal sitting there, she nearly burst into tears. For one thing, it was good to see her best friend from school. Sulu helped get her through those awful years, and Jane truly did enjoy her company even if no one else did. Sulu's personality was an almost irresistible concoction of misanthropy and sarcasm.

She looked exactly the same as she did in high school. Unlike Jane who had progressed and drastically improved, both in appearance and personality, Sulu had remained static—and stagnant. She wore ill-fitting tan khakis, red and white running shoes, and a purple blouse that wreaked havoc with her skin tone. Sulu wasn't overweight in school: she was thin and wore thick glasses and had greasy hair. Now she'd picked up some weight, enough so that she looked plump. After Jane's initial joy at seeing the familiar face, Sulu's appearance depressed her. Nonetheless, she plastered a big smile on her face and greeted her.

Sulu stood uncertainly as Jane approached the table.

"Hi, Sulu." They embraced in an awkward half-hug—minimal contact was allowed—and quickly pulled apart to avoid breaking any rules.

"How are you? Are you working?" Jane asked once they were seated.

Shaking her head, Sulu put her hands on the table as she was probably instructed to do by the prison guards. "No, I left my last job two months ago… actually, it's been more like three now… and I haven't been able to find another one. I really should have finished my degree."

"It's never too late, you know."

She rolled her eyes and Jane had to bite her tongue to keep from saying anything unkind. Sulu always saw the downside of everything. Always.

"So what do you need to know?" Sulu asked her once they'd gawked at each other for a protracted minute.

Jane pressed her lips together, abruptly realizing the futility of this meeting. What did she really hope to glean from Sulu anyway? She cleared her throat and forged ahead nonetheless. "Let's start with what kind of person I was. How did I treat other people?"

Screwing up her face, Sulu said nothing for a minute or so. "You were like me, Jane: sarcastic and bitter, but it's not like we didn't have reason. People were mean to us, and every day was like running the gauntlet. We had to survive by growing claws."

Jane leaned in closer and then remembered herself before the guard had a chance to reprimand her. "So I was mean to other students?"

"Only if they were mean to you first. You were OK, Jane. Like I said, we needed to survive."

"Su, what about Mason Caldwell?"

"What about him?"

"How was I with him? I mean, I remember having a huge crush on him, but he never knew I even existed, right? I just want to know if there's anything I'm not remembering."

"You were obsessed with him. You'd just talk about him for days, analyze everything you saw him do or say, the minutiae of his life. It was incredibly pathetic and annoying."

"Well, thank you. OK, so I was obsessed and annoying. Anything else?"

"Like what?"

"Did I ever threaten any of his girlfriends or say anything like that?"

Sulu's nostrils flared as she looked all around her. "Jane, I don't think this is the time and place for this conversation. I really don't think it will help you."

"Sulu," Jane started, feeling her desperation climb as she began to perspire, "do you understand the dire straits I'm in right now?

The other woman just stared back at her old friend with a stony expression. If she heard the tremor in Jane's voice, she gave no sign of it. "Yeah, I understand. What I don't get is why you think I can help."

Sucking down her agitation, Jane mustered all of her self-restraint to deal with the infuriating person in front of her. "You can help," she began in artificially calm voice, "by assisting me in filling in some of the blanks. You have to understand, Sulu, that I'm operating completely in the dark here. I've been arrested for a murder that I don't even know if I committed or not. I'm pretty sure I didn't, but since I have no memory, I can't be certain. You and my parents are the only ones who know who I was—am—exactly."

The homely woman shrugged her shoulders in an

exaggerated manner. "You could be a nasty bitch when pushed, but I don't think you'd kill anyone. People were shitty to us, so we returned it in full measure. But you liked Mason, and I don't think you'd hurt him… or his wife. That's all I can say really, Jane. I'm sorry you're in this awful predicament…"

It was no use. Jane took a deep breath, folded her hands on the table in front of her, and changed tacks. "So what have you been up to?"

Sulu smirked. "Filling out paperwork and applications to finish my doctorate. I already did a lot of the course work while I was pursuing my master's. Mainly I have to take about three more classes and do the dissertation. Almost an ABD."

"Oh, when you said you should have finished your degree, I thought you meant your bachelor's."

"Of course not," she sniped. "What kind of a loser do you think I am, Jane?"

Jane ignored the comment. "Wow, good for you. What exactly are you going for?"

"Applied sciences. I'm focusing my research, though, on biochem. I think it's the best fit for me. I'd like to get a job with the CDC."

"You'd have to relocate then, in all likelihood."

"Yeah." She shrugged her narrow shoulders. "But New York has lost its edge anyhow. It looks like Any City, USA. It's a little more interesting but not by much."

Jane nodded. "I really appreciate your coming here today, Sulu. I hope I'll be able to put this nightmare behind me soon, and if so, I'll take you out to dinner."

She pushed her chair back and the legs scraped the tile floor. "I guess I should be going. Are your parents here?"

"No," Jane shook her head. "I don't know if they're

even planning to come. But then they've never been the greatest parents."

She turned a level gaze at Jane. "No, they haven't."

Chapter 34

Jane's Journal, late December

MY FATHER'S attorney came through for me and got me out of Rikers within an hour of his appearance on Friday evening—after I spent thirty-six hours in that hellhole. I took a cab to the city and checked into a Midtown hotel, afraid to go home. I texted Mel to let her know I was out and that I'd call her in the morning, and then I ordered room service, ate everything in sight, and went to bed exhausted. I slept ten hours straight without waking up once. After I took a shower and had coffee, I called Mel.

"Jane, where are you now?"

"Still at the Marriott. The one in Midtown. On 40th Street. I have an hour until checkout but I might stay a bit longer if the room is available."

"Uh-huh. I have your journal and I'll meet you for breakfast and bring it to you. Let's go to Artie's—it's about halfway between my place and the hotel."

So we met and that's when Mel told me about the

furniture. It was such good news that I almost actually cried. I left a message for my attorney while we were still in the restaurant.

My hotel room was booked for the next week and I would have had to move to a different room so I decided to just buck up and go home. I'd have to do it sooner or later. Depending on how bad it was or how unsettled I felt would cement my plan to list the house for sale sooner rather than later. I hated the thought of selling before I even had a chance to live in the charming home, but if I didn't feel comfortable there, what was the point? There were tangible reminders everywhere of this traumatic experience, and all I wanted now was to move on as quickly as humanly possible. The double whammy of car accident and murder arrest was savage on my psyche—I had to get away.

I woke up in my own bed on Sunday morning, but I'd slept drastically better in the hotel. I probably should have stayed a little longer. I didn't feel safe in my home. The graffiti painted on my driveway scared me, and right next door was a man who believed I contracted a hit man to kill his wife. How safe could I be?

I hired someone to clean off the spray paint and repaint my front door but the words wouldn't erase in my mind. There were people out there who wanted to do me harm. That's not something that's easy to get used to.

One week after my arrest I was lying in my bed on the cusp of sleep when a riptide of memories began swirling madly around my head, causing chaos in my brain as they streamed in from wherever they'd been dammed up. Like flotsam in a river, I saw flashes of faces, words, smells, songs—everything associated with them. Most were of my life in high school, the minutiae of it, the miseries; it all came flooding back into my conscious.

And I realized something that everyone else seemed to take for granted already: along the entire odyssey of my adolescence, I watched Mason Caldwell. Watched him… and adored him from afar.

It's astonishing that I ever forgot who he was.

Mason Caldwell, the third. His friends called him alternately Tri, Trey, and Three Sticks.

Stalker. That's what they're calling me, what the police labeled me since my arrest. I hate the word. I don't see what's so terrible about showing interest in a person who practically demands it? It's not too much different from his being a celebrity and my following his career, except that maybe public people have an expectation of this sort of thing and he doesn't. But, in any case, he didn't know—couldn't know.

Now he does. Now the world knows. Now I'm a pariah.

Most or all of the top tier of popular kids in any high school aren't kind—they're by and large the polar opposite of kind—but Mason, he was. He was kind and relatively decent even to the lower castes in the school. He never went out of his way to be cruel. Occasionally, he might have laughed when one of his friends was bullying a weak student—I never said he was a saint—but Mason himself never went there.

For that reason, I forgave him for a multitude of sins I might not have otherwise overlooked. In the main, for his very pedestrian taste in girls.

True, they were beautiful; he dated the glossiest girls in school. Sarah Needham in ninth grade: 5'6", blond hair, pale eyes, big white teeth, cheerleader. I loathed her. Tess Gardner with shiny dark red hair and giant boobs in tenth. Shannon Graham, Barbie doll, in eleventh. She lasted until twelfth and graduation.

Then again, out of a graduating class of over two hundred, Mason was without question in the top five of the most perfect males. In my book, he had no peer.

And another memory: Mason went to Tufts. I remember that. I wasn't too far from him at Brown and it made me happy. I think I even remember seeing him at Brown events. Boston and Providence. Yes… that's right. He was dating a girl who went to my school. I hated her for it. I guess I lost track of him at some point, probably after we both finished college.

Meantime something extraordinary happened in my life. I finally found appreciation.

AT MY HEAVIEST I tipped the scale at 189, not too bad since I'm five-eight. Probably about forty or fifty pounds overweight.

I was also in the top five percent of my class.

Ergo, I had only two friends, both of whom were outcasts like me. For fun, we worked out math problems.

People like me are invisible. I got my job because of my talent with numbers, but I never expected to ever get far. My first day was awful. The train was eleven minutes late; the subway had problems too. I got to 1850 Broadway at ten after nine when I was supposed to check in with human resources at 8:45. The woman behind the desk gave me an ugly scowl and practically threw the papers I had to sign at me. I almost did an about-face and left, but my misfit-girl stubborn streak kept me there, filling out the paperwork.

Then the stars realigned and my fortune changed dramatically. Thank God I stayed that day. Now I'm earning six figures and have a cushy job while that scowling HR bitch was let go a few months after I started. Plus, I'm appreciated at MT.

It was a whole new concept for me.

UP A LITTLE AND now down even further. I might go to prison for the rest of my life, for a crime I may not have… no, I probably didn't commit. I don't feel like a killer. I cannot imagine being so coldhearted as to pay someone to kill another person, especially someone innocent like Cate Caldwell. The motive the police and prosecutor are assigning to me is a feeble one.

I keep thinking about it, contemplating the possibilities versus the probabilities. I suppose if I hated someone enough, hated him or her with everything I have in me… I suppose I might want to kill that person. I think every human being has that capacity but the majority are able to temper it. Logically, if I ever would have been pushed to murder, it would have been when I was miserably bullied in high school—and yet I never committed murder then.

So what could Mason's wife have done to me to push me far enough to want to kill her? If somehow I did hate Cate Caldwell with such ferocity as to pay to have her executed, I don't remember it at all.

In fact, I don't remember ever meeting the woman. I've seen photos of her and her face is not at all familiar to me. I just cannot conceive of the possibility that I'm guilty of this crime, and my predicament makes me want to bang my head against a brick wall.

Chapter 35

For the past three weeks Mason Caldwell kept crossing paths with his high school friends. He'd been staying at his parents' Pleasantville home pretty much since his wife's death, finding it easier than being alone in the house he shared with her, albeit for only a few weeks. An old football buddy, Todd Tennant, was the first one he encountered. They ran into each other at the local coffee shop.

"Duuude," Todd called out from the back of the queue. Mason turned around and jolted when he saw his old bud's face. He waved him up front, risking filthy glares from everyone behind him since Todd was now effectively cutting the long line. One older blonde's eyes blazed with fury, but she kept her lips stitched closed. Good thing. These days, Mason's nerves were overwrought. He didn't need any more grief from anyone.

A high-school star running back, Todd had kept himself in football-ready shape. Tall, broad-shouldered, with Nordic blond hair and piercing green eyes, he'd been in serious demand with the teenage girls and had run in the same circles as Mason. He wiped his hand on his pants before shaking Mason's hand—he looked like he'd just been exercising. "Hey, man."

"Bike ride?"

"Exactly. A quick ten-miler with a colleague."

"Where are you working now?"

"My dad's BMW dealership."

"Does he still sell Porsches too?"

"You know it, bro. Come see me; I'll fix you up. So... howya holding up? God, I can't believe that double-Dalmatian bitch did what she did. For fuck's sake, it's a shame we lost the death penalty in New York. She should be strapped down and injected. Poison for poison." He snickered. "Probably take a lot of dope to kill that fat bitch."

Mason bobbed his head, trying to refrain from making any comment. It would only spur Todd on even more, and there were people all around them. He'd just as soon keep his private life just that although it was impossible now. His whole life was smeared on the front page of every local publication, print and online.

"Did you have any clue the crazy bitch was stalking you?" he persisted. "Or was it, like, out of the blue?"

Mason casually eyed the knot of people standing around them—to his relief none seemed to be paying attention to Todd's big mouth. Or they were pretending not to, more likely. Outside the sky had darkened as a storm approached. Shit, he'd left some tools outside his father's garage. He needed to hurry. "We moved in to our new house and discovered she had just moved in next door a few weeks before."

His blond eyebrows arched. "She moved there first? Either bad luck or talented stalker."

Nodding absently, Mason muttered, "Mm-hmm. Have you seen Jane recently?"

"Me? No. Not since high school. Why?"

He couldn't help a smirk. Some things never changed, and Todd was still an asshole. Good football player, though. "She's become… well, let's just say a *lot* more attractive. And I hear she makes bank."

"No shit? Why do it then? If all is going so well for her?"

Mason just shook his head. "No clue. I'm not even sure she did it."

"Whaddya mean, bro?"

"Uhhh." His grunt landed on the tail end of a freighted sigh. "The police do sloppy work, real sloppy. I guess we'll learn more at the trial. Oh, we're up," he said as the pretty dark-skinned barista waved him over and he stepped up to the counter to place his order.

AFTER THE RAIN let up a few hours later, he went for a run—he despised running, but it was a necessary evil—and stopped at the local market for fresh fruit on the way back. He had just finished paying for it when he heard his name called.

"Mason, it's great to see you, man. How've you been?" An awkward pause ensued when Tom Henley realized his gaffe. "Oh shit, sorry. I'd forgotten what's going on with you. God, I'm so sorry about your wife."

"Thanks. It's been really tough. A nightmare."

"I can only imagine." He dropped his voice to a lower volume. "Do you really think Jane Jensen did it? What the police say she did?"

Screwing his pursed lips to one side, Mason shook his head. "No idea. It's hard to wrap my head around anyone doing such a horrible thing…"

"Yeah," he said, nodding, "especially Jane. She was

such a sweetheart. I got to know her a little in our senior year when we had an AP chem class together. She was just so nice and…"

"And?"

Tom hesitated, but his dark eyes never left Mason's. "… well, pretty. I spent some time talking with her, you know, and noticed that she was actually very pretty once you looked beyond the extra weight and ugly clothes. Smart too. She let me cheat off her test when Braden wasn't hawking us."

"Pfft. Fucking Braden. What a dick he was." Mason shrugged. "I don't know. The police are saying she was stalking me, which is too weird."

"It is weird because she's really fucking hot now. Saw a recent photo of her online. Wouldn't mind her stalking me." He closed his eyes and shook his head, grimacing. "Wow, I can't believe I just said that to you. Sorry."

"No, it's okay. I mean, it's hard, you know, but it's nothing I haven't been thinking myself."

"And I read in one of the articles that she's wealthy. Is that true, do you know?"

Mace rolled his neck, stiff from falling asleep on the sofa during the storm. He had to get into better shape. "So they say, but who knows if it's true? Apparently, she's sought after in her field, but that doesn't make her loaded." He stopped, looking down at his shoes as he kicked an errant penny around on the floor. "She is kind of beautiful, isn't she? Wonder why no one noticed back in high school."

"I think people were just so brutal to her that she sort of withdrew, you know. Made herself inconspicuous in order to survive. It happens." He hooked his thumbs in his jeans pockets. "But it's funny to think how someone like Kendra Ortalano, who was smokin' in high school is such a used-up slut now, and Jane, who was practically invisible, is a total babe—that is, if she's not guilty," he added quickly.

Mace nodded and barked a laugh. "Yeah, my gut tells me she's not, but what do I know. The police and the DA are so certain. So what's up with Kendra? You've seen her?"

"Yeah, about a month ago, I guess. Oh, man, it's all been downhill for ol' Kendra. I heard she was prostituting herself… became a two-bit porn actress… into drugs… just a total skank. I take it you haven't kept in touch?"

"Nah, we lost touch after high school. I wondered what she was up to. Drugs and prostitution? Wow. I can't imagine why she'd go that route." He grinned. "Then again, she did, like, the whole football team junior year. Everyone but me and Bondi, who liked dudes."

Tom chuckled and scratched his barely-there beard. "I'm guessing it was all about money. Some people try every which way to get big money without working for it. Not that anyone can get rich by just slogging away at a shitty job day after day. But still… it's got to be better than prostitution and porn." He laughed. "Oh, and remember gorgeous Shannon Graham?"

To Mason's nod, he continued. "Duh, of course you do. How could you forget, right? You dated her for a long time. Have you seen her lately?"

"No, I haven't seen anyone lately. I don't live around here anymore. What's up with her?"

"She married Joe Riley… remember him? He was valedictorian the year before we graduated? He's doing really well for himself with some online start-up he co-founded, and Shannon married him before she even finished her degree at Sarah Lawrence. Her parents were massively pissed but it was shotgun. Anyway… she got huge when she was pregnant with her twins, hasn't lost the baby weight. It's hard to believe she's the same girl as that Baywatch babe we used to know." He surreptitiously checked his watch. "Well, I don't want to keep you, Mace. It's great seeing you and if you need anything… just let me know. I'm really sorry about your pretty wife. So damn tragic."

"Yeah, thanks, Tom," Mason replied but he wasn't really listening anymore; his attention span was always limited and for the last few minutes his mind was traveling, his thoughts drifting through the aspects of the murder case. The tide had to start turning soon. But as long as Jane was the suspect, the pressure was off Mason. If things changed, that could bring the heat back onto him. He didn't want that, but he could sense something was coming. He just didn't know what it was or how to be ready for it.

Chapter 36

Jane bolted upright, her pajamas drenched in sticky sweat. A dream jolted her awake from a deep slumber. Or was it a memory?

Yes. It was a memory… *the* memory. It had infiltrated her subconscious, a dream she knew had its roots in reality. As soon as she regained consciousness, it all came hurtling back. Her hands flew up to her head, holding both temples to keep them from exploding.

One moment there was no other car in sight on the parkway and despite the ominous clouds growing pregnant with the coming storm, she found the late-afternoon drive soothing. She took her eyes off the road for one moment when something off the shoulder caught her eye.

It stood out on the green swath of lawn and brush: a bald eagle. Was it even possible? She'd never seen one in New York, never seen one anywhere but photographs. But there it was—unmistakable with its black body and snowy white head and shoulders. Forcing her eyes back to the road there was barely enough time for the event to register in her brain before it was already in the past. The split second of horror as a car intentionally swerved in front of her, cutting her off so severely she had no choice but to veer violently, sending her car over the narrow grass median. The momentum of the car—she usually drove between 65 and 70—jettisoned her into oncoming traffic. Bluish-white headlights bore down on her, and then the horrid, terrifying, unforgettable screech of metal twisting was all she'd had time to process as her body flooded with adrenaline.

Her memory shut down there as if a black curtain dropped over her brain. The last image she had was a face in the other car, a man's face, dark-skinned yet pale, reflecting her own horror back at her. But there was one thing she did clearly remember, one thing she never should have forgotten.

Someone had forced her off the road.

It wasn't that a car just badly cut her off as the police had led her to believe. That car, that black SUV, had dogged her for miles. She'd been trying to evade it when she came upon a slow-moving vehicle and shifted into the left lane to pass it. That's when the SUV bore down on her, intentionally causing her accident.

It was definitely personal.

SHE COULDN'T GET BACK to sleep. Battling with the bedcovers and unable to get comfortable, she finally ripped them off her and got up. One in the morning. She went downstairs and curling up on her new sofa, she turned on the television and found an old movie. Jane figured she should indulge in this kind of thing as much as possible. Her autonomy might be taken away from her soon—and forever—her daily schedule determined by other people.

Why would someone intentionally run her off the

road? What was she involved in before her accident that may have pushed someone to attempt to kill her? Or that she may have wanted to kill someone else? And why couldn't she fucking remember?

It was easier for her to accept that someone hated her enough to do her in than it was to think she could be a killer. Moreover, the accepted theory as to her motive was downright stupid. Why would killing Mason's wife get her any closer to Mason? He'd have to be in on it with her… an astoundingly unlikely scenario and judging by the interactions they'd had since Mrs. Caldwell's death, there was nothing there between them.

It was all just so freaking stupid and it made Jane want to scream. Unable to keep her attention on the movie, she got up and made herself a cup of tea. Mason followed her into the kitchen. He shadowed her as she made the tea and came back into the living room with her. She couldn't wipe her mind clean of the man and it was driving her insane. If nothing else could cure her of her adoration for him, maybe this would. She laughed bitterly. Maybe it took being accused of his wife's murder for her to get over her childhood crush.

The real question facing her now was how this would ever be resolved if she didn't recover all of her missing memories. She didn't like the answer—she hated the answer.

Chapter 37

Jane's Journal, January

I'VE BEEN HOME for over a week now. I came home to a mess, though Melanie, bless her kind heart, did her best to clean the driveway of the spray-painted slurs. A professional cleaning crew got rid of the rest.

Since all my new furniture is here, I can at least distract myself by arranging and rearranging it. My boss is coming to see me tomorrow and I want the house to look good. He and the number-two at the company want to speak with me, and I'm hoping and praying they'll stand by me no matter how bad things look.

Though my father got me my attorney through a friend, my parents have been less than supportive. My mother was especially horrified when I called her from the holding cell.

. . .

"JANE, I simply cannot believe you got yourself into this situation. Do you realize how grave your circumstances are?"

"Yes, Mom, *I do. Why do you assume I 'got myself' into these circumstances? Is it so difficult for you to believe I'm innocent?"*

"If you are, then why have you been arrested, Jane? Usually the police don't go around just arresting innocent people."

"Do you think I'm capable of orchestrating a murder-for-hire scenario? Tell me the truth. Do you?"

I could hear the stutter of hesitation across the line before my Betty Crocker mother began speaking again. *"I wouldn't think so, Jane. You were never the sweetest child, but I never saw any real venom come out of you."*

I'd closed my eyes, somewhat relieved. *"Well, thank you for that atomic particle of confidence. I don't have my full memory back and likely never will, but I'm pretty damn certain that I am not a killer. The big problem I face is proving it."*

"Thank goodness we're not in New York anymore. The trial would be sheer hell and such a public disgrace. Just complete mortification."

"Are you saying you're not coming to support me?"

"I'll try, dear. Your father will be coming for certain."

"It's good to know I have backup." She didn't even notice my sarcasm or if she did, she chose to ignore it.

MY MOTHER COULDN'T WAIT to get off the phone and back to her drought-resistant garden or her turquoise-and-sterling jewelry. Yeah, Tammy Jensen was never the most original person, and most aptly fit the definition of a sheeple—only the pretentious bourgeoisie kind.

I have no illusions about my parents and their love for me. It's basically zilch. Harold and Tamara Jensen are the kind of shallow social climbers who have no business whatsoever procreating. As their only child, I have suffered such benign neglect that I'd almost rather have been actually maltreated. At least that's the more honest way of abusing a child.

I don't know if I'll ever be lucky enough to fall in love with someone and have children with him but if I am, I know everything not to do—courtesy of the Jensens of Sedona, Arizona.

I hope they both drop dead.

Chapter 38

"Captain Branson? This is Mason Caldwell. Yes, sir. Thank you, sir. It's been difficult. How are you? My parents are well, thank you. Yes, thank you, sir, it's been hellish, as I'm sure you can imagine."

He stopped to listen to the long response.

"Actually, that's why I'm calling, sir. I need to report a possible miscarriage of justice..." He began to explain to the police captain.

"That's correct, sir. Her name? It's Kendra, K-E-N-D-R-A Ortalano, O-R-T like Tom-A-L-A-N like Nancy-O. Yes, sir. Someone phoned me... a woman, I'm pretty sure it was. I honestly don't remember exactly when, sir. I haven't been sleeping well. Yes, sir. I guess someone from high school... gosh, I can't remember who it was. I didn't pay it much attention right away... I've gotten so many calls.

"Anyway, someone claimed to have seen her in Poughkeepsie on the day the police say the killer was getting paid. She said she recognized Kendra. I should have told her right then to call the police directly. I was in such a fog of grief, and I dismissed it as another nut-job. I've gotten a lot of crank calls. Yes, sir.

"I do agree that it bears investigation. If Kendra was there, I'm sure you'll be able to confirm it somehow, right? Of course, I understand.

"Yes, sir. I'll tell my parents that you send your regards. Oh, and Captain B.? Much appreciate your discreet assistance."

He reached into his pants pocket and took out the other phone, tapped in the only number the phone ever called. It rang and rang. Where was the stupid bitch? On the fifth or sixth ring the line clicked open… there was a loud noise—she dropped the damn phone. Must be high or drunk. He waited for her to speak.

"Hi, handsome. What's up?"

"Listen to me carefully. I need you to destroy this prepaid phone you're on. I'll do the same to mine. We have to cut off contact for a couple of months. The cops are going to start leaning on everyone—they've already started. They'll get to you soon."

"How will I contact you?"

"You won't. Not for a while. When things cool down, I'll be in touch."

"Tsk, I hate that. Is it really necessary?"

He took a deep breath through clenched teeth and spoke very slowly, enunciating every syllable. "Yes, it is necessary. That's why I'm telling you to do it. Now, once we hang up, you have to crush the phone. Stomp on it—or use a hammer. Then take the broken pieces outside with you and throw each one into a different garbage can. Do exactly as I'm telling you. Unless you *want* to go to jail?"

"Of course, I don't. I'll do what you said, Mason."

"Good. I'll contact you as soon as it's safe to do so. Take care in the meantime."

"You too. Love you."

He disconnected the phone and leaned back in his office chair. He almost moaned in contentment. The Aeron chairs were pricey but worth every dollar. He closed his eyes and smiled, finally having a reason to do so.

"SHE LOOKS DIFFERENT," James Pernod told the prosecutor's assistant right after he left the courtroom. I don't think that was the same woman who gave me the money."

Jax Altamont, the ADA working as Harmon's number-two rolled his eyes. *Voir dire* had been a monumental pain in the ass, trying to choose twelve supposedly impartial jurors out of a pool of nearly three hundred. They did their utmost to save their peremptory challenges but had to use them up pretty quickly. It seemed as if every potential juror either was a jilted lover, a stalker of some kind, or had some agenda that would potentially invite bias. After nearly two interminable weeks, they finally seated a jury of twelve and two alternates, and the case was on track to move forward. He and Harmon believed they would get an easy conviction considering the plethora of evidence. Now Pernod was pissing him off with this bullshit spewing from his mouth.

With the exaggerated calm usually reserved for a child, he turned to him and explained. "If she looks different, it's only because she lost a lot of weight after her car accident… then went out and bought new clothes, got a new haircut, etc. You know, like a makeover. That's all it is."

Pernod shook his head. "Still… I'm pretty sure it's not the same woman. I'd swear to that in a court of law." He chuckled at his own joke.

Jackson's jaw tightened so hard he almost cracked his

teeth. When Rhett got a whiff of Pernod's doubt, she'd blow an artery on the spot. He had to try to talk him out of it before she returned.

Thing was he was a killer who was going away for a long time anyway, plea deal or no plea deal. Harmon would be damned if she'd let the bastard ruin their airtight case. His testimony was their ace in the hole, one that the defense didn't know was coming for them. Anyway, it was almost a certainty that Pernod didn't recognize Jensen because of the change in her appearance, not because she wasn't the same woman who paid him for the hit. And why was this the first time he'd seen Jane Jensen? He knew for a fact they'd only had a grainy photo of her when they'd first arrested him and he'd provided a detailed description of the woman who hired him. But why hadn't anyone done a photo line-up long before they got here today? Slipshod work on the part of NYPD. This kind of crap work had to stop.

"All right, look, Ms. Harmon will be here momentarily. You can express your misgivings to her, but I guarantee that she won't appreciate it—to put it mildly. Personally, I think you're just confused by the defendant's changed looks—it's not that she's a different woman. You'd be surprised at how altered a person can look after losing weight. Add to that some makeup and nice clothes? Voila, a completely new person."

His eyes more than skeptical, Pernod swung his head back and forth. "Yeah, but, this is not that," he said, punctuating his opinion by jabbing the photo with his index finger. "That lady is not the same person I met up with who handed over the envelope and I'm certain of it. It's not the haircut or the weight—it's that she's not the same person and I'm pretty damn sure of it."

Stupid lowlife piece of shit. Jackson wanted to choke

him. The bastard could sink their whole case at the eleventh hour, and he didn't want to have to hear Rhett when she got wind of this new development.

She was going to fucking detonate. DEFCON-1 here we come.

Chapter 39

Benny "Wink" Rodell sat in the waiting room at the DA's office, twisting his baseball cap, his knee bouncing up and down rapidly. Proximity to any kind of law enforcement made him edgy, but this was the last part of the job he'd been hired for and he wouldn't see the big payday until he testified in court. He thought he could just give his witness testimony to the local cops in Riverdale, but they'd directed him to the district attorney prosecuting the case.

Months before he'd been hired for a job, a cream puff of one, and been paid half the money upfront. All he had to do was follow some bitch as she made a cash drop to a sandman, and then afterward until she got back to the city. The only critical requirement was that he couldn't be made by the woman. If she saw him tailing her, he had to abort the job and he wouldn't get the rest of the cash.

Easiest money he ever made. Ten bills for two hours' work, plus the dude rented him a car for the day. Benny was just sorry to have to bring it back to the rental agency the next day; he'd had some fun with that machine.

Watching the payoff was nothing much, but it was

what happened afterward that took him by surprise. The bitch ran someone off the road and then calmly sped away like it was nothing. Apparently, they were now prosecuting the same lady who got run off the highway, and he was here to tell them about the bitch who made the payment and then caused the accident. They weren't gonna like it 'cause it trashed their whole case. But it was the truth. Let's see what they did with it.

Benny didn't have much faith in the criminal justice system. He'd been on the wrong side of it a few times and knew lots of peeps who'd gotten royally screwed by corrupt cops and overzealous prosecutors. Sometimes the truth is the last thing prosecutors wanted to hear—they're after convictions, wins that build up their careers, and they generally don't give two shits about sending innocent people upstate, not if those people can give them a leg up in their careers—a leg up by stepping on their damn backs. And cops, shit, he didn't want to get started. Those fuckers need to fill the prisons—it keeps the machine fed that makes everyone money. The holy prison industrial complex that makes a for-profit industry out of taking people's freedom away and locking them up behind bars. Forcing them to do slave labor for pennies and the slop they're given to eat.

Yeah, the truth don't much matter in the criminal justice system. Benny had to admit he was curious how his testimony would fly with the DA and affect the case. Probably they would just ignore it and keep on going with it as if he'd never came to them. If they did, he'd have another job coming his way: taking his story to the good ol' media.

Maybe he'd get his fifteen minutes after all? Wouldn't that just make his day?

~

WHEN PERNOD TOLD ADA Rhett Harmon that Jane Jensen was definitely not the woman who gave him the money—though she had similar height and coloring and was wearing an obvious wig and big sunglasses—the tension in the conference room was about a foot thick before the lawyers began a concerted interrogation of the assassin.

Three of them went at him from all angles for over an hour, grilling him, trying to get him to second-guess himself, sowing doubt wherever possible, giving him alternative narratives to explain any discrepancy. As the clock ticked past lunchtime, Rhett, Jackson, and Ezra Johansen, an investigator who was attached to the DA's office, threw questions and comments at him, made suggestions, offered various scenarios, showed him different photos of the defendant, and did anything and everything they could think of, and still he didn't budge from his belief that they had the wrong woman.

"Can you fucking believe this?" Rhett screamed once she and Jackson were back in her office. "I'm due to give my opening statement to the jury in two days and he tells us this now, the little rat turd?"

Jackson very quietly cleared his throat, hating to deliver her the next blow but he had no choice. The guy was out there and Jackson couldn't ignore him, much as he'd like to do so. "Rhett, there's someone in reception waiting to speak with us."

Blazing eyes flicked to his, fiery enough to incinerate his courage. The black fury in her gaze forced him to take a step back. "And?" she spat.

"He says he has information on the case. Kelly quizzed him and it doesn't sound good. He's implicating someone else in the hit and saying she was the one who ran Jane Jensen off the road."

Rage transformed into disbelief. Rhett just stared at him, her mouth gaping open. "You have got to be kidding me. Tell me you're kidding me, Jax. Please."

"I'm not kidding, Rhett. I'm sorry."

She dragged her hands through her hair, ruining her careful styling and giving zero fucks about it at this point. "Could this really be happening?"

OH MY GOD. Rhett's head swiveled back and forth, listening to the latest story to cut gaping holes into her case. Benny Rodell was a heroin addict with an eye twitch who just happened to be witness to the cash transaction between James Pernod and the woman who hired him. He told them a fantastical story of how he followed the woman, thinking she would be a good blackmail target.

Why would you think you could blackmail her? Couldn't she just be paying a debt to someone who loaned her money? is what they all asked him.

No, he'd said. He'd been around enough to know a shady deal when he saw one.

Why didn't you follow the man instead? they asked. *You might have prevented a murder.*

His answer was that he was afraid of the man, that he could tell he was some kind of assassin and the woman was a safer bet. Plus, the murder didn't happen for weeks after, he pointed out helpfully, so following him wouldn't have saved the lady. He said he followed the cash lady right onto the parkway and saw the whole accident unfold.

How did a heroin addict have a car? they asked him next.

"Oh, come on," he'd replied. "I'm not that much of a loser." But then he had to admit it was a rental.

"Who rented the car and why?" they wanted to know.

"A friend rented it and I borrowed it to make a buy."

"What friend?"

He gave them the name just as his employer told him to do. Benny highly doubted it was his real name.

They brought him back a few hours later to show him photos of ten women, two of whom were Jane Jensen and Kendra Ortalano. He picked out Kendra with absolutely no hesitation. Zero doubt.

When asked why he didn't come forward sooner, he'd said he wanted to clean up his act first. Bringing this to their attention was part of his 12-step program of righting old wrongs. Again, it was a line fed him by the boss man but in a weird twist of fate, Benny'd joined a program and he was really liking it. Having a captive audience to bitch to every week was habit-forming.

In effect, Wink gave the investigators the truth, at least as he'd rehearsed it with the chap who paid him off. Because Wink had only been paid half the money upfront, the other half would be his after he completed the job by bearing witness in court. A lot more was coming and Wink couldn't wait to get his hands on the hay.

He had plans, motherfucker.

KATHY ELLISON CARTER was the motorist who called in the accident. She'd claimed that she thought it was a woman who was driving the black SUV. She had pulled over just ahead of the accident site and had a quick glimpse of the black-SUV driver through the windshield that was only slightly tinted, but she thought it was a Honda CRV. She said it looked like a woman with a baseball cap pulled down low. Granted, she got only a fleeting glance as the woman drove by very fast. It was all on the police accident report that was never further investigated since it was considered nothing more than a collision caused by reckless driving.

It was very easy to verify Ms. Carter's story once they had Kendra's name. All it took was a search on Kendra Ortalano's credit cards. They quickly determined that Kendra Ortalano had rented a black Honda CRV the day before the accident. GPS showed the car was in the vicinity of the accident at the same time and day. A letter ostensibly written to Mason by Jane was found in Jane Jensen's dresser drawer during the search conducted immediately after her arrest. It was covered in Kendra Ortalano's fingerprints and none of Jane Jensen's, obviously something she planted to incriminate the latter. The evidence kept mounting against Ms. Ortalano and exonerating Jane Jensen. In the space of a day and a half, their rock-solid evidence disintegrated into dust, and weeks of hard work went down the toilet.

Their case was now as dead as Cate Caldwell.

After having watched in utter dismay her airtight case unravel strand by strand, Rhett excused herself to go to the restroom. Once there, she checked all the stalls to make sure she was alone. She wadded up a bunch of paper towels, went into a stall and locked it, then screamed into the paper. The paper muffled the noise but it still probably could be heard outside.

She could hardly care. Her case had gone to shit and that was all she could think about at the moment.

"I wasn't prepared. Motherfucker," she muttered. "I wasn't fucking prepared enough."

A WEEK later the charges were dropped and Jane was legally unencumbered. News articles reported that new information had come to light in the form of new witnesses. Actually, two were new and one was revisited—an interview someone took when they were preparing the case against Jane Jensen. A Metro-North rider by the name of Rachel Carson, who came forward and gave a deposition about her conversation with Jane on the train, and it was considered irrelevant and buried in the mound of ever-growing paperwork associated with the case. Truly, Ms. Carson's information didn't prove anything but helped bolster Jane Jensen's innocence when the other witness testimony came to light. Jensen had shown Rachel Carson the text summoning her to Poughkeepsie for a job interview. If she were planning a murder, she'd probably keep her trip to meet the hired killer under wraps.

To say Rhett Harmon was peeved was the understatement of the year. Being a realist, however, Harmon had done her grieving for her dead case and moved on. And just when the night was the darkest… well, she was gifted with a new shining beacon in the form of a culpable suspect, gifted to her with the same information that exonerated Jane Jensen. ADA Harmon was all about making lemonade.

~

LESS THAN TWO weeks after all charges against Jane Jensen were dropped, Aaron Rinder was with Kendra in her apartment and still asleep, having spent the night. The evening before they'd gotten home late from a cabaret show, and he hadn't felt like making the drive to Greenwich. Aaron's wife hardly noticed when her husband didn't come home these days. For one thing, their house was so big that even when both were home, they didn't necessarily have to be aware of the other's presence. Besides, Lydia really didn't care where Aaron stuck his dick, as long as it wasn't in her. She loathed him and only stayed married to him to spite him.

The Rinders also had a condo on the Upper West Side, a two-bedroom, but his college-age son was living in it right now and Aaron didn't dare just show up unannounced, never knowing what or who he might find there.

The banging on the apartment door was loud.

Aaron bolted up in bed and poked at the dead-to-the-world woman beside him. "What the fuck is that all about, Kendra?" He glanced at the clock: it was barely eight a.m. "Deal with it."

She unstuck her eyelids, glued together by remnants of mascara, and looked at him through bleary eyes. "What?"

The word had just left her lips when the banging started again. She threw her arm across her face, blocking out the sunlight. "Someone's at the door."

"Very astute observation, dear. Get up and go see who it is, but don't open the door until you're sure it's safe."

Kendra rose, reaching for her kimono, and shouted toward the door, "One minute please," as she quickly wrapped the cobalt and pink satin robe around her naked body.

She peered through the peephole and saw a police officer staring back at her. Leaving the chain lock engaged, she opened the door slightly. When she looked out now, she saw three cops—two men and a woman. "Yes? May I help you?"

The big one in front spoke. "Are you Kendra Ortalano?"

"Yes. Why?"

"I'm Officer Robards, NYPD. Ms. Ortalano, I need you to open the door please."

"Can you tell me why first?"

"Ma'am, I need you to open the door now."

Aaron had come up behind her now, wearing trousers with his shirt flapping open. "What's the problem here, Officer?"

"Who are you, sir?"

"I'm her friend."

"Sir, you should instruct your friend to obey my directive and open the door before we have to batter it down."

"That really won't be necessary," Aaron replied, his cheeks flushing. "May I see your badges please?"

All three pulled out their badges and held them aloft for Aaron's inspection. He carefully read each one, comparing the information with the faces in front of him. "What precinct are you with?"

"Sir, two of us are attached to the 24th precinct. Officer Romano is with the Riverdale station."

Aaron looked at Kendra. "Go put on some clothes. I'm letting them in."

Kendra retreated to the bedroom as Aaron shut the door to unchain it, quickly opening it again to give them entrance.

"Come in, Officers. I'd offer you coffee but this isn't my home, and it's probably not stocked with any provisions if I know Kendra. She's dressing and will be back in a moment."

The cops just nodded in unison and stood in the hallway awkwardly.

"Would you like to sit down? There are chairs in the kitchen."

"No, thank you. What's your name again?"

"I never provided it to you before. But it's James Sinclair." Rinder just hoped they didn't ask him for identification.

"Do you live in the vicinity, Mr. Sinclair?"

"No. I'm just visiting the young lady and we had a late—"

Kendra's entrance into the room interrupted his explanation. Still barefoot, she now wore worn-out jeans and a relatively transparent T-shirt. "OK, so what's this all about?"

The largest one moved closer to her and again spoke up. "Kendra Ortalano, you are under arrest for the premeditated murder of Catherine Caldwell. You have the right to remain silent—"

"What? Are you serious?" Aaron interrupted. His head whipped toward Kendra whose face had turned ghostly pale. "Kendra, don't say a word. I'll call my attorney and have someone meet you wherever they take you."

"…anything you say can and will be used against you in a court of law. You have the right to an attorney…"

Aaron pulled the female officer to the side. "Where are you going to be taking her?"

"Riverdale station, sir. Could you get her a pair of shoes, please?"

Aaron Rinder nodded, his ashen face pinched. After grabbing a pair of sneakers he found in the bedroom closet and having to put them on her himself because of her state, he felt ill. He watched as they took a nearly catatonic Kendra away, considering whether using his own personal attorney to help her was wise. Maybe Kenneth could recommend someone? After all, it was a criminal case and Ken was more of a corporate litigator.

His next thought was less altruistic as he wondered how he could keep his name out of the press. If he abandoned her now, she could drag his name through the mud as this case was getting a lot of media attention. It was probably in everyone's best interests to try to help her. Damn

Kendra for putting him in this unenviable position. He really could strangle her.

BY DAY'S end Kendra Ortalano had been charged with one count of first-degree murder, one count of second-degree murder—since the death of the male driver in the car accident she caused constituted felony murder—and a charge of attempted murder in the case of Jane Jensen.

She was processed at Rikers and met her attorney in the same room where Jane had discussed her own case with her legal representation. Aaron Rinder paid her bail and cautioned her not to do something stupid. As far as he was concerned, the attorney and fees he paid constituted the last of his dealings with Kendra. He paid her rent for the next three months, gave her a check for living expenses, and wished her good luck.

Kendra didn't blame him. She knew he had a reputation to maintain, and he at least hadn't abandoned her. The person guilty of that treachery was Mason Caldwell. He wasn't answering his phone when she tried to call him, and he hadn't gotten in touch with her. Kendra hadn't even realized the charges against Jane Jensen were dropped until she read about it in the news.

The press enjoyed it immensely, headlines screaming about the case all day long. Yet another unexpected twist in the case of the killer stalker. What would surely make Rhett Harmon's heart glad was the fact that Kendra made a much less sympathetic defendant than Jane Jensen.

Over the next few days, Kendra sat captive in her apartment—the press camped out just outside the front entrance of her building—and plotted her revenge. She knew there was no evidence against her and didn't even know how the cops had traced it back to her unless it was merely because of her lifelong friendship with Mason. How would they build the case against her, though?

First off, there was no way she'd have that kind of money to pay off a contract killer. There was no money trail at all—Mason had left the cash in a manila envelope and slipped it under her apartment door, ten stacks of one-hundred-dollar bills, lined up side by side so they'd fit under the metal door.

Plus, she had nothing to gain from Cate Caldwell's death—nothing that they would know about. She and Mason had been nothing more than friends, and they hadn't been in contact in years before he called her about this plan.

By the end of the week, Kendra had convinced herself there was nothing to worry about. The charges couldn't possibly stick.

Chapter 40

Rhett Harmon leaned back in her leather chair, tapping a pen against her lips, and looked in her colleague's eyes for a protracted moment… and then smiled. "Here's the way I see it going. Then you can tell me your scenario."

"You're on," Jackson Altamont said. "Shoot."

"Poor choice of words, Jackson. All right." She stood up in her black Manolos and began to pace as she spun her tale, her version of how it all went down.

"In high school they got together. Spent a lot of time with one another; they'd go to her house—both parents worked—smoke pot, screw their brains out, and when they were too tired to do any more, they'd settle on the sofa with an oversized bowl of popcorn and watch old movies."

She leaned back against the front of her desk, grasping the edge with her hands. "Hitchcock was a favorite of both. Especially *Strangers on a Train*.

"Looking back, neither could remember whose idea it was, couldn't remember the conversation that spawned the idea and started them on the path. Both knew that great reward only comes attached with great risk. Both of them accepted it.

"They didn't start planning it right away. After all, Mason hadn't even met his wife yet. But both Kendra and Mace knew that eventually they'd meet the right person and when they did, they'd know it. Mason met Cate in his junior year at Tufts. She'd graduated three years earlier and—"

"Actually she took a few years off so she graduated the same year as Caldwell," Jackson interrupted.

Harmon waved her hand dismissively. "Whatever. She was in town for a dog show, decided to attend the alumni-student mixer or whatever was going on. Cate was dressed all in tight black. Kickass, in other words.

"Caldwell took one look and…" her hand sliced through the air. "… was instantly smitten: lean, long-legged, and golden, and the fact that she was older and more sophisticated than he added to her allure. So smitten, in fact, that they were married for over a year before it occurred to him that Cate was the target that he and Kendra had been waiting for. She was perfect. He already had the life insurance policy—each of them had taken one out on the other. She was already starting to massively annoy him with the stupid dog and all the pretentious dog shows she put her in.

"Not to mention that Cate didn't give a flying fuck that he wanted kids—all she cared about was her preening canine. When she began making noise about adding an Afghan puppy to their household, he called Kendra."

"How do you know she wanted a puppy and not kids?"

"Her mother told me." Rhett placed her hands on Jax's chair arms and leaned in close. "Kendra was ready, waiting, and absolutely willing."

She straightened and again started pacing. "Kendra

had been patient, waiting all these years for that phone call to come from Mason. In the interim, she'd quit her education after high school, done some catalog modeling, and then some lean days forced her to do a little prostitution and porn on the side. Ultimately, she found a sugar daddy, and the creepy old bastard paid her bills, but she wasn't living large by any measure. As far as sugar daddies go, hers must have been relatively cheap, considering her apartment and clothes," she added. "No high-end life for Kendra. So despite having a pretty nice setup, she wanted out, away from his wrinkled old body and imperious I-own-you attitude, and Mason's insurance policy would help—well, her half of it. She was starting to age—and badly at that—and was looking a little dog-eared. Two million bucks split two ways? She could live on it nicely for her lifetime if she was smart.

"And Kendra believed she was smart."

Now Rhett sidled back around her desk and sat down, her eyes on Jackson with a laser focus as only Rhett could do so well.

"They needed a fall guy. Or girl, as it were.

"'*Who would kill a wife if not the husband?*' Kendra asked him over lunch one day.

"'*A lover?*'

"She considered the situation. '*Maybe. Who else? Maybe someone a little less obvious?*'

"Now he shrugged. '*I don't know. Got someone in mind?*'

"Her eyes gleamed with joyful malevolence. '*As a matter of fact, I do. How about...*' and Kendra leaned across the table to get closer to him, '*...a stalker?*'

"'*Stalker? There's a slight problem, Ken. I don't have anyone stalking me.*'

"'*Not yet you don't. But if we make it irresistible, you will. We just have to think on it for a while,*' she said, and took a bite of her burrito. When her mouth was full she made a noise at the back of her throat and Mason looked up from his meal. '*Do you remember back in high school… there were like… those scary girls who used to just swoon over you?*'"

Jackson smirked. "How do you know they were eating burritos?"

Rhett shrugged. "Everyone eats burritos. Don't interrupt me; I'm on a roll."

"You're on a burrito," he grumbled. "Go ahead."

"OK," she smiled. "Now, where was I? Oh, right. So… Mason smirked and said, '*Vaguely. What'd they look like?*'

"'*One was fat and wore brown clothes all the time. The UPS girl,*' Kendra laughed at her own joke. '*She had a friend who was real tall and thin and had really bad eyesight. Her glasses were the thickest I'd ever seen. Those are our best candidates.*'

"'*All right,*' Mason said and leaned back in his chair so Kendra could notice that chest of his with all those tight abs. He was all in now."

Jackson shook his head slowly as his eyes rolled up.

"The next week when they met again for lunch, Kendra had a copy of their yearbook. They selected the three potential candidates but before too much time, they both realized that one out of the three was more than perfect. She had been obsessed with Mason, and they knew she'd be perfect. Her name was Jane Jensen, the girl in brown.

"The plan was to have it look like she was stalking him… or even entice her to actually stalk him. They would place him on her train several times, talking loudly in her presence about buying a home in Riverdale. They did their homework and knew Jane had become unexpectedly successful since she graduated college. Knowing she'd have the money to afford it, Mason talked up the house. They hit pay dirt when Kendra's realtor friend informed them there was a buyer for the adjacent townhome to Mason's—a buyer named Jane Jensen.

"Finding the two houses for sale had been nothing short of serendipitous. Both had been for sale concurrently because the contiguous homes were owned by the same estate. It was another crucial part of the plan, and this was one that had required Cate's approval. But Mason knew his wife would love the Riverdale home, so it wasn't too hard to talk her into it. Jane, true to her past behavior, fell in line and purchased the house.

"From there they needed to set up a hit, and Kendra would pretend to be Jane. But they also needed to draw Jane out that way. Kendra pretends to be a professional headhunter with a company who wants to steal Jane from MT. Jane turns her down, time and time again, but through mettle and sheer determination, Kendra convinces Jane to at least make the trip to speak with her. Now they have Jane where they want her—in Dutchess County.

Jane gets there and the headhunter is a no-show. She cannot believe the audacity of the woman. She decides to have lunch and then go home. That takes about an hour. Meanwhile, Kendra is meeting up with Pernod disguised as Jane Jensen.

"The hit is paid for in the minutes before Jane gets back on the highway. Kendra plans to run Jane off the road and hopefully she'll be killed. The highway Jane uses is known for fatal accidents because of its winding, narrow lanes, which is a gift from the universe for Kendra. The plan works perfectly. At the right moment, she cuts Jane off on the left and Jane has no choice but to veer toward the oncoming traffic, thus having a head-on with a vehicle on that side. Kendra drives away.

"Setting up the few clues was a breeze. Mason saw Ms. Bartholomew taking the photos of the house. He searched for them on the internet and found one on Ms. Bartholomew's social media account where she tends to display her photographic talent. Copied it, put it in his drawer.

"Prior to that, he'd tailed Jane for a few weeks, saw her buying the furniture… went in after her. The owner, flush with all that cash, mentions to him that he loves customers who pay cash. Mason turns on the charm and learns Jane withdrew seven grand in cash to pay the store. He arranges to pay the hitman as soon as possible after the withdrawal so it seems to implicate Jane. It's all going so well.

"But someone saw the whole thing—the active parts of the plan. Benny didn't go to the police because he was drunk and high, and he knew he'd be arrested. But a few months and full sobriety later, he's part of a 12-step program. He has to go to the authorities to tell them what he knows as part of his pledge to make amends and right wrongs."

There was silence in the room when Rhett finished her version of the story. After a minute or so, Jackson got up and poured himself a whiskey from the bottle that Rhett kept in the back of a filing cabinet. At nearly four o'clock it was almost after hours so it was sort of acceptable.

"Want to hear my version? It's a lot shorter, and Mason isn't a leading character in it."

Now Rhett rolled her eyes. "He's as guilty as sin. Why can't you see that?"

"Because I don't think he was involved. You have him planning it in high school, even before he met his wife."

"My gut says he's involved—don't let his slimy charm fool you, Jackson. I think my scenario is close to what happened… with some dramatic embellishment. Maybe it didn't start in high school but it did at some point. You have to see that Kendra Ortalano is too stupid to plan and carry it out by herself. She had to have help. She claimed that she contacted her co-conspirator at a number that turned out to be a dead end, but that could easily have been a prepaid phone."

"Agree on all points, but it wasn't Caldwell. Maybe we should cast around for someone else?"

"Like who?"

"I thought I had the one with Mason's cousin Jake Emerson. After all, he dated Cate in college."

"And?"

He shook his head. "Didn't pan out. No real motive. I had Detective Kelvin interview him, and then I myself met with him. According to both Mason and Cate's mother, Jake and Cate dated casually, and Jake wasn't at all upset when Cate preferred his cousin. Mrs. Cobb called Jake a delightful young man with a lot going for him—it was clear that she preferred him for her daughter over Mason. Plus, Cate was a silent partner in his firm, and though when she died her shares reverted to him, he turned around and immediately gave them to his cousin, making them fifty-fifty partners. That sort of dissolved any financial motive. Nothing stuck."

Rhett pursed her lips. "Hmm, that's a shame. It would've made for a sensational trial."

"Yeah, well… *c'est la vie.* Take Caldwell out and I'm all in; we'll go after Kendra Ortalano with all our guns."

"We already are. She was taken into custody this morning. We are fast-tracking the case against her too. I want that killer behind bars fast." She paused. "Tell me one thing, Jackson: why do you insist that Mason's innocent?"

"Why do you have such a hard-on for him?"

She pressed her lips together, refusing to rise to his bait. "I have a close friend who's an FBI profiler. I'm wondering if he could shed any light on Caldwell for us. I can set up a meeting under some guise so they could talk. It would help to figure out what makes him tick."

Jackson shrugged. "Call him. It can't hurt, but my money says he's not involved."

Rhett crossed her legs, admiring how they looked in her high heels. When she was walking in them, the heels made her calves flex and they looked seriously good. But even when sitting the shoes did wonders for her legs. There's no denying that shoes make the woman as well as the man. "Tell me why you're so sure."

"For one thing, Cate Caldwell was much hotter than Kendra Ortalano. And she came from money. Why kill her for a paltry two mil that he has to split down the center? Put himself at a disadvantage with a used-up shrew like Kendra? Someone like that is so easily prone to resort to blackmail if she runs out of funds.

"Also, he seems like a genuinely nice guy. I don't get any sociopath vibes from him. Your scenario, while fascinating, seems farfetched to me, Rhett. And way too complicated with too many things that could have gone wrong. Simple is best, and that's how we'll convince the jury. Honestly."

She stood up, snapping defensively, "I don't think it's at all farfetched, and if I find enough to prove it, I will do it." Rhett Harmon had a very low threshold of tolerance for any kind of criticism, constructive or otherwise. She had a plan for her life, and there would be no deviation from it if she had anything to say about it. She reached over and picked up the receiver of the desk phone. "Yes, Bennett, get me Luca Derricks at the FBI. Quantico, Virginia. Let me know when you have him on the line. Thanks."

Chapter 41

It happened fast.

Kendra Ortalano was tried and convicted on three counts: first-degree murder, felony murder, and attempted murder. Although she'd had a decent attorney, he wasn't able to counter the overwhelming evidence, and the prosecution was so confident of a conviction that they offered his client no plea deals. Zero. She was given two sentences of twenty-five years-to-life to be served concurrently and one of five-to-seven years to be served consecutively. Until they dragged her from the courtroom, she was loudly insisting she'd been set up by Mason Caldwell. Some of the jurors may have believed her—especially the middle-aged brunette at the far right who seemed way too sympathetic for Rhett's taste—but since Mason Caldwell wasn't on trial, it was a moot point.

On the first day, Rhett Harmon strolled into court wearing a cloak of confidence and what her colleagues called—behind her back—her court-cunt clothes. It was an identity she'd carefully crafted over the first months of her ADA career. Every accessory was elegant and expensive, creating the serious yet stylish persona of winning assistant district attorney. High heels that wavered between sensible and sexy, matching two-piece suit, the skirt hemline just teasing the top of her knees as she walked, and a pale silk shirt. Her straight black hair worn either pulled back or up, subtle makeup, one strand of either freshwater or sterling silver pearls, and her Omega De Ville wristwatch. From the first words of her opening argument she owned the room, and she sensed it, never letting the momentum go sluggish. There was no way she was leaving this courtroom without a conviction.

The jury was conflicted initially and took three days to finish deliberating. On the first day, the count was seven-five and on the next, nine-three. The three holdouts—which definitely had to include fiftyish brunette—caved on the third day of deliberations. Of course, the defense had the jury polled—Rhett held her breath for those interminable moments. Already-won cases had fallen to mistrial many a time over jury polling by sore-losing attorneys on both sides. Although Rhett and Jackson were confident in their win, the three-day wait still didn't make for good sport, and the polling prolonged the agony for a few more elastic minutes. Ortalano's attorney, Ian Waterhouse, endured worse than they did—and he wasn't accustomed to losing. Rhett had eyeballed the extremely fit attorney with appreciation throughout the trial. Maybe she should console him for his loss?

The prosecution had proved its case with a believable narrative: Kendra had been rejected by Mason all throughout high school. She'd been jealous of his girlfriends and was always hanging onto his coattails. She also hated Jane Jensen, bullying her so much in high school that she once chased Jane into traffic where the latter got hit by a car. That incident had caused Kendra to lose friends and status, and apparently, she had nursed a grudge all these years. Resentment heated into violence recently when she'd run into a high school friend who caught her up on how well Jane Jensen was doing lately. Kendra wasn't doing well at all, the opposite of well, in fact, and the old jealousy and insecurities alchemized into toxic venom.

Though Kendra denied having any money—actively using the lack of it as part of her defense—the detectives had managed to locate a PayPal account under the name of Kendra Olson but with her tax and address information, into which funds were direct-deposited on a monthly basis by a phone-sex company operating out of a Newark warehouse that had her—or Kendra Olson—on its payroll during the time frame in question. For six months, varying amounts of money came through her PayPal account until just over ten thousand dollars was accrued. That entire amount was withdrawn the week before the hit man was paid and a check was cut to K. Olson. It was cashed a week later at a check-cashing store in the Bronx, and its surveillance footage showed a woman very closely resembling Kendra Ortalano cashing the check. The woman wore a distinctive red coat, and the cops found the same coat in the defendant's closet.

The prosecution siphoned off any remaining faith in the defense with the strongest evidence against the defendant: Ms. Ortalano had been identified by Benny Rodell in a lineup and then again in the courtroom as the woman who paid off the killer. She'd also been identified by Pernod, the hit man. Unfortunately, Kathy Carter, the driver who witnessed the auto accident, didn't get a long or close enough look at the driver to be able to definitively ID the defendant, but her testimony helped in placing Kendra at the scene of the accident as well as the payoff.

As for Caldwell, he was in court nearly every day,

reprising his role of the grief-stricken husband. He never went alone, always surrounded by an entourage of friends and family, and a retinue of security in case any wackos came after him. His handsome face appeared on the front page of news outlets all week, and women began calling and emailing him. One Twitter user had dubbed him the worth-it-widower and the moniker stuck for a while. The press coined a sobriquet for the defendant too: Triple-K for Krazy Killer Kendra

Rhett Harmon mined every lead and peered into every shadowed corner but could never could dig up enough to try Mason Caldwell as a co-conspirator. The profile Luca Derricks compiled on him showed him to be a narcissist with some sociopathic tendencies but still within the normal range. There was no concrete or circumstantial evidence to tie him to the crime. In fact, other than the DA's instinct, the only other suggestion of his guilt came from Kendra and her vehement accusations. It just wasn't enough.

One person who was not in attendance in court was Jane Jensen. Rhett wasn't at all surprised, and she didn't think anyone expected her to be. After all, the woman was arrested and spent two or three nights at the Rikers hotel before finally getting released. Rhett had learned that Jane had already leased out her newly acquired home to a young family, put all her belongings into storage, and went into self-enforced seclusion. She did, however, keep her job and faithfully showed up each and every day. News reporters would camp out in the lobby of the building during any high points of the trial, and Jane would be spirited in and out through other entrances and exits. One thing was for sure: her employer backed her every step of the way.

Rhett couldn't bring herself to feel any remorse for

what happened to Jane Jensen, though she believed she should. It's just the way things happen to people sometimes, and it was nothing personal. The one aspect that did give her pause was how the whole arrest and subsequent trial prep tailgated Ms. Jensen's ghastly accident—courtesy of one Kendra Ortalano, or inmate 304468962 as she was now known. Jane Jensen's longtime bully had finally been put of business.

Justicia fiat.

~

AFTER THE CONVICTIONS CAME DOWN, there was a celebration in the DA's office. The champagne had not yet lost its bubbles when Jackson Altamont made his way over to Rhett Harmon's desk.

"Got a minute?"

Rhett skirted her desk and nearly collapsed into her chair. She was bone-tired, having spent the day on her feet in court. All she wanted now was a hot bath, a cold glass of vodka, and a warm man. Unfortunately, she'd probably get only two of the three. "What's up?" she answered Jackson.

"Something interesting came up with the Caldwell case. Want to know?"

Rhett sighed. This case nearly drove her insane, taking so many turns that it confounded all of them at times. At some point, each and every player was considered a guilty party. Rhett's mentor, the incomparable DA Evan Bond, told her something the first day she began working for him that she took to heart and would herself pass on to a newbie someday. She could still hear his graveled voice as he cautioned her, sitting on the edge of her desk, elbow propped on his crossed arm, and gnawing on a pencil—he was always chewing pencils, a substitute for the cigarettes he never stopped missing. *"Rhett, there are going to be cases that stick in your craw. Cases where you'll know someone is as guilty as sin but you can't prove it. And if you can't prove it, you can't prosecute. He'll walk. Or she will. And there's not a single thing you can do about it. So celebrate the victories and do not dwell on the failures. Just do your job to the best of your ability. That's what the taxpayers are paying us to do—not to pontificate and definitely not to waste their money."*

Now she looked up at Jackson's earnest face. The important thing for their office was that they won a conviction and Cate Caldwell received a measure of justice. Though Rhett believed with every molecule in her body that Mason Caldwell was complicit in his wife's murder, and Ortalano had consistently maintained that he helped her plan it, the evidence just wasn't there. They'd pored over phone records; they'd checked every one of his alibis for the points of the murder plot. Zilch and nada. He came out as squeaky clean as a rubber fucking ducky.

The insurance company balked at paying out the policy as long as there was a shadow of a doubt over his innocence and kept postponing the payout, but ultimately it had to cough it up when threatened with a lawsuit. It still pissed off Rhett massively. And it scorched Cate's mother's ass for sure. That woman was out for blood and guts, and she didn't get enough of it. She shared Rhett's belief of her son-in-law's guilt. Mason had better watch his back.

Snapping out of her thoughts and back into reality, she finally answered Jackson. "I probably should say no, but you're most likely aware that it's just not in my DNA to decline information of any stripe. Go ahead."

"Well, I was combing through the case, preparing the transcript for the civil suit when I stumbled upon an interesting fact. Remember when I told you that Cate Caldwell took some time off from school? Well, Jane Jensen and

Cate Caldwell attended Brown at the same time for a year. I dug a little further just for the sheer fun of it, obtaining official transcripts for both and they were in at least one class together."

Her glare practically neutered him on the spot, and he almost reached down to protect his junk. "Cate was three years older than Jane," she snarled. "How much time did Cate take off?"

"Apparently, she left school during her junior year because her brother was ill, and she returned a few years later to finish her degree."

Her eyelids dropped shut as she sighed. "God, I hope it's just one of those bizarro coincidences and not another twist in that fucking case. I hate the damn thing."

Trying to de-escalate her stress, he chuckled. "You and I both. All right, just thought I'd let you know. Probably doesn't mean anything."

"Yeah. Probably. Thanks, Jackson, for losing me sleep tonight."

"You bet. Goodnight, Counselor. I can't believe you're absconding to the other side. A slimy defense attorney? Really?"

Laughing, her mind floated to her new cushy office and a way higher number in front of the zeros of her annual salary. She'd just accepted the law firm's offer about an hour ago, though the partners had been courting her for months. "I can't believe it myself, Jax. Remember Luca Derricks, the feebie who helped us with Mason's profile? He began his career as a defense attorney and he's going back. He talked me into changing sides with him. His silver tongue helped convince me." A rush of heat blossomed in her face when she realized her last comment sounded dirty. Or did it? Maybe her mind was the only one in the gutter.

Jackson shook his head. "He was the deciding factor?

Well, when you can't sleep tonight, if you need something to do, give me a shout. I'll keep you company in that big lonely bed of yours." Eyebrows arched, a mischievous gleam in his eye—he was serious about the proposition.

No, her mind wasn't solo in the gutter. She tilted her head, studying him. Jackson had never come on to her before but he probably considered her fair game now that she was leaving the DA's office. She wondered what it would be like to sleep with him. She cleared her throat. "I will be certain to keep that in mind. Goodnight, Jax, and thanks for your great work as always."

Chapter 42

"You've already rented it out?" Mel asked.

Jane grinned at Mel's surprise. "Yes. When and if the O'Briens decide to move out, I'll list it for sale. I love the house, but I'll never feel comfortable there again, you know?"

"Bad juju. I think it's the right thing. Hey, why don't you move to Manhattan close to me? For what you'll get for the townhouse, you can probably afford at least a hundred square feet in Soho."

Jane laughed. "Trade in 1750 square feet for a hundred, huh? I don't think so."

Mel's eyes widened and she grabbed both of Jane's hands. "Oh, come on, Jane. We'll have so much fun."

Jane's head tilted back as she laughed. Mel's enthusiasm was infectious. "We'll see. Maybe..." She was about to say something else but stalled, a strange expression crossing her face.

"What?" Mel asked, blunt being her personal art form.

"So… um, are you still seeing Fitzgibbons?"

Mel held onto one of Jane's hands and tugged her

forward. "Let's get a table first, and then we'll talk. I'm starving."

They were at Mel's favorite bistro, located around the corner from her apartment. It had a great brunch menu and served pitchers of Mimosas or Oyster Marys, which kept Mel coming every chance she got. The brunch crowd was just starting to arrive so they were able to get a table right away, a total score in NYC. Once they were seated and the waiter brought their lattes, Jane looked at Mel expectantly. "So?"

Mel scrunched up her nose not really wanting to answer the question. That barely-there relationship had been a casualty of the case. It had been, what? Three weeks since Kendra Ortalano had been convicted but more than six months since she'd last seen Rob, and she hadn't heard much from him beyond the few text messages he'd sent during the trial. She had no plans to initiate contact since he was the one in the wrong. It very much looked like it was a done deal at this point, though, since he hadn't gone out of his way to return to her life. "You know we stopped seeing each other after your arrest, right?"

"Mmm, I figured as much. Suddenly you stopped gushing over him."

"Tsk." She squinted her eyes. "I never gushed. I don't gush."

"You did."

"Well, whatever. I liked him—a lot—but if he wants to ever see me again then he's got to make the first move. He was wrong, and I'm dead set on the sinner making the atonement." Her remark earned her a funny look from Jane. She sniffed. "I would consider forgiving him for being a suspicious jerk about you… if he groveled for at least a week."

"Well, *I* don't forgive him."

Mel wasn't sure if Jane was joking or meant it, but she decided to slough it off. "Well, that's because you weren't boinking the dude—he has a giant dick, Jane. Do you really expect me to just give that up with no regrets?"

Scowling at Mel's words, Jane finally had to laugh. "Well, when you put it that way… but though he might have a giant dick, I still maintain that he *is* a giant dick."

"Only fair." Mel agreed, taking a sip of her latte. "Mmm, God, I love coffee. I would feel exactly the same if I were you, Jane. Please take note that I, however, never faltered in my loyalty to and belief in you."

Sighing, Jane reached across the table and took her friend's hand. "I have taken note, Mel, more than a few times. I would never have survived the whole ordeal without you. I hope you know that."

Mel's eyes prickled. "I do know, chica. I do. Now…" She clapped her hands. "…let's eat."

ONE FOOT on the couch and the other stretched out and propped on the coffee table, Mel lounged on her over-stuffed purple velvet sofa watching a French comedy and polishing her toenails. Two days before, she'd helped Jane find a small studio sublet around the corner from Mel's own apartment. Jane had four months in the apartment to decide where to go from there. When the doorbell rang just as she was about to begin doing the last toe on the first foot, she figured it was her brand-new neighbor.

"Perfect timing, Jane," she muttered and carefully placed the brush back into the bottle of Sally Hansen 401, a lustrous dark cinnamon. "One min," she yelled as she screwed the lid closed.

Getting up, she gingerly used her right foot that had four toenails gleaming with fresh polish and one sad, naked pinkie toe. Jane must have slipped in behind a resident to get upstairs because Mel hadn't buzzed her into the six-story limestone building.

When she peeked through the peephole, Mel sucked in her breath. It wasn't Jane.

"Are you going to let me in?" The deep timbre of his voice rumbled through the door and right into Mel's body, sending a shiver pirouetting up her spine.

Smiling, she leaned against the door. "Depends."

"On?"

"Are you here to apologize?"

"Something like that. Open the door, Mel."

"Fine," she sighed loudly, flinging open the door, "but you better be here to admit you were wrong about Jane and apologize to me for your pigheadedness—and also the long delay in getting back in touch."

Rob Fitzgibbons stepped across the threshold and replied lightly, "I'll apologize, but we're going to have to leave it at that." He smiled broadly, and his eyes scanned her head to unfinished toe. "It's good to see you—you look good."

Mel turned, her gait airy, and led him into the living room. "It's because my life is finally back to normal—well, what I call normal anyway." She plopped back onto the sofa, her toenails forgotten. "And I've finally caught up on my sleep deficit that was months in the making."

"Good, I'm glad to hear that." He stood stiffly at the end of the sofa, just looking at her.

She motioned with her arm toward the empty end of the couch. "Have a seat?"

Nodding, he inhaled audibly but didn't speak as he lowered himself to the sofa. Mel figured he had something to say and waited for him to spit it out. Meanwhile, she checked him out thoroughly. The detective was one fine specimen of the human male, and Mel did appreciate ogling him. Though broad in the shoulders, Rob was lean with lots of definition. Ripped. His light eyes and tanned complexion provided nice contrast and his brown hair was silky to the touch.

"Are you all Irish?" she blurted out.

Rob's head popped up. "What made you go there?"

She hitched her shoulder, unable to hide her grin. "I was just… admiring… your appearance, and I realized that your complexion isn't as fair as most Irish. There's gotta be something else mixed up in there."

"Yeah, as a matter of fact, I'm a quarter Italian—but I told you that already—and an eighth Native American. Cherokee."

"Ah, that 'splains it. You're very pretty—but you know that."

"Pretty?" He huffed a laugh. "I don't think most men would appreciate being called that, Melanie. But, hey, I guess the sentiment is well intentioned."

She tucked one foot underneath her, stretching out the one with the polished nails. "All right, Detective. Say what you came to say. I'm in the middle of my pedicure."

He looked down at her unfinished foot and pressed his lips together. "OK, look. I'm sorry for some of the things I said and did, but I honestly had little choice. Your friend was a defendant in a case I was involved with and there were few choices to be made. Now she is no longer a defendant, so there's no reason for us to keep apart, and I'd really like to see you again, Mel. I've missed you."

"Hmm. Most of that doesn't sound like an apology. What about the way you treated Jane?"

Contempt fleeted across his face before he wiped it

clean. "I treated her the way I treat anyone who has been arrested and charged with a serious crime. Why should I apologize for doing my job?"

"You were wrong, that's why, and you refused to take seriously the information I had that partially exonerated Jane."

"Point taken, but we had so much more against her."

"It was all manufactured," Mel jumped in, volume rising. "If I could see that, you should have been able to see it. You're a trained detective."

"Right, except I still don't believe it. It smacked of a setup."

"A setup?"

"Of Ortalano." His voice was grim.

Mel bolted up from her seated position. "Wait a second. Are you telling me that you didn't believe Jane was framed, but you do believe that Kendra Ortalano was set up?"

"Bingo."

Mel's hand was itching to slap him. "What are you talking about? Jane was vindicated."

He sat there, chewing his cheek and looking straight ahead. Without shifting his gaze, he added, "Let's just move on. I've apologized to you for how I treated *you*. That's what's important." He reached out to grasp her hand and finally looked her in the eye. "Can we just try to pick up where we left off? I really like you, Mel, and I told you already that I think we can have something good together."

Growling, Mel spun around in a circle before stopping to look at him. For a pregnant minute, she just stood there in front of him, saying nothing but staring at his face, infuriated and yet immensely turned on. Throw him out or kiss him breathless? Then she held out her foot. "Do you like my nail polish?"

Rob shook his head, laughing, as he stood up and pulled her into his arms. "Yes, I love it. Want me to finish your other foot? I used to polish my sister's nails all the time because I had a steadier hand."

"Game on, babes. Do a good job and I just might buy you a couple of burritos for your trouble."

"It's got to be a chimichanga. It's fried or it's not worth eating, right?"

"Deal," she agreed and winked at him. He was just too hot to turn away.

JANE HAULED in one of the larger boxes from her new car. Once it was filled, she wouldn't be able to budge it, so she figured she'd pack it near the door. The O'Brien family had rented the house with most of the furniture so Jane was taking only her personal belongings and the sofa. She absolutely adored her new sofa and the O'Briens had their own, as well as a couple of bedroom sets. Jane had only furnished the master so their own stuff would come in handy. The sofa along with all but two of the boxes would go into storage as Jane was staying in a fully furnished sublet for a while until she decided what was next. She was taking only her clothes, laptop, and a few of her books and smaller possessions.

Pretty sure I could fit everything into three—maybe four—large boxes, she thought, as she got the other two big ones and placed them side by side. Crouching beside them, she started to pack the heavier items in the largest of the three boxes. Her stereo was blaring though it was only ten a.m. She had the volume cranked up for two reasons: first, to keep her energized as she was packing up her life that she'd barely unpacked a few months ago. Second, because she felt very unsafe here, thinking some people still believed her guilty of Cate Caldwell's murder. Didn't matter that all charges were dropped and two other people were tried and convicted for the crime. Some people were like dogs hanging onto bones once they got their teeth into something juicy, false or not, and it couldn't be yanked out of their snarling mouths for anything. The music kept her mind off of her fears.

Radiohead was singing her high school theme song 'Creep,' and she was trying to rearrange the box to maximize the fit when she caught a swift movement in her peripheral vision, and her head whipped around so fast she hurt her neck. When she saw the man standing in her living room, she choked on her own saliva when she tried to shriek and gasp simultaneously.

He held out his hands in supplication. "Sorry, Jane," he almost yelled to be heard over the music. "I didn't mean to frighten you. I just thought I should come by…" He pointed with his thumb toward the front door. "You didn't hear me knock and the door was unlocked." He jammed his hands in the pockets of his jeans. "I heard the music… from down the block," he added with a grin. "So I figured you were home."

She stood up and brushed the dust off her hands, unsure what to do next. "Yeah. For a little while… I…" Her words stuttered as she scrutinized him. What were his intentions? Did he still believe she'd taken out a hit on his wife? She spun around to lower the volume on the music but angled her head to keep him in her line of vision.

"Um, no, it's fine, Mason," she assured him, turning back around, and wiped her sweaty hands on her thighs. "What can I do for you?"

He looked around. "Moving again?"

Feeling her face flush, she nodded. "Yeah. My reputation got kind of trashed here." She tried to muster a smile. "I just want to say—"

"Don't think that you—"

They both began to speak and then both dropped silent and chuckled. "You first," Mason said, pointing his thumb at her, his other fingers still thrust in his tight pockets.

Though she still wasn't sure of his motive for the visit, she wanted to give him the benefit of the doubt. Still, it was scary to be all alone in an empty house with a man who very likely had his wife killed. The prosecutor who won the conviction of Kendra Ortalano was convinced the woman had Mason's help, even if she couldn't prove it. Jane knew this because Detective Fitzgibbons had told Mel, and Mel had told her—it wasn't a big secret. Plus, there were Kendra's hysterical rantings, claiming Mason planned the whole crime and then framed his old high school bestie. Maybe he came here to finish the job that framing Jane for murder hadn't achieved?

It was more than a little difficult to believe her high school crush was capable of such atrocities, but then who knew who Mason had become in the last seven years. It was possible that he'd turned evil, she supposed. Schizophrenia doesn't develop until young adulthood… maybe the same holds true for psychopaths?

Jane took a deep breath and tried to ingratiate herself with him. "I'm just really sorry for everything you went through. I hope you can find peace enough to move forward…" The acoustics of the emptying house echoed her voice.

He stepped closer to her and her pulse leapt like a panicked rabbit. It took every iota of control Jane had in her to refrain from physical retreat, or a few steps back at least. She was certain he could hear her heart pummeling her ribcage for it sounded deafening to her.

He was standing in front of her, hands held out, eyes wide, emotional strain etched into his expression. "That's very generous, considering what you went through. And, Jane… same goes. It's unreal the lengths that crazy woman went to so she could continue to bully you. Just insane."

"And obsessing over you," she said softly, "even after all these years. You're the one who has a lot of pieces to pick up. Me, I travel light. God, I'm so sorry about your wife, Mason."

He shrugged, a frown contorting that handsome face of his—a blessing and curse, no doubt. "You know, I've spent a lot of time mourning Cate. It's time… I'm trying to get on with things," he murmured. "I'm only thankful I have my family for support. There are a lot of people who think I had something to do with Cate's murder. Kendra's wild accusations didn't help."

"Mmm. Are you going to keep your company going?"

He rubbed the back of his head, stretching his long, muscular back and Jane couldn't keep her thoughts from going to erotic places. The man was just too seriously hot. "It's really my cousin's company—and Cate was a silent partner. You remember Jake, right?"

"Yes, I think I do. I think… in fact, I'm pretty sure we met up again in college and sort of became friends."

"Huh. He never mentioned that to me."

"Yeah. Well, my memory is still spotty about the last five or six years or so. But… bits and pieces, fits and starts. Anyway…" she said, her eyes focused out the window to avoid looking at him. A noise brought her gaze back to him.

He was twirling his key fob around his finger, looking

around at the large empty room. "Well, I suppose I should let you get back to your packing. I have to go anyway. I borrowed Jake's Porsche—again—and he'll probably be ticked that I took it without asking," he said with a feeble chuckle. "I think I need to buy my own soon. My Audi feels too tame in comparison."

Jane smiled. "Jake rebuilt that 911, didn't he? I seem to recall his telling me it was a mess when he got it." As soon as the words were out of her mouth, Jane stood there immobilized, brought up short by the new memory. Every day was an adventure in life with a TBI.

Mason looked surprised too. "Yep, he did. Jake's a jack of all trades." He started backing up toward the door and pointed his keys at her. "Be well, Jane. Take care of yourself."

"You too, Mason. Hey, tell Jake I said hello."

"Will do." He winked at her as he smiled and started to turn. "Goodbye, Jane."

After he left, Jane's legs quit holding her and she dropped back to the floor, just sitting there for a long minute. She hadn't eaten anything since early last night; her blood sugar levels must be plummeting. Grabbing the arm of her chair, she pulled herself up and went into the kitchen, scrounging around for a sleeve of crackers or something she could scarf down fast.

She felt off-kilter, way off.

She found a package of oatmeal cookies and stuffing one into her mouth, she tried to focus on chewing and swallowing, not on her queasiness. A few minutes passed before she felt better enough to resume her packing.

It was sad, so sad. Mason's life was ripped apart, Kendra would spend the rest of her miserable days behind bars, and Cate Caldwell's promising future was snatched from her, cut down in the prime of life. And for what?

Jane knew she'd probably seen the last she'd ever see of Mason Caldwell III. It was bittersweet, but she was good with it. He wasn't ever a part of her life, just a fantasy of hers, one that she was forced to create by the wretchedness of her childhood. But hey, she was no longer that child. And what happened between them was not much more than a fantasy. He didn't even have the faintest clue that she was that girl Janine who he had the briefest of flings with, one night of intimate fun. And he never knew that the condom broke, never knew about the baby son, never knew what that first accident had stolen from her.

Jane had a good life now: an excellent job, a loyal friend, well, really two now that she and Rachel Carson—her older British train friend—started getting together. Someday soon, she'd have a new home too. Something to look forward to.

And isn't that really what anyone needs to be happy in life? Just something to look forward to?

Epilogue

One year later

"IT'S SO BEAUTIFUL HERE, isn't it? We should just sell our places in the city and buy a home on the water. Don't you think, love?"

Jane picked up her head to look at him. Even the bright morning sun didn't diminish her husband's phenomenal good looks. She could hardly believe that life led her here, together with the man of her dreams.

Leaning her head back against his shoulder, she murmured, "Long commute," as she once again stared out over the expanse of blue, watching the gilded light tremble on the water's surface. It was like staring at the most brilliant of jewels.

"They love you at your job, Janey. You can ask if you can work from home two days a week and only go in for three. I can stay up here with the kids when we have them. I'll sell my company—"

"What about your cousin?"

"Mason wanted to sell all along, but when Cate's share reverted back to me and I cut him in as an equal partner... Who knows? Maybe Mason will buy me out—he's taken a much stronger interest in the business since it became his and not Cate's." He shrugged. "If instead we both sell, he stands to make some nice coin."

His fingers gently pushed her long hair away from her face. "You can get a studio apartment in the city to use for the three days a week you're there," he added as he lifted her chin with a bent finger and lightly kissed her lips. "Doesn't that sound good, sweetheart?"

Jane closed her eyes. It sounded more than good: it sounded sublime. She could do it—*they* could do it. Her house in Riverdale was worth a lot and so was his loft in Harlem where they lived now. Pooling the money would buy them a paradise up here. She could easily afford to buy a small place in Midtown, close to the office. It would be kind of fun to live as a married woman four days a week and a single one the other three.

She still had a hard time believing the extreme turn her life had taken since the twin nightmares of her car accident and the murder charge against her. About two months after the trial had ended, she chanced to sneak out of her office building to run some errands at lunchtime and who of all people did she run into?

Jake Emerson, Mason Caldwell's cousin and partner.

Jane had already begun to recall their friendship during college and seeing him again made her ridiculously happy. From there it just took off. It was as if they'd been together their whole lives, not just a few months. Six months later they stood before a justice of the peace in Hawaii with Jake's parents as witnesses and made it official.

. . .

SHE LOOKED up to find him still watching her. "So," he said with a tentative smile, "what do you think?"

She nodded and returned the grin. "I think, actually, it's a great idea." She angled her body to touch him, running her fingers over the architecture of his perfect face. She couldn't get over the flawless symmetry of his features and took photos of him day and night, in light and darkness, in clothes and without. Harsh light, flashbulb—it didn't matter. He was so photogenic. Sighing, she grasped his chin and turned his face directly toward her. "Life would be perfect if only I could get the rest of my memory back."

He reared his head back to look her in the eye. "Maybe it's for the best if you don't ever get it back."

"Why, Jake? That makes no sense." She studied his expression. "At one time I was afraid of remembering everything, but since Kendra..."

"I know you were. I just think... well, sometimes, Janey, the truth hurts and ignorance—"

"—is bliss, right?"

He guffawed. "Right. Follow your bliss."

IT WAS the week they closed on the house—a two-story 1874 clapboard and stone eyebrow Colonial on six acres of waterfront, meadow, and wooded land. The property included a two-bedroom guesthouse and an old red barn, and the main house sat on a hill with a green swath of lawn leading right down to the water's edge and their own private dock. Jane was sitting at home reading a blog by a doctor whose specialty was amnesia recovery. She had come to terms with living with large gaps in her memories, but it couldn't hurt to keep trying to get them back. Dr.

Ziegler listed various mental exercises designed to keep the brain agile and recommended using popular music and comfort food from the lost time period to help jog and recapture the slippery memories, and Jane had printed out the blog for future reference.

While she was waiting for the printer to prime and spit out the documents, she headed to the kitchen for an iced tea. Jake was sitting in his favorite chair, watching some idiot adult cartoon. On the way to the kitchen she veered toward him to place a kiss on his head, and his arm snaked around her, pulling her down onto his lap with a plop. She laughed, a lock of her long hair stuck to her lip and he looked at her with—well, Jane would have sworn it was love. When he looked at her like he was doing right then, she could believe he adored her, and it made everything she went through to get here worth it.

"What are you watching?"

"Some stupidity." He switched to the news, and immediately his attention was caught. The crawl said 'Breaking News: Westchester fire guts restaurant and adjacent bakery.'

"Oh shit. Look at that, Jane. That's Rasputin's."

"Rasputin's? Did we go there?"

He looked at her and smiled slightly. "Yes, we did. More than once. In fact, you wore those sexy Louboutin heels for me the last time we were there, the ones I bought you?"

Jane chuckled. "Yeah, Mel has had some serious designs on those shoes, but I beat her off them. Actually, I had to buy Mel her own pair. I thought she was going to faint when she opened the box." She tapped his nose playfully with her finger. "Maybe if you're good, I'll wear them again for you. Maybe even tonight?"

"Mmm, with nothing else, I hope."

She was just about to lean down to kiss him, really kiss him, when a memory hit her sideways, its ferocity making her gasp—not just the way it materialized without warning but also because of what it consisted of. She jolted, almost falling backward in the process. He grabbed her with his right hand and her eyes were drawn to the delicate tattoo on his middle finger: the Buddhist symbol of the eternal knot.

Her gaze caught Jake's and he looked at her with discerning eyes, almost immediately understanding what was tripping over in her head. Various emotions skittered across his face but his eyes remained static, flat… determined. After a long minute transpired, his face split into a grin, a grin that was more knowing than any other, a grin as malevolent as any could be.

"You remember, don't you?" he asked, his smile baring all his teeth.

She nodded slowly, seeing him through a different lens, one with a backstory she lacked before. Emotion clogging her throat, she finally answered him. "Yes, Jake. I-I think I do.

"I ALREADY KNEW I met you again in college." There was no question mark attached to her words but he treated it like one nonetheless and nodded. "But we became close. Very close."

"Yes. Yes, we did." His voice shook with emotion—the emotion of someone who's been profoundly alone and suddenly isn't anymore.

"She left you to marry your best friend. Your cousin. She broke your heart."

Again, he nodded, his eyes darkening with the echoes of betrayal.

She kept going, possibly even oblivious to the emotional turmoil her words might be causing him. "Cate Cobb treated you like a piece of dirt, as if you were dispensable, the socialite bitch. I couldn't bear to see it anymore. One of the most wonderful men I'd ever known, and she acted as if you were less than spit."

His pupils dilated, darkening his polar-blue eyes. "She signed her own death warrant when she insisted we make Mason a full partner. Why should I give such a valuable chunk of my assets to the man who stole my fiancée, my so-called best friend? So much for blood being thicker than water. I worked so hard to build the business from scratch. Plus, I knew they both wanted to sell, and if we made Mason a partner, they'd be able to overrule me. This way, I kept the whole company, and it was my choice to eventually split Mason in."

He winked at her. "For you there was also Kendra. That afternoon at Rasputin's… I saw steel in your determination to pay her back."

"She made my life a living hell in high school. And for what? I never did anything to her."

"And when I contacted her, pretending to be Mason, with the plan to pin the hit on someone else, she honed right in on you as the scapegoat—I needed no manipulation there." He grinned. "Not to mention she never doubted that I was my cousin."

"She's a horrible person."

"True dat, baby. And she'll rot in prison. She deserves to after what she did to you, causing the accident—as if all the bullying wasn't enough."

For an uncomfortable moment Jane hesitated. She remembered something else. That night. The car accident. The ambulance. The kids all standing around watching.

She was pretty certain she'd never told Jake, never told

anyone, about her and Mason's baby, and she never would. Mason never even found out about the baby or even that Janine was Jane.

But like a cracked egg, the truth of Jake's words broke open in her sluggish brain—he meant the *recent* car accident—and she realized she could have just made a huge mistake. If she'd mentioned the miscarriage… Jake wouldn't like that, knowing that Mason was the one who took her virginity. No, he would never know, but all the same Jane had avenged her poor baby now. Ven, she called him, to remind herself of a vendetta that would never expire. But Jake was referring to something Kendra did that… she almost retched as the truth dawned upon her.

Both her hands clutched her head. "The car accident. *She* was the one who ran me off the road."

Granite-jawed, he nodded. "That was never part of the plan obviously. She saw you at the gas station…. You never checked in with me… I couldn't get any information at all. My friend Kurt has access to a police scanner. I called him, and he told me about the accident. You have no idea how much I suffered when I heard. Even though I took a huge risk, I went to the hospital to try to get information. I couldn't stand it any longer."

Her eyes widened. "You were Ed Jensen."

He nodded. "I was sure the cops would get the security footage of that day, but it never occurred to them. I guess, why would it? The… *event*… hadn't even occurred yet. Just my paranoia."

Jane was quiet for a moment and Jake rushed to fill the void, as if any silence would turn her against him. "It came out during Kendra's trial about her running you off the road—she was actually charged and convicted for it. The state pressed charges since you refused to speak to the cops or anyone from the DA's office. And you called a blackout on the trial. I guess it's come as a shock now?"

She nodded, swallowing back the lump that lodged in her throat.

"The DA won two murder convictions against her for Cate's death and that of the gentleman involved in your crash. And then one for attempted murder. Of you."

"Where did the money come from? The cash paid to the killer?"

His smile stretched from ear-to-ear. "A big chunk of it came from Cate herself. Her loan for the company. I needed less than I thought, but I never gave it back since she insisted on my making her a partner. The rest you and I put in over many months, a few hundred here and there. It wasn't all that difficult. We kept it in a shoebox."

"We placed the photo of me in Mason's drawer?"

"Uh-huh. Mason had given me the key to their old place, the condo. You and I went there and you put your fingerprints all over it. Later on, I slipped in the photo. When it came time for the happy couple to move, good ol' Jake helped them pack things up. Cate didn't trust the moving companies with her precious antiques. I made sure to wrap the dresser myself with moving blankets, preserving the prints."

"Why did we do that anyway? We wanted the police to suspect me?"

"You don't remember?"

Jane shook her head, feeling bad about the disappointment shading his eyes. "There are gaps…"

"First, we found a reliable hitman. Pernod was a professional assassin, and we never thought he'd be sloppy enough to get caught. We'd figured the testimony from the one paid witness—the guy we had watching the money exchange—would be enough to exonerate you, and I also had another trick up my sleeve if that didn't prove enough. What we didn't count on was Pernod getting arrested and becoming a witness for us. Not at all. But he became the star witness, and it was all unplanned. His testimony was the coup de grace for the case against you. I mean, Kendra was the only person he'd dealt with, either by phone or in person. He couldn't give anyone else up in a plea deal.

"We tried to stay three steps ahead of the police. Since I had something to gain—monetarily—coupled with my history with Cate, we wanted to divert attention away from me. We figured we'd throw the suspicion on you initially. By making it look like someone was framing you, you would soon be excluded once the exonerating testimony came to light. That was set up in advance, for Benny to wait until you were charged before telling the prosecutor it wasn't you.

"Everything went perfectly according to plan… when Mason told me the house next door to the one he'd just purchased was for sale, I knew it was meant to be. Every single piece was plotted meticulously… except for your car accident."

Jane watched his handsome face as he explained, trying to stitch together all of the individual memories into one coherent quilt. She still had holes but the beauty of the design was now apparent.

"C'mere, baby." He held out his arms and she went right into them with no hesitation. He was her safe harbor, and she guarded his tender heart. Nothing would ever make her turn against him. Nothing could.

JAKE CAME BACK from a walk on the water's edge to a silent house. He found Jane asleep on the charcoal chenille sofa in the study. It was the one from her Riverdale house, the only piece of furniture they took with them, and she loved it. Even her favorite brown velvet chair had been left behind. Jane had chuckled, saying no more brown was allowed in her life. He tiptoed out of the room, quietly closing the door behind him.

Making a cup of coffee, he took it and went out on the deck with their dog. Jane had learned that the man who was killed in the car collision had a dog with him that survived the crash. Unfortunately, there was no family member available to adopt the poor little guy. That's all softhearted Jane had to hear; in a heartbeat, she was in New Jersey, knocking on the door of Barkingham Palace—the shelter housing him—to adopt the pup. She also made a large donation to the NAACP, the organization where the man worked.

Unlike his feelings for his former girlfriend's Afghan hound, Jake loved this dog. He was a garden-variety mixed breed, maybe a shepherd and husky blend. His name was Hugo, and they liked it so much they kept the name. Hugo was about four years old and a great pal, following Jake everywhere he went, and Jake enjoyed the fact that he could feed him whatever and however much he wanted to. There were no shows in Hugo's future.

They were a little family, and they'd gotten their happily ever after, and if and when they were lucky enough to have a kid or two, it would get even better. He'd never give up on Janey, and he'd never let anyone or anything get between them.

Janey wouldn't either. Of that he was as certain as he was that the sun would rise in the morning.

END

Author's Note

Dear Reader:

Thank you for taking the time to read THE GIRL NEXT DOOR. If you enjoyed it, please consider telling your friends or posting a short review on Amazon and Goodreads. Word-of-mouth recommendation is an author's best friend and very much appreciated!

Thank you,
Lisa Aurello

Amazon link:
The Girl Next Door

Made in United States
North Haven, CT
27 September 2022

24620168R00183